LadySmith

Ty Spencer Vossler

This is a work of fiction. Names, characters, places, and incidents are products of the author's imagination or are used fictitiously and are not to be construed as real. Any resemblance to actual events, locations, organizations, or persons, living or dead, is entirely coincidental.

World Castle Publishing, LLC
Pensacola, Florida
Copyright © Ty Spencer Vossler 2023
Paperback ISBN: 9798891264076
eBook ISBN: 9781960076076
First Edition World Castle Publishing, LLC, April 18, 2023
http://www.worldcastlepublishing.com
Cover: Karen Fuller
Editor: Maxine Bringenberg

CHAPTER 1
COLLECTIVE CONSCIENCE

Greeks didn't consider One a number. Euclid defined numbers as an aggregate of units. Numbers begin with two. One is both male and female, odd and even—the least misogynist.

In the United States, there are signs posted everywhere proclaiming #1. Sometimes the number is traded for claims such as World's Best. Other noteworthy examples of one: Elsie Eiler is mayor, head clerk, and tavern owner in Monowi, Nebraska. She's the only resident living there. In all of Shakespeare's works, there's only one hiccup. It's found in Twelfth Night. The perpetrator is no other than Sir Toby Belch.

Many words begin with a unifying prefix—Uni and mono—unicycle, monogamy. The dromedary has one hump, a cyclops one eye. Many humans believe in one God. Yet there's really only one bonafide unifying element in the universe. That's where I come in. Consciousness has outsourced since the dawn of humanity because man isn't born with it. My job is to try and balance ego with consciousness. Without me, ego runs amok.

CHAPTER 2
ARRIVAL

I arrived on Earth from the heart of creation. Think of my kind as the Collective. We filter dark matter into energy. No need to pull into a filling station when we travel. Mandatory social service is a Collective requirement. I'm charged with making clients into critical thinkers. Many factors determine the effectiveness of my efforts. Man has free-will, which either closes borders or opens superhighways.

My client's name is James. He goes by Jimmy. My arrival was accompanied by a sunrise, glowing yellow, orange, softening into a delicate pink as it emerged from the highest peaks of the Sierra Nevada mountains, floating to the surface as if from a fiery lake.

Dawn emerges along with the odor of weeds, walnut leaves, dirt, and skunk. It smells of new beginnings.

Words are codes often used to camouflage truth. Politicians make a living doing this. I try my best not to hide behind empty words. Truth is sacred. I entered into the fray with perfect timing—a shot in the dark, so to speak. Navigating five layers of the atmosphere surrounding Earth, descending the exosphere, thermosphere, and mesosphere, I pierced the stratosphere's ozone layer before easing into the troposphere.

At 5:31 in the morning, I hovered at ten-thousand feet to focus on one hundred-and-sixty-eight acres of farmland in the central San

Joaquin Valley. The main entrance was a gravel lane about a quarter mile long bordered by dozens of palm-trees. There were two barns, one for hay, another used as a workshop/storage. Close by was the heart of the farm—a modest three-bedroom house painted beige with brown trim topped with asphalt shingles. The surrounding land had a voice, whispering as sweetly as a dove in the early morning.

Nothing is impermeable. Eventually, something always gets in. I passed through a crack in the front door of the farmhouse, drawn by the delicious diversity of human sounds. I paused next to the fireplace in the living room to listen.

A four-year-old twitched her feet beneath clean sheets. Steady breathing issued from her eight-year-old brother on the other side of the bedroom. A black dachshund stirred in a wicker basket and farted. Noises from another bedroom drew my attention. I passed beneath it.

More breathing—heavier this time. I floated above husband and wife. They've chosen this fine morning to indulge in the most pleasurable pursuit available to humans. Sighs, muffled moans, and a few gasps built toward a crescendo. And then my moment arrived.

It is 5:57. Millions of sperm swam toward a homeless shelter. Only a hundred and forty-six made it to the door. They crowded forward. Those who simply knocked at the door were rejected. Others tried a forced entry and were denied. One slipped in. I followed before the portal closed. In that instant, sex was determined. Jimmy was now more than just a twinkle in his father's eye. At that moment, I was clueless as to how difficult my job would be.

***

In Meadowland Memorial Hospital, April 3rd, 1956, after eight months, two-hundred and ninety-six days of solitary confinement, Jimmy arrived. His voice was spanked into being. How strange that life should begin with pain instead of wonder. Doctor Parkinson, the family doctor for over twenty years, handed Jimmy to the nurse.

"Nice big boy," says Parkinson.

Jimmy is swabbed clean and placed in Mother's arms. Father is allowed in. Parkinson accepts a cigar and slips it into a shirt pocket. The nurse hands Jimmy to Father. Everyone smiles, including the baby.

"See that?" says Father proudly.

"Gas," explains the doctor. The doctor tickles Jimmy's feet, takes vitals, and pronounces him fit as a fiddle. "Gotta name picked out?"

"James," says Mother. "James Irwin Koch."

"After James Dean," Father clarifies.

"Oh," chimes the nurse. "I just saw *East of Eden* at the Meadowland Theater. What a wonderful actor." She moves to a Remington typewriter that sits on a small table off to the side.

"James Irwin Koch." Parkinson pronounces it Kock.

"Koke, not Kock," amends Father.

The doctor, fluent in German, knows better. "Koke it is."

"K-o-c-h?" The nurse is typing birth information on the official certificate.

"Yes," Father says.

She finishes typing and hands Jimmy back to Mother. Fifteen minutes later, Jimmy opens his eyes. He can't see very far, but his mother's face is close.

"Blue eyes," she announces.

"Yep," agrees Father.

The nurse retrieves Jimmy to place him inside an incubator. There are two other encapsulated babies in the care center. She returns and, with a click-clack-clickety-clack, adds the parent names to the birth certificate—Barbara Eileen Koch, William Lester Koch.

***

Magnets have a north and south pole. North and south are mutually attracted to one another. North-to-north, south-to-south are repelled. James Irwin Koch and I were East of West Eden.

CHAPTER 3
THORNS

Perceptions have reference points. From the air, farmlands are geometric—squares, circles, and rectangles. Closer inspection shows ragged edges, imperfections. The same is true of human consciousness.

Sibling rivalry causes perfidious behaviors. James Irwin Koch had a sister, Karen (five) and a brother, Michael (eight). They were with Grandma Dobbs when Jimmy was born. Leora Dobbs lived close to the hospital where her daughter was recovering. The children called her Grandma Dobby to her face. Behind her back, she was the *Mud Dauber*.

They would have preferred staying with Grandpa and Grandma Koch. As the crow flies, they live across a prune orchard from their house. They walked there nearly every day. Children in those days were often barefoot. The biggest worry was bull's-head sticker patches. If you stumbled into one, someone with shoes had to lift you out. For kids, wearing shoes was like using gloves to play a cello.

Grandpa and Grandma Koch loved the kids yet exercised little control over their activities, which were often dangerous. Their middle-aged son, Uncle Ed, lived there too. Today he would be labeled as mentally challenged. Yet, in 1956, people referred to him as slightly retarded. Ed's love for the children was borderless and all-encompassing. His laughter could be heard a mile away, expressed in three syllables,

"Uh huh-huh!" He played with the children, attended their sporting events, and listened to whatever stories they had to tell.

When Uncle Ed was school-age, special classes weren't offered. He was mainstreamed into regular classes. It was rumored that when he was born, the doctor held him up by one leg and made it longer than the other, which was why Ed walked with a bad limp. It was also thought that Gladys left baby Ed in the sun too long while she was gardening one day, causing a diminished mental capacity. Both theories reflected the ignorance of the time. Truth is, Ed was blessed. He didn't need to wrap his brain around complex issues. He lived a day at a time, and his basic instinct for love served him well until his dying day.

Sometimes the children called him Special Ed, but never to his face. He was a capable farmhand, able to drive tractors, irrigate crops, and prune trees. When instructions were explained slowly and carefully, Ed could do almost anything asked of him. He always carried a pack of Wrigley's Spearmint gum in his pocket for the children.

Undoubtedly, Uncle Ed's greatest talent was the uncanny ability to fart at will, followed by his trademark laughter, "Uh huh-huh!" The children debated how it was possible to expel gas so long and so loud.

"Can fart anytime I wanna," he joked. When challenged to do so, he replied, "Don't wanna." This always drew snickers from the children. Then he'd ask them to pull his finger.

The only time Karen and Michael saw Grandpa Andrew angry was the previous Thanksgiving held at his house. Grandma Dobbs was there, too, bringing austerity to the table. Before feasting, Grandpa said a prayer of thanks.

"Father, bless this food to the nourishment of our bodies—"

At which point Uncle Ed, sitting across from the prayer-giver, lifted and let one rip.

"For Chrissake, Ed!" Andrew's face turned crimson, and his hands closed into fists. He was so upset he knocked over his wine glass.

"Sonofa—"

"Andrew!" admonished Gladys before he concluded the expletive.

Sitting between Dobby and his father, Michael covered his mouth with a cloth napkin to hold his laughter. Karen copied him, and tears streamed down their cheeks. Uncle Ed saw them and was unable to control himself. His laughter erupted in three loud blasts, "Uh huh-huh!" Andrew stood, leaned over, and slapped Ed hard across the face.

Bill glared his children into silence. Barbara dabbed a napkin at the corners of her mouth. Dobby did the same, her face becoming a mask of disapproval. Uncle Ed sobbed. It's frightening to see adults cry. Gladys went to him and put gentle hands on his shoulders. Then she stared straight into Andrew's eyes.

"Should be ashamed! What're you teaching the children? C'mon, sweetheart." She coaxed Ed out of his chair. "Let's get you cleaned up."

Ed followed his mother into a bathroom, where she dabbed his face and soothed him with kind words. Andrew picked up his wine glass and then stared at his dinner plate. Michael lowered his napkin, and Karen drew screeching sounds from the plate with the tip of her fork. Bill broke the silence.

"Pass the mashed taters, would yuh?"

Happy for a respite from the storm, Andrew quickly complied, and there followed a flurry of clinks and clanks as dishes were shared, plates filled. Michael looked at his sister and moved his lips to form one whispered word. "Amen."

***

There was a reason Michael and Karen weren't allowed to stay with Grandpa and Grandma Koch when their mother began labor. On the grandparent's property, there stood a large, dilapidated red barn. The sliding door was always open. Michael devised a plan to scare fruit bats out from behind the door. He knew they were there, evidenced by piles of guano beneath. Karen rattled the door, and Michael smacked escaping bats out of the air with a broken shovel handle. Karen called out the results in the universal language of baseball.

"Single…strike one…single…double…strike two…steeerike three. My turn!"

"Naw, I got one out left."

Ed found Michael and Karen. He stood with hands on hips. Michael was giggling like a madman, clobbering one bat after another. Ed laughed, "Uh huh-huh!" until a bloodied bat smacked his chest. "Dammit to hell!" Uncle Ed often used unfiltered language.

"Sorry, Unk," Mike called out.

"Home run!" exclaimed Karen.

Later, recalling how funny it had been, Uncle Ed told his brother. Bill told Barbara, but she didn't think it was a bit humorous.

"That's the last straw. What if they'd been bitten?"

"I'll talk to 'em," Bill said.

"Your parents, Bill. That's who you need to talk to. The kids are just being kids. It's your parents. If they can't look after the kids when they're there, then…." She left the rest hanging.

Bill sighed and nodded. "Yeah, I know."

"Well, if you know…." She pursed her lips.

Bill walked away, not wishing to reopen old wounds. His parents had never approved of Barbara. She and Bill married fresh out of high school.

As a result, Mike and Karen were banished to the Mud Daubers when it was time for their mother to push Jimmy into the world. There was nothing to do at the Daubers. Being used to roaming the ranch, they felt like caged birds there. Grandma Dobby found a stash of Tinker Toys and building blocks and procured crepe paper and crayons to occupy them. On top of that, she had a manicured miniature white poodle named Princess that bit Mike on the arm soon after they arrived.

"What did you do to provoke her?" Dobby accused.

"Not a goddamn thing!" Mike answered.

"Watch your language, young man."

Princess cowered and then twisted around to lick her butt.

The phone rang. Grandma Sally picked up. "Hi! Oh, that's so exciting! Congratulations. Yes. James Irwin Koch. How's Barb? Good. The children are fine…."

Michael motioned his sister outside. They sat on the front porch facing a street. Cars raced by. There was a small patch of lawn and an elm tree there. They heard the shush-shush-shush of traffic, the sound of a lawnmower, someone shouting in the distance, dogs barking. It was all mixed up, so you couldn't distinguish one from the other.

In the past few years, Michael and his sister had forged a truce. Michael realized it was better to have Sis as an ally rather than an adversary. Jimmy was a monkey wrench tossed into the cogs of their alliance.

"There goes the neighborhood," Michael said.

"What's that mean?"

"Means shit's gonna hit the fan."

"How?"

"That little bastard's gonna cause nothin' but headaches. Mark my words. You and me gotta stick together. It's us against him, understand?"

"Mommy says the baby will be a blessing."

Michael shook his head and stood up to stretch. He was tall for his age and towered over Karen. "He'll be a pain in the ass."

"Mom says you shouldn't use words like that."

"Wait 'n' see. When the little blessing gets home, we'll be invisible."

"Why?"

"You'll see."

The front door opened. Grandma Sally smiled down at them. "There you are. Guess what? You have a baby brother!"

Michael nodded and glared at his sister.

"Michael says that—"

"What's its name?" Michael interrupted.

"*His* name," she corrected. "James Irwin. Jimmy. Always liked that name."

Jimmy, he thought. *Stupid-ass name.*

"Tomorrow morning, you'll go home with your new brother. Excited?" She beamed.

Karen looked pleadingly at Michael. He offered Dobby a fake smile. "Course."

"Pick up the Tinker Toys before dinner."

"Can we watch Gunsmoke later?"

"So violent. Lawrence Welk's on tonight. I think you'll enjoy it." She started back through the door.

As the door closed, Michael stared at his feet. "Fuckin' Dauber."

"What're we gonna do?"

"We'll figure somethin', don't you worry."

Later that evening, Karen and Michael sat on the loveseat while Dobby took up the entire sofa to watch Lawrence Welk. She wore a worshipping smile for the entire show. The maestro lifted his baton, "And uh one-uh and uh two-uh and uh three-uh…." Dobby was remembering happier times, when she was sixteen, pretty, passionate about life—before getting pregnant, miscarrying, the boyfriend's denials—before her world came toppling down. Less than a year later, she was pregnant by another man, who quickly skedaddled. This time she carried Barbara to term. To get by, Leora Dobbs learned to sew quilts. She did housework, babysat, whatever she could do to earn a dollar. She survived. Yet the journey took its toll. She never married, never had another child. Her dreams were stitched into quilts to comfort others.

Bobby and Susie were smiling and dancing a waltz as Lawrence Welk waved his baton. Princess was snoozing on Dauber's lap. Michael glared at the disgusting pink warts that showed beneath the dog's white curls. The glow of the television made the dim room seem smaller. He tried to concentrate on a Superman comic, reading it to his sister. He had taught her to read utterances such as oof, ahhh!, and grrr.

"Go ahead and hit me, Superman," he read. "The more you hit me, the stronger I get!" He pointed to the next bubble indicating Superman's response.

"Oof!" Karen cried out.

Grandmother shot daggers at them, and he fired back. "Yeah," he whispered. "Oof."

CHAPTER 4
ZEMO MEANS BAD

The dry summer heat of the central San Joaquin valley is mummifying. Circumstances feed from the inside out, leaving behind a leathery outer shell. In the end, it's all that's left. Four years after his birth, one mid-morning, James Irwin Koch was kneeling alone beneath a large walnut tree in the front yard. He examined a June beetle being eaten alive by tiny red ants, who crawled in and out of an invisible opening. The beetle kicked one rear leg in protest.

Mother multitasked between the kitchen and the laundry room. On a line in the fenced backyard, clothes dried rapidly beneath the unrelenting valley sun. When Jimmy was born, Bill built a four-foot fence around the entire house. He also constructed an A-frame play set with halved tires hanging by strong ropes for swinging and a full-sized tire to twist around on. Jimmy didn't use the tire because Michael claimed a black widow lived in the hollow. The backyard was also where the washroom was. Barbara used the Whirlpool Bill bought her for Christmas.

"Stay inside the yard," Mother warned Jimmy.

"But I wanna go with Karen and Mike."

"When you're a little older."

Michael was twelve. Karen was eight. Jimmy wondered how old

he'd have to be to roam the farm as they did.

"Not fair."

Jimmy found a garden trowel and dug at the foot of the walnut tree. He imagined treasure buried there. His father had been reading Treasure Island to him a few evenings a week. It was slow going. Most nights, Bill was wiped out, unable to muster the energy to see what Long John Silver was up to.

"Yo-ho-ho and a bottle of rum," Jimmy intoned as he excavated deeper. *Nothin'*, he thought as his search encountered stubborn roots. On a whim, he found a faded yellow plastic Indian and a blue canoe laying in the brittle brown grass close by. They had been part of a cheap bagged set, along with cowboys, a brown wagon, and other Indians. The Indian held an upraised tomahawk. Jimmy laid the yellow Indian inside the canoe, placed them into the hole, and covered them. He didn't know why it felt satisfying, but it did.

Two cats named Louie and orphan Annie were fighting on the rooftop. Like most farm pets, they just showed up one day. An Australian shepherd named Joe accompanied his father in the back of the pickup wherever he went. Gretchen, the black dachshund, was mostly Barbara's. It padded around on stubby legs traveling from wicker basket to dog dish and back again. At night it slept in Karen and Mike's room. During the day, the basket was moved into the living room.

This morning, Bill was using the John Deere to cultivate a field of black-eyed peas. Joe slept in the shade beneath the yellow F-100 pickup parked close by.

"Look, Karen, there's a monkey in our yard." Michael approached the front gate and pointed to Jimmy. Karen giggled. "What you doin', monkey-boy?"

"I'm *not* a monkey!"

"Sure you are. Doc Parkinson chopped off your tail when you were born, but they couldn't do nothin' about the rest of yuh."

Jimmy pursed his lips and focused on the freshly covered Indian grave.

"He's burying a banana to eat later," Karen added.

Michael cackled and squatted next to his little brother. "Ooo-ooo ah-ahhh!"

"Lemme alone!"

"Bet you could climb this ol' walnut tree, lickety-split."

"Shut up!"

"Mmmonkey."

"Shut up!"

Karen added, "Roses are red, violets are blue, you look like a monkey, and you smell like one too."

Jimmy stood to face his adversaries. "You're both monkeys!"

"What's going on out here?" Mother was standing in the front doorway.

Jimmy's face was pinched with anger.

"Nothin'," Michael answered.

"Doesn't sound like nothin'," she said.

"Jokin' around."

"Be nice to your brother."

Monkey, Michael thought. "Okay."

"You too, young lady."

"All right."

The door closed. Jimmy was facing Michael. His teeth were clenched. "Hate your guts and wish you were dead."

Michael pitched himself to the ground and lay still.

"See what you did?" Karen said. "You killed him."

"He's not dead."

"Look at 'im."

"Mom!" Jimmy yelled.

"Shut up. I can bring him back. Anybody in the club has the

power." She bent over Michael. "Trizzle-trazzle-trozzle-trup, time for Michael to wake up." She waved a hand over her big brother's limp body.

Michael sat up. "W-what happened? It was so dark."

"See, it worked," Karen said. Then they sang in unison. "Camp'n'wee is Carl. Carl means good, Zemo means bad."

"What's that supposed to mean?" Jimmy wanted to know.

"It's a secret," Karen said.

"Hey, Sis," Mike continued. "Should we initiate Jimmy into the club."

"Think he's ready?"

"What you think, monkey? Got what it takes?"

Jimmy stared at the dry grass. Whatever he replied would be twisted one way or another until he'd forget what the question was. He knew very little about the *Camp'n'wee* club. Only that they bragged about the benefits of membership, inventing new words to describe the various aspects of the club. For instance, *Karl* meant good, and *Zemo* was bad. Zemos were evil entities to be avoided at all costs, and the only way to kill them was with a *Cue-wiz* stick. Those were made with a rifle-length of wood. A long nail was hammered through about a quarter of the way to form both trigger and hammer.

"How 'bout it, wanna join?" Mike asked. "Make your mind up. We ain't got all day."

"What do I gotta do?"

Michael nodded toward Karen. "We'll have to have a meeting to decide. Stay here."

They sequestered themselves on the opposite end of the yard. Whispers were punctuated by giggles. While he waited for the verdict, Jimmy dug up the Indian and reburied him. After five minutes, they returned.

"Okay. Ready?"

"What do I gotta do?" He repeated.

"You'll find out soon enough. I'll go ask Mom if you can come with us."

Michael went into the house. The windows were open to diffuse the heat inside. Screens kept out the flies and mosquitoes. Jimmy heard his mother say, "Okay, but stay close and keep a close eye on him."

"We will."

"Back in an hour for lunch," she added.

Karen and Michael led Jimmy out of the yard. There were various zones on the farm, one for farm implements that scratched, gouged, or combed the earth's surface—lows, rotary harrows, disks, ripper-blades. Heavy work was done with the B-3 John Deere. It was usually stored beneath a large open port next to the diesel tank. It was called a B-3 because it rode on three wheels. Jimmy called it the *dat-dat* because that's the sound it made. Another area was set aside for scrap iron. There were often lizards scurrying around in there. There was a wood pile, a canvas-covered hill of silage to feed the cattle. They only had three Herefords in a small pasture next to the house, keeping them as a reminder that they'd once been cattle ranchers. There was also an old horse named Fern, walking stiffly as she grazed on grass.

The red barn was off-limits to the children. Inside was an acetylene torch, arc welder, drills, sanders, saws—all tools with maiming potential. The white barn had two tall haystacks on either side of the large open entry.

"What we doin' here?" Karen asked. "You said—"

"Shhh!" Michael pointed to a large, centered crossbeam twenty-five feet above, spanning the width of the barn. "Okay, monkey, you gotta go from one side to the other."

"Quit callin' me that!"

"That's not what we said," argued Karen. "We said he's gotta stand barefoot on a mound of red ants for two minutes."

Jimmy stared up at the crossbeam. "I'll do it."

"If you make it," explained Michael, "yuh have to sing the Camp'n'wee song perfectly before we let you in."

Karen began singing, "Camp'n'wee is Karl, Karl means good, Zemo means bad."

"This's the easiest way up." Michael showed Jimmy where bales formed a crude staircase to the top.

Jimmy began his ascent. Last time he'd been up there was with his father, who'd shown him where four newborn kittens were hidden.

"Can we keep 'em?" he asked his dad.

"Fraid not, buddy. Got 'nough animals to feed."

"What'll happen to 'em?"

"I'll find 'em a good home."

Later in life, Jimmy discovered that *home* was a gunny sack filled with rocks and kittens tossed into a nearby irrigation canal.

Jimmy was at the top. The beam stood at chest level and was a yard wide. He climbed up and crawled until he could see over the edge. A sick feeling welled up instantly, and beads of sweat broke out on his forehead.

"Go on!" Michael yelled.

"Don't make him," said Karen.

"Chicken out, and the Zemos'll get you tonight when you're asleep!"

Jimmy focused on the other haystack across the way, yet the empty space between looked like pictures he had seen in Life Magazine of the Grand Canyon. He thought of the Indian in the canoe and wondered where the rest of the tribe had gotten to. His hands gripped the edges of the support beam. His knees moved—left, right, left, right. His hand slid correspondingly along the rough edges as he went. Left. Right, left, right—a bit more, and he'd be in Camp'n'wee. *I'll get a Cue-wiz gun.*

Jimmy felt a sharp jab as a large splinter entered the palm of his left hand. He screeched and looked down. Dizziness filled his head, and he felt like throwing up. Lying flat, he wrapped his arms around the beam as far as they'd go.

"Oh God, Michael!" cried Karen.

Mike stood below. "I'll catch 'im if he falls."

"Let's get Mom!" Karen started toward the open end of the barn.

"No, wait!"

Karen stopped, and her voice trembled. "Gotta get help!"

Michael lifted his head. "You're halfway there!" he coached.

Karen joined him. "You can do it, Jimmy!"

Mike's words were muffled by the beating of Jimmy's heart in his temples. He began sliding himself along with his hands. More splinters entered his chest and arms. He inched forward, opening his eyes every few moments.

Michael heard it first—the sound of Father's pickup turning onto the dirt road leading past the white barn.

"Dad!" Karen turned to rush out.

"No!" He gripped her by the arm.

The crunching of pebbles and dirt beneath tires was closer.

Jimmy looked—so close. With a mighty effort, he closed his eyes and dragged himself, ignoring the splinters. "Hide!" Jimmy heard his brother say. He opened his eyes and saw that he was directly over the haystack. Father's pickup cruised past slowly to minimize the dust. Jimmy rolled off the beam to drop down into the hay, knocking the wind from his body.

Michael and Karen heard a wheezing sound above them and scampered up the stack. Jimmy was on his back.

"What's the matter with 'im?" Karen was crying now.

"How the hell should I know?"

Jimmy's breath slowly returned. He stared at the rafters. There were pigeon nests in each corner, rimmed with bird shit. The metal roof of the barn snapped and popped beneath the heat of the sun. He heard a Hereford call out in the distance, followed by his mother's voice.

"Michael! Karen! Time for lunch! Jimmy! Lunchtime!"

Jimmy took a deep breath and sang, "Camp'n'wee is Karl, Karl means good, Zemo means bad." Exactly as his sister had.

"Let's go. It's lunchtime.

They climbed down, and as they walked home, Jimmy picked at a splinter in his hand. "When do I get a cue-whiz gun?"

Mike glanced over to Jimmy. "You sang the song wrong."

"Did *not*! Said it just like her!" Jimmy pointed to Karen.

"Nope. You said, Camp'n'wee is Carl with a C. It's spelled with a K."

Jimmy furrowed his brow. Karen shook her head at Michael's mendacity.

"Did what you said. I'm in the club." Tears rolled down his cheeks.

"C'mon Mike, 'nough's 'nough," Karen tried.

Michael shook his head. "Yuh almost did it."

"Liar! Hate your guts and wish you were dead!" Jimmy ran toward the farmhouse, where macaroni and cheese was in the beginning stage of rigor-mortis. His father was washing in the bathroom, and his mother waited in the kitchen.

Karen was sullen. "We're gonna get it now."

"Naw. He won't say nuthin'. You'll see."

"Why don't we let 'im in?"

"Me and you, remember? Thick as thieves."

Michael was right. Jimmy didn't say a word about the fiasco. When Mother saw his arms festooned with slivers, she glared at his siblings.

"What in God's name?"

"The woodpile," he said.

"How in the world...?" She examined his arms and lifted his shirt. "Good Lord! I told you to watch over him!"

Mike and Karen glanced at each other as Bill joined them.

"What's going on?"

"Look at this." She lifted Jimmy's shirt. "I'll get tweezers and alcohol." She stalked toward the bathroom.

"What the hell?" was Bill's two-in-one phrase when he wanted to know *what* and *who* to blame.

"We was makin' a fort in the woodpile. Mom said he could play with us." Michael expertly put the blame on his mother as she rummaged.

"Doesn't even hurt," Jimmy said bravely.

"It will," Bill warned. "specially when the ones your mom can't get fester up. Shouldn't be playin' in that old woodpile. Black widows, snakes, lizards, opossums...." He left the rest to their imagination.

Michael tried his father's method of combining sentences. "Sorry, won't happen again, promise."

"Yeah, well...." Bill mumbled something else under his breath as his wife returned with tweezers and a bottle of isopropyl alcohol.

"C'mon, Jimmy." She led him into the bedroom. The silence at the table was punctuated by sharp cries and Barbara's admonishments. "Never in my life. Christ, this one's too deep. Be still!"

Karen stabbed a macaroni with each painful burst. Michael rounded his up with a spoon and shoved piles into his mouth. Bill did the same.

Afterward, Michael cleared the table, and Karen washed dirty dishes. Nothing much was said. She averted her eyes when Michael tried to get her attention. Jimmy hollered.

"Sounds just like a monkey," Michael whispered. Karen didn't laugh.

CHAPTER 5
FORTRESS OF SOLITUDE

Two weeks later, Michael convinced Jimmy to try again.

Holding up minimalizing fingers, he said, "You were this close. I know you can do it," Mike encouraged.

"Liar."

Mike shrugged, "Okay, if you don't wanna join—"

"Did what you said."

"Yeah, forget it." He lifted his cue-wiz stick. "C'mon, sis, let's go kill some Zemos. Too bad. Could'a used Jimmy's help. There's a lotta 'em."

Jimmy felt a sudden attack of anxiety. Four-year-olds trust blindly. He knew nothing about Abraham Lincoln, yet he decided to believe in the better angels of Michael's nature.

"Wait up!" he yelled. "Tell Mom I'm comin'."

Michael stopped, stared straight ahead, and smiled. Without turning, he said, "Naw, had your chance." He resumed walking.

"Maybe we oughta," advised Karen.

Michael stopped and nodded slowly. "Okay. Your turn. Mom don't trust me no more."

Karen ran past Jimmy and into the house. Barbara was ironing clothes in the living room. She smiled at Karen. "What yuh up to, sweetheart?"

"Can we take Jimmy?"

Barbara put the iron down and pursed her lips. "After what happened?"

"Just gonna walk around. Jimmy wants to come real bad."

Barbara paused, nodded, and lifted a warning finger. "Tell your brother he's on thin ice."

"Thanks, Mom." She did a pirouette and skipped to the front door.

"Back in a couple hours. Don't make me come lookin'."

"Okay."

"What'd she say?" Jimmy asked.

"Said you're on thin ice. What's that mean?"

"Can't imagine," lied Michael.

Jimmy swallowed hard and followed them. As they walked, Mike hung an arm around his brother's shoulder.

"Gotta give it to yuh. You're a brave little monkey."

"What do I gotta do?" Jimmy asked.

"We'll show yuh."

He and Karen lifted their cue-whiz sticks and led the way.

***

The woodpile was a short distance away. Six cords of oak logs were stacked in the merciless heat for firewood. It was covered with a black plastic tarp in winter to keep it dry. Thoughts of sitting close to the fire and drinking hot chocolate made Jimmy miss the bitter chill. Jimmy remembered the previous winter when Father sat an old pair of Mike's cowboy boots in front of a blazing fire. He had doused them in water so they might shrink enough to fit him. It didn't work, but Jimmy stuffed the toes with socks and wore them anyway.

A small, whitewashed shed filled with scraps sat next to the woodpile. Bill had exceptional carpentry skills and whiled away rainy days in the red barn, building birdhouses, dog houses, and wooden containers for his wife's flowers. The strong A-frame swing in the backyard, and bed frames for the children, all resulted from hours spent in the red barn. It rained just enough in the central San Joaquin valley for weeds to thrive. In the red barn, Bill sometimes collaborated with his hired hand, Mister Loftus, to build original equipment. They welded together a frame with wheels to hold a large water tank. At the height of the dry season, when roads were covered in fine gray powder, they used it to soak them. Barbara hated when her freshly washed '53 Buick Special was covered in dust simply from driving to the mailbox and back.

In the woodshed were unused shingles, kindling, plywood sheets, two-by-fours. It was home to a variety of spiders, lizards, insects, and an occasional gopher snake. Possums and skunks squeezed in through a wide crack in the crude doorway, which was locked with a primitive drawbar like the ones put in place to keep enemy soldiers from breaching castles.

Michael hadn't thought up a new initiation. He stood there looking around. The ranch was flat. Bill and Uncle Ed rotated black-eyed peas, cotton and planted alfalfa in between to keep nitrogen in the soil. There were forty acres of prune trees separating them from Grandpa and Grandma Koch.

The three of them were barefoot. They had developed calloused layers of protection over the years. Nineteen-sixty was a good time to walk barefoot. The US government had just sent thirty-five hundred men to Vietnam. Thirty percent of them were black. John F Kennedy was president, Chubby Checker started the twist craze, aluminum cans were popular, and Xerox introduced the first photocopier. All of this was a million miles from the three children gathered for an initiation.

"Stay there. We gotta prepare for your test."

Jimmy stood as his siblings parlayed out of earshot. A series of pinpricks brought attention to the fact he was standing on a colony of red ants. He hopped away, stomped his feet, and brushed off the rest. His fingers carried the acrid smell of dead ants. Itchy bumps were rising on his feet. He was glad Mike didn't notice, not wanting to relive the experience as part of the initiation.

He saw blue-bellied lizards facing off on the outer wall of the woodshed. They bobbed heads and did pushups until one was intimidated enough to skittle away. From where he stood, he noticed ground squirrels peeking from holes. When he was old enough, his father would buy him a bee-bee gun. Michael had his confiscated after being caught shooting the Herefords in the flank to watch them jump.

Michael and Karen returned. Mike towered over Jimmy. He smiled and put a hand on Jimmy's shoulder and nodded toward the woodshed.

"We decided to take it easy on yuh this time. Just have to catch a blue belly in the wood shack. Oughta be easy 'cause they're slower in the shade."

Blue-bellies were common lizards in central San Joaquin. They preferred wood and concrete piles to live in and around. They were difficult to catch, yet Jimmy was relieved. He'd caught them before, storing them in a Bell-jar to study before releasing them. Compared to traversing the crossbeam in the barn, this was a piece of cake.

"Okay." He lifted the bar from the entrance.

"Watch for nails," warned his sister. "They give yuh a shot in the ass if you step on one."

"Mom says you shouldn't use such language," taunted Mike.

"Shut up, you do all the time," she retorted.

Michael opened the door and then added more incentive.

"Catch two, I'll make you the best cue-whiz gun you ever saw. Better'n mine." He lifted his and nodded.

Jimmy nodded and stepped inside. Unlike the woodpile, nothing was organized here. Odds and ends lay everywhere, covered in dust and cobwebs. The door let in enough light for him to see. He lifted a square of plywood close to his feet, and a blue belly skittered out. Jimmy lunged and missed. The lizard disappeared beneath a pile of kindling. As he bent to search, the door slammed, the drawbar was replaced, and Jimmy was plunged into semi-darkness. His eyes adjusted as slivers of light made it through knotholes and cracks in the walls.

"Hey!" Jimmy cried out. "Open up, can't see nothin'." He heard Michael giggling.

"That's cruel. Open it," said Karen.

Mike raised his voice, "You want out, Jimmy?"

"Open up!"

"Ten minutes. Start practicing the Camp'n'wee song, and you better get it right this time."

Jimmy closed his eyes. Sweat poured from his face. Within the darkness, he imagined eyes all around.

Loud enough for Jimmy to hear, Michael said, "Don't think I told yuh, Sis. Last winter, Dad sent me out here for kindling, and swear to God, seen a giant black widow hangin' on a web in the corner. Never seen nothin' like it."

"Lemme out! Don't wanna be in your stupid club!" Jimmy's ears were ringing, and his left eye was ticking.

"Mike…," Karen protested.

"Shit, thing's belly was the size of a baseball, bright ol' red hourglass—"

"Lemme out!"

"Mike," Karen tried again.

"Started creepin' toward me real slow-like. Grabbed an armload of kindling and got the hell out."

Jimmy was sobbing. "Lemme out! Lemme out!" He kicked at the door.

"Jimmy, stop! You'll draw its attention. Fucker's got 'nough juice to kill a horse."

"Let 'im out, Mike."

"Ahhh-hahhh! Lemme out! It's comin'!" Jimmy's voice was raw. His head jerked up and down involuntarily.

Michael pulled out a matchbox and lit three at a time. Then he blew them out next to a knothole. "Oh shit, the shacks on fire!"

"Michael!" Karen tried to open the door.

Michael blocked her. "C'mon, Sis, this'll make a man out of 'im."

Jimmy squatted with fists on his knees. His voice was hoarse now. He took deep gulps of air to let out tiny squeaks. Then he pitched forward, so his head rested on a piece of plywood. He closed his eyes, and darkness crept deep inside.

"Dad's comin'!" Karen distracted Michael long enough to make it past. She lifted the bar and swung the door open. Sunlight spilled on Jimmy's inert body.

He heard voices coming from somewhere. "Get up, faker!" Mike's voice. "Fine. We won't even make you do the song."

As consciousness returned, Jimmy sang it in his head before opening his eyes. *Camp 'n' wee is Karl, Karl means good, Zemo means bad.*

Jimmy developed his first nervous habit—a nod reminiscent of blue-belly lizards challenging each other beneath the hot sun. Michael noticed it right after the second initiation.

"What you doin'?"

"I don't know," said Jimmy.

"What?" asked Karen.

"That thing he's doin' with his head." Mike pointed. "Wait for it."

As if on cue, Jimmy's head nodded.

"Watch this." Mike rubbed his chin as if he were thinking deeply. "Jimmy, are you a monkey?"

Jimmy couldn't stop it. He nodded.

"Knew it."

"Hate your guts and wish you were dead!" Jimmy ran toward the front yard.

"Hey, stop!" yelled Mike after him. "You gotta black widow on your back!"

Jimmy tore off his T-shirt and threw it to the ground.

"Think he'll tell?" Karen asked.

"Jimmy!" Mike yelled. "Rat, and you're outta the club."

"Zemos love rats!" Karen added.

Jimmy paused, picked up his shirt, and disappeared inside. His mother was reading a thick book with a scantily clad couple snuggling on the cover. She looked up for a moment, adjusted in her seat on the couch, and continued.

***

Jimmy's nervous nod persisted for nearly a year. His parents discussed taking him to Dr. Parkinson yet deferred to a higher power—advice from farm wives like Mrs. Cloninger.

"Matthew picked his eyebrows 'til he hardly had any. Finally grew out of it," she said. Zeb Granger's wife Clarice confessed that her daughter "Ate boogers 'til she was seven."

Jimmy eventually conquered the first habit on his own.

CHAPTER 6
LIKE MIKE

When Jimmy turned six, he entered kindergarten at Woodland Elementary school. Suburban schools were K-8. After that, you took a bus to Meadowland High School, home of the Panthers. Michael was a sophomore there. Karen was in sixth with Mister Ganns, and Jimmy began his education with kindly Mrs. Kitchener. The principal at Woodland was a mild-mannered fellow named Mr. Johnson, who went around smiling and nodding as if he, too, suffered a nervous habit.

Jimmy was happy at school. The teacher called out his name every morning, and it made him feel important. He played with other children, and some had good imaginations. When he returned home, he was virtually invisible. Mother had a snack waiting, then she shooed him outside to play so she could read another chapter.

Since Michael was in high school, he and Karen weren't as close anymore, separated by a distance that couldn't be measured with numbers. Karen still slept with stuffed animals. Michael fantasized about Candy Schubert. Jimmy thought of his new friends at school. Children in kindergarten are too young to don the masks humans create for themselves as they grow older.

Woodland Elementary was a labor-camp school. With the exception of a few white farm kids, most pupils were Chicano or

Mexican. Most of Jimmy's friends had brown skin and names like Beatrice, Arnulfo, Nelda, and Samuel. He knew the other white farm kids, but they didn't play with the same enthusiasm. Yet he did like Matthew Cloninger. Their two families had been friends for three generations.

Boys and girls usually played separately because boys were naturally rough. They built roadways in the sandbox, girls busied themselves pretending to be housewives in the classroom's play kitchen area. On weekends and during the prune harvest season, Jimmy saw some of his Mexican friends accompany their parents into the fields. Father rarely let him talk with them. Cultural distancing was practiced long before social distancing was required.

Years later, Jimmy came to understand racism is like chewing gum hidden beneath desktops. You don't notice it until you run your hands over it. He was never allowed to have a Mexican friend to sleep over. It had to be a farm kid, and even that was rare. Matthew Cloninger lived on the next farm over. His father, Bert, was an alcoholic. Cheap beer was his poison of choice, and he kept a supply tucked away in a workshop. On hot days he drank it warm.

Jimmy and Matthew worshipped their fathers for the same reasons boys everywhere did. Even if they were sloppy drunks who used a belt or the back of a hand, sons found reasons to forgive. Jimmy never questioned the off-color remarks his father made around other farmers regarding Mexicans and blacks. They were convenient patsies for anything they considered wrong in the world. According to farmers, people of color were lazy, thieving, ignorant, dishonest baby-making factories. In 1986, Martin Luther King Day was proclaimed, followed by Cesar Chavez Day in 2000. Farmers collectively shook their heads and rolled their eyes, adding more gum beneath the table.

Early Saturdays, Jimmy went to Woodland with his father to pick up a few groceries. The small market was owned by a middle-aged couple named Jack and Larue Ashworth. They were both very serious, having swapped a marriage relationship for a cooperative one. They seldom spoke to each other and rarely made eye contact. Jimmy often heard Uncle Ed call the husband Jack Assworth, followed by his trademark laughter, "Uh huh-huh!"

Jack and LaRue depended on the Mexican community. Yet, if the store was empty and Bill went in, he and Jack would end up gabbing about the good-for-nothin' Mexicans getting out of hand. The United Farm Workers Union had recently been formed.

"Damned beaners," said Jack.

"Yep, getting' pretty bad."

"First the niggers, now the greasers. What's next?"

"Canadians," Bill joked.

"Dad, what's a beaner?" Jimmy had asked.

Bill turned red. "Never mind, son. Get yourself a root beer."

Jack and Larue only had one employee, Zeke, the butcher. He ran the meat counter in back and was an expert in providing the cuts of meat Mexicans used for carne asada. He always carried an adult magazine in his back pocket to look through when things were slow. Zeke was short for Ezekiel. He was a muscular Chicano and had little love for his own race. Jimmy saw him reading a magazine when he went to get a root beer from the refrigerator.

"What you readin', Zeke?"

He lifted the cover. Three Nazis surrounded a panicked, voluptuous, half-naked blonde bound and gagged in a chair. One Nazi was preparing a hypodermic. The others were unbuttoning their shirts. The name of the publication was Man's Magazine.

"What they doin' to 'er?"

"Terrible things, Jimmy. Terrible."

"Let's go, Jimbo!" his father called.

Sometimes Bill took Jimmy with him to check on irrigation. If a siphon pipe wasn't running, he let Jimmy restart it. Siphon pipes were specially shaped to curve over the contour of a ditch bank.

To water field crops, a special blade was pulled by a tractor to create a V-shaped ditch parallel to the furrows. Siphons were laid out by hand, one to a row. The ditch was filled with water using an irrigation pot, and when filled, siphons were started by covering the opening with a palm and pulling it over quickly. An experienced farmer could accomplish the task quickly and easily, one-handed. Some were able to do two at a time.

Jimmy's hands were small. To start a siphon, he held it in his left hand and put his right palm over the end. Then he pumped it back and forth until it sprayed. If he was lucky, water would keep flowing when he pulled it over the bank. Bill got a kick out of watching Jimmy try. The final task was to adjust valves on the pots, so the water level in the ditch remained constant. His father often let Jimmy wear his straw cowboy hat as they moseyed along in the pickup, searching for stopped pipes. Occasionally a half-drowned gopher would emerge from its burrow, and Joe would set upon it.

"Can I take it home?" Jimmy asked when he saw one before Joe.

"How would you keep 'im?"

"Cardboard box."

"Chew right through. Gotta metal box in the red barn I'll loan yuh. Fill it with dirt and make sure he don't get out."

Following Bill's advice, he kept it in the laundry room and named it Go-go Gopher after a cartoon with a similar name. Yet there was too much dirt in the box. The first night, Go-go escaped, squeezed beneath the Whirlpool washer, and chewed through some wiring. The result was a fried Go-go and a washer that needed fixing. Go-go was the front-runner to a series of exotic pets Jimmy had over the years.

The winter of his sixth year brought a dusting of snow one February morning. Mrs. Kitchener let the kids play outside, and they managed to build a small snowman. It was a magical time. After all, this was the central San Joaquin Valley, where thermals lifted buzzards and red-tailed hawks to unimagined heights, and seedless grapes became raisins in twelve days. Winters were mostly dry and cold, and the legendary Tule River fog sometimes blanketed everything in a white, impenetrable veil.

Jimmy's father told the story of, "Halfway to Meadowland, I got caught in pea soup so thick, had to drive with the door open just to see the centerline. Shut off the engine at stop signs to listen for cars." Dozens of fatalities were listed in the Meadowland Recorder the following day.

February 1962. The children threw snowballs, and Mrs. Kitchener took a picture of the entire class posing with the melting snowman. Clouds broke, and soon the sun erased all evidence of the miracle. They returned to the classroom and were given sheets of crepe paper and safety scissors to make snowflakes.

Karen's class had no such luck. "You'll catch your death," said Mr. Ganns when students begged to go outside.

At high school, Mike's English teacher Mrs. Otto said, "You act like you've never seen snow." Matter of fact, not many had. It covered the snow-packed Sierra Nevadas, yet parents rarely deigned to take children to roll in it, toboggan down it, or create snow angels. Michael and Karen stared helplessly as flakes covered the ground and turned into slush with the first rays of the sun.

Mike complained at dinnertime. "What're the chances that'll happen again? Slim to none, and Slim left town."

Jimmy didn't brag about his frolic in the snow. No use in tipping the boat. He had sat next to Matthew on the bus ride home that afternoon. They carried ABC worksheets with coveted gold stars stuck to them. They also had crepe snowflakes to give to their parents.

"Watch *Bonanza*?" Matt wanted to know.

"Sometimes. Little Joe's the best."

"Hoss's better."

"They don't look anything alike."

"Yeah. Maybe they got different moms."

Floyd, the bus driver, began his show. He swung a microphone out in front of him. It was to be used for announcements or to admonish rowdy boys, but Floyd had other ideas. In a pleasant baritone, Floyd unleashed his own version of "Ain't She Sweet?"

"Ain't she sweet, see 'er walkin' down that street, yeah I ask you very confidentially, ain't she sweet?"

Kids sitting on the bench seat in the very back rolled down side windows to spit on stop signs.

"Ain't she nice, look 'er over once or twice, yeah I ask you very confidentially, ain't she nice?" Before the next verse, he added, "Boys in back there, roll up that window!"

In addition to being an all-purpose janitor/maintenance expert, Floyd umpired sports events, coached Little League, taught boys how to shoot a basket, throw a spiral, and square around to bunt during the lunch break. His slenderness made him look taller than he was. Quick with a smile, his kindness never wavered.

Floyd was first to notice Michael Koch's golden right arm. Occasionally he played catch with Mike during lunch and had to use a sponge in his glove for cushioning. He talked Mike into playing Little League with a team he coached on weekends. He taught Mike everything he knew about pitching mechanics.

"When you gonna teach me a curveball?"

"Gotta let your arm mature more. Believe me, you won't need one for quite a while." He assumed a crouch and watched Mike carefully as he delivered the next pitch. The ball smacked leather-to-leather.

Mike smiled with satisfaction when he saw Floyd wince.

Floyd stood and walked over to Mike. "Hold the ball across the seams," he demonstrated. "Push off on your back leg, and follow through. Follow through's real important."

Little League games were played at Woodland Elementary. There were three fields that could be used at the same time. The smallest was for Pony League, players younger than nine. Then you tried out for Little League, which took up the other two diamonds. Each field was riddled with gopher mounds, and Floyd had mostly given up trying to control them. When he cut grass with the tractor mower, gophers peeped out of their homes, and Floyd imagined hearing their taunting laughter.

First game Mike pitched, he went the six-inning distance, striking out fifteen, walking ten, and hitting two batters. Despite the fact that the opposing team didn't get a hit, they lost five to three. In the stands, Uncle Ed menaced the poor umpires. While Mike was pitching, Ed disputed every close call and was asked to leave several times.

"God*damn*, right down the middle. What's wrong with you, ump?"

Umpires were usually volunteer fathers. Some tolerated Ed's comments. Others didn't.

"Ed, I'm 'bout to whoop your ass!" warned Mr. Ramirez, who helped Floyd with maintenance.

If Bill was there, he'd tell Ed to hush. Sometimes another farmer was there watching his kid, and he would assume Ed duty. Usually, after a warning, Ed calmed down with a finishing, "Dang it to hell anyway."

After a particular game in which Michael completely dominated despite losing because of wildness, Jimmy's father treated both teams to snow cones. Floyd talked to his father about Mike.

"Boy's gotta cannon, Bill. Kids 're afraid to hit against 'im."

Jimmy was eating a snow cone with lime-flavored syrup.

"Yep." Bill took the cigar he was chewing out of his mouth. "Seen 'im bring down a rabbit with a rock."

After hearing that, Jimmy began throwing stones at everything he could think of—Herefords, dogs, cats, lizards. His success was limited to breaking a front window to the house. Jimmy wanted to be just like Mike, but it wasn't working out.

Mike was a good student too. He graduated eighth grade as salutatorian, a tick away from Janice Johnson, who was valedictorian. She was also the principal's daughter. Michael started his graduation speech with, "We stand at the threshold of discovery."

Mike's success continued in high school. He was a top scholar/ athlete and got noticed by Candy Schubert, who took him off the singles market his sophomore year.

In high school, Mike took German, which was strange considering over half the population in Meadowland spoke Spanish. German class was filled with white kids—further evidence of gum stuck beneath the table. There was an unspoken understanding about segregation. His honors classes also reflected this fact.

Jimmy's goals were cemented by his brother's words, *We stand at the threshold of discovery.* He was determined to follow whatever path Mike took and replicate it as best he could. He even memorized the first passage in Mike's German text. Wo ist Monika? Im bot.

CHAPTER 7
ROPE VAULT

You'd think living on a ranch would offer abundant opportunities for staying busy, yet Jimmy and his siblings grew bored with the routine— visiting grandmas, riding bikes, hunting for lizards, swimming in the muddy water of an irrigation canal. Mike couldn't drive yet, so his romance with Candy Schubert was put on hold. When he wasn't on the phone with her, he invented solutions for filling time slots beneath an unrelenting sun.

The Tule River canal was a mile and a half from the farm, a wide man-made trench designed to carry rain, snow melt, and reservoir water to thirsty farmlands. It was bordered by thick strands of weeds, brush, and bamboo. Kids simply referred to it as the river. Farm parents didn't allow their children to play there often. The place was infused with urban legends.

Although the news never appeared in the Meadowland Recorder, there were rumors of murder, rape, and beasts roaming the river at night. One thing for sure, marijuana was grown in coffee canisters and hidden inside the bamboo. Transients lived at the river too. Empty bottles of Thunderbird gave evidence, and they were often spotted wandering the banks. Coyotes called the river home, along with feral cats, stray dogs, and an occasional mountain lion or bobcat.

Michael's persistence was finally able to wear down his parents' reticence. He was soon to be a high school junior, had played varsity baseball as a freshman, and set a school record for strikeouts in a seven-inning contest—nineteen. Baseball scouts noticed the tall, lanky kid with the blazing fastball. Along with success came an increase in parental trust.

"Okay," Father relented one Saturday morning. "Pick you up on the bank in three hours. Don't wander off too far, and wear shoes."

"Think it's a good idea?" questioned Mother. "You heard what happened to—"

"They'll be fine, honey. Give us some time to smooch."

The children cringed as their father grabbed his wife and peppered her with kisses. She giggled and pushed him away, yet her imagination had already set the plate.

A dirt road took the children there. From a distance, the river banks loomed large and foreboding. The closer you got, it was apparent the so-called river wasn't much more than a giant V carved into the ground. Muddy shallow water flowed lazily during summer months, surrounded by hot sands that burned your feet if you went barefoot. Occasionally, heavy winter rains threatened to spill over the banks and damage surrounding farmlands.

It was over a hundred degrees when they began the two-mile journey to the river. Michael regaled them with tales of terror along the way. Yet he mostly directed his talk toward Karen.

"Know Pepe Reyes?"

"Yeah."

"Told me he found a dead body at the river last year. Some guy. Said it was all bloated, full of maggots and shit."

His sister wrapped arms around her shoulders and shivered despite the heat. "Gross."

"Mountain lions, too," he added, as if the two subjects were somehow related.

Secretly, Jimmy wished Joe was with them even though there was little evidence to prove the dog was an effective deterrent against anything but gophers. Jimmy didn't cotton to the idea of stumbling on a mountain lion.

"Fuckers'll tear you up. Dad said he saw one in the white barn a few weeks back."

"Liar," Karen said.

Michael embellished further. "Heard him tellin' Loftus. Didn't wanna worry us."

"Such a liar."

"Swear to God."

Swearing to God meant nothing, yet somehow instilled veracity to extraordinary claims and was often used effectively to sew doubt.

"Suit yourself. Don't say I didn't warn yuh."

That afternoon they discovered spent shotgun shells, empty beer cans, a transient nest, and a dead ground squirrel. They built a bamboo fort by mashing down trails. Then they made spears out of dried shoots and practiced throwing them at a massive oak tree. It was fun until Mike recreated a scene from the movie, Lord of the Flies.

He pointed his spear toward Jimmy. "Hey, Sis...kill Simon, kill Simon! He's the *real* monster!"

Karen played along up to a point, raising her spear half-heartedly.

Jimmy dropped his spear and backed away. Michael pulled his arm back as if to throw. Jimmy scampered up the embankment, running and screaming. Mike pursued him, growling, "Simon, give it up. You can't outrun me! I have the conch, I have the conch!"

Dust from Bill's truck warned of his arrival.

"Dad's comin!" Karen called.

Michael stopped chasing and cast aside his spear. "Jimmy, wait up!"

Jimmy kept running, sobbing, gasping for breath. He met his father's pickup and hopped into the back with Joe before it came to a stop. Mike was there a minute later. His father got out and put hands on hips. "All right, what the hell?"

"Nothin'," Mike explained. "We're just playin'."

"Don't look like it to me."

Michael narrowed his eyes on Jimmy. Karen still carried her spear.

"Whatcha got there, sweetheart?" Bill asked.

"Spear. We made 'em."

"What's your brother upset about?"

"Don't know. Ask 'im."

"What's wrong, Jimmy?"

"Nothin'. Twisted my ankle."

"Lemme look."

"Naw, it's okay

"Sure?"

"Yeah."

"Let's go have lunch. I'm so hungry I could eat a coyote."

***

Despite the incessant bullying, Jimmy was impressed by Michael's ingenuity. The next day he came up with the idea for a new sport. It was an incredibly torrid mid-July afternoon, which infected the three of them with lethargy. Yet, children have a tremendous capacity for finding things to do under adverse conditions. On triple-digit days, they sometimes wandered to the grandparent's house for tomato fights. Andrew's tomato garden was his pride and joy, yet on blazing days he sheltered in the house. Gladys occasionally checked on the children if she wasn't busy. Ed was the only one who sometimes hung around with the children.

There was a dog named Ike there. It had showed up one day

with a broken front leg that flopped around uselessly when he ran. Ike was the reason the word mutt resided in the lexicon. He was covered in dirty dreadlocks and spent a great deal of time crapping, pissing, and munching on his butt.

Most folks in the farming community thought Gladys was a bit odd. Instead of purchasing new furniture, she changed colors with spray paint. Ed put his foot down when she offered to repaint his pickup. Usually, she left the kids to their own devices. She wasn't there when Michael roasted ants with a blow torch made with a Lysol can and matches. Nor was she present for the unveiling of Ike's new haircut. Michael found electric sheep shears in a tool drawer kept in the garage. Jimmy and Karen were in charge of holding Ike still as Michael went to work. He'd only finished one side when Ike broke free and disappeared for two days.

"What the hell?" Ed wondered aloud when Ike showed up looking like the yin-yang of mutts.

Bill was there and figured that Michael was involved somehow. Yet, he couldn't bring himself to reprimand his son. After all, *The boy had good intentions.* Parents want to believe in their children even when evidence is stacked against it.

Tomatoes leave an uncomfortable stickiness on the skin. Jimmy didn't like playing tomato war because Mike and Karen ganged up on him. Their T-shirts were covered in tomato juice, skin, and shards. After playing, they rinsed T-shirts beneath a garden hose and put them back on. Heat dried them within a half-hour. They knew if Grandpa roused from his easy chair to face the mummifying heat and saw the ravages of war, his jovial demeanor would be replaced by the one they'd seen once on Thanksgiving.

Michael was able to hurl at the speed of light, once knocking Jimmy out cold with a green tomato to the temple.

"Faker," Michael said.

"Don't think so." Karen shook him by the shoulders.

Jimmy heard a ringing, followed by the shushing of ocean water as it reached the shore. Then he opened his eyes. Mike was turned away with hands stuffed in his pocket. He closed his eyes again.

"Get Grandma."

"Hold your horses. He'll be all right. Remember the woodshed?"

Jimmy opened his eyes again and saw Uncle Ed hurrying over, yelling, "What the hell?" He and his brother's favorite inquiry.

"We were messin' around," Michael tried.

"Jimmy, you okay, boy?"

Jimmy's head cleared, and he sat up. "Think so." He blinked hard.

"Better clean this mess. Grandpa'll shit fire if he sees what you done with his tomatoes."

Jimmy giggled when he pictured someone shitting fire and knew it was a possibility if his uncle ever let one go around an open flame. He made it to his feet, bent over with dizziness. Michael and Karen picked up shrapnel and tossed it off into the distance. Uncle Ed stayed with Jimmy until he was able to join in the cleanup. Then he spun a long creative fart with a wet conclusion.

"Damn near shit myself!" he announced, grabbing the back of his pants. "Uh huh-huh!"

On this particular summer day, Michael came up with a brilliant idea. He was fifteen and stood six feet four. He was slated to grow another two inches before he was finished. He looked more like a giraffe than a boy. That Halloween, his girlfriend Candy painted him green, and he attended a school costume ball as the Jolly Green Giant. She dressed as Tinker Bell. Not yet able to drive, Bill took them to the dance and picked them up afterward. Mike couldn't wait to get his license. He already had plans to borrow his father's truck and use the bed for something other than hauling a shovel and Joe around.

Although he was good-looking, acne dotted Mike's face and back. Mother wouldn't allow him sweets, and she spent many evenings squeezing zits he couldn't reach. As they walked back to the farm from the grandparent's house, Mike had an epiphany.

"Got 'n' idea," Mike said. There were patches of Clearasil medicine on his face that looked like the makeup their mother used.

"Long as it doesn't have tomatoes in it," Karen said.

"How 'bout we tie a rope in the barn to swing on?"

"Where?"

"The beam, dummy. There's a pulley thing up there. If we get a rope around it...."

Four feet above the beam was a one-foot diameter metal pulley with a grooved rim for a rope to pass through. It'd been years since it was used for hoisting hay bales.

"How you gonna do it?"

"Climb up and toss it through."

Jimmy was in awe of what his brother suggested—risking life and limb for the creation of a new diversion.

"I know where there's rope," Mike added.

They snuck into the forbidden red barn. The filthy cement floor was strewn with bat guano, and the metal roof popped beneath the blazing sun. There was a long wooden table with drawers filled with implements of various sizes to fit any need. Many tools were strangely shaped and used exclusively for the John Deere. Also residing in the barn was a cutting torch, arc-welder, and a cement pit covered with wooden slats to work on the undercarriage of trucks or tractors. Hung on corner walls, dried stiff from disuse, was every manner of leather harness, reins, buckles, harkening to days when horsepower ruled. Creaky stairs led to a loft where a horse buggy was stored in pieces. There was a neatly coiled length of rope at the edge.

"I'll push it over." Michael gingerly made his way up the stairs.

At the top, he weaved through stored items—an old steam cleaner, a defunct power generator, an aged saddle with mouse holes, and a dusty magazine laying atop a buggy wheel. He picked it up and brushed off the cover, revealing a naked woman holding her boobs in the palm of her hands, licking the tip of a nipple.

"What's takin' so long?" Karen shouted.

"Hold your horses." Michael slipped the magazine down the front of his pants and went to the rope. He pushed it over the edge, unleashing a cloud of dust when it landed. "Told yuh. It's perfect."

The hemp rope was over an inch thick. Michael descended the stairs, feeling the edges of the magazine digging into his upper thighs. *Hide it in the hay*, he thought.

When they got there, Mike ordered Karen and Jimmy to uncoil the rope.

"I'm gonna go up there to check it out." At the top of the haystack, he lifted a bale and put the magazine under there. Then he stood at the edge next to the beam and looked up at the pulley.

"You're gonna kill yourself," warned Karen.

"Naw." He climbed to the beam and slowly crawled to the center. Then he straddled it and called down. "Throw it up."

Karen grabbed an end and measured out what she'd need. "Look out, Jimmy."

Jimmy backed away as his sister twirled the rope a few times before tossing it. Her first try was way off.

"Christ, Sis."

She tried and failed again.

"Tie a knot to the end, make it heavier."

"Shoulda thoughta that before," she complained.

"Wanna trade places?"

"I will," Jimmy said, feeling brave.

"Remember last time," Karen reminded him.

"Wasn't *my* fault."

"Shut the hell up and try again," Mike said.

Karen tied the knot, and her subsequent throw was perfect. Mike snagged it. Then he wound it, so he had a good length to work with. From a sitting position, he tried to cast the rope over the pulley. After five failed attempts, he stood on quivering legs.

"Just tie it to the beam. Good enough!" Karen was frantic.

"Yeah, Mike," added Jimmy.

"Shut up! Lemme concentrate!"

Though the beam was a yard wide, it looked thin from the ground. Michael swung the rope and slung it upward. He missed. His heart was pounding. He tried again. This time a pigeon took flight with a whirring of wings, and Michael swayed dangerously. Missed again. He swallowed hard. His next toss looped cleanly over the pulley and settled into the groove. He let out slack, grabbed the knot, and sat down, drawing it with him.

"You did it!" Cheered Jimmy.

Mike looked down and smiled. "Told yuh!" He tied a knot that slipped up snug against the pulley. Then he crawled back to the haystack, pausing to stare at the bale hiding his new treasure.

By the time he got down, Karen was already dangling from the rope with ten feet still dragging on the dirt floor. Mike took out a folding knife and sawed off what wasn't needed.

"Lemme try," he demanded. "Later, we'll tie knots for hand-holds," he explained. Yet before he could get in his first good swing, Mother's voice cut through the air.

"Michael, Karen…," and as an afterthought, "Jimmy! Lunch!"

***

1962. The new wall in East Berlin was completed. Throughout history, walls are built to keep people out or in. Walls go up, get torn down, and are rebuilt. Humans build emotional walls that can prove impregnable.

Ego is the strongest.

The kids wolfed down lunch so they could return to the barn. Michael was jam-packed with ideas. He tied a cow halter to the rope so they could swing from the top of the haystack with their arms out like Superman. The first time Jimmy tried, Michael had a field day.

"Look, Sis, a flyin' monkey!"

The joy Jimmy felt as he flew through the air evaporated into shame.

When they grew tired of that, Mike set up markers. You took a running start toward the mouth of the barn and let go at the return. Distance measurements were taken. Of course, Michael was always champ.

Karen and Jimmy pumped Mikey up with retellings of his brave effort to get the rope up. His brain functioned better when heaped with praise. That's when, late afternoon, sweaty with exertion and tired of the new games, he had another epiphany.

"Got a better idea," he announced. Karen and Jimmy followed him to the scrapyard. Piles of metal lay akimbo—channel iron, curtain weights that looked like rusted turds, worn disc blades. "Here," Mike lifted a rusty disc and handed it to Karen. He found another, and they set them aside.

"What you want with these?" Karen wondered.

"You'll see. Let's go to the wood shack."

Jimmy cringed. "You go on. I'll wait at the barn."

"Chickenshit." Mike knew how to get to his brother.

"Fuck you."

"Did you hear that?" Karen was aghast. It was the first time Jimmy used the word in front of her.

"Not tonight, darling. I have a headache," Mike answered, and kept walking. He lifted the drawbar. "Gotta find somethin' to stick in the disk holes." He slipped into the shack, followed by Karen. For a moment, Jimmy thought of revenge, yet Karen was in there, too and didn't deserve it as much. He joined in the search.

Karen found what was needed. "What about these?"

She pointed to a stack of fifteen-foot poles used for knocking prunes off branches before modern harvest methods made them redundant.

"That'll do the trick."

Without thinking, Jimmy let Karen and Michael out first, and an instant later, the door was shut and barred. His left eye instantly began ticking, and a ringing started in his ears. Yet he was determined not to give Mike the pleasure of knowing how frightened he was.

"Did you see that black widow? Bigger now. Swear to God there was a fuckin' mouse in its web."

Jimmy squeezed his eyes shut. His body trembled, yet he held his silence. After a few minutes, Michael grew tired of the game and let him out. Without a word, they took the poles and discs into the red barn. Michael found a hammer and gathered dozens of long, loose nails from a metal bin. He handed Karen a metal tape measure, a black coal pencil and told her to measure off inches, starting at four feet until she reached fourteen feet.

Lastly, they rummaged for a crossbar—something to span the distance between the poles. Jimmy found a long shoot of yellow bamboo. No one could figure out what its purpose had been, yet it was perfect. Mike hammered nails into the hash marks to hold the bar. The end result was a decent likeness to a high-jump stand.

Michael gripped the rope and walked toward the closed end of the barn as far as he could. He kicked some dirt to mark the spot. He set the disk blades about seven feet apart and slipped the poles into the niches. They fit almost perfectly. Lastly, he laid the bamboo across at the five-foot mark.

"Watch." He grabbed the rope.

Michael ran toward the barn opening and swung, using momentum to take him in the other direction toward the bar. When he got close, he pulled himself up, lifted his feet, and dropped to the other side.

Rope vault was born.

As the bar was moved upward, records were broken, and landings became more painful. They put down a square of brown canvas and covered it with hay for cushioning. Then they covered that with another square. Father surprised them by pulling up. He gawked at the spectacle, amazed by the ingenuity. After admonishing Michael for his fool-heartedness in getting the rope attached, he shook his head and smiled.

"I'll be damned." He sat on the tailgate and watched. Inspired, Michael soared ten feet one inch for a new record.

"Try it, Dad!" He challenged.

"I'm fine right here. You kids be careful. Mom finds out she'll have my hide."

Bill took out a chewed Roi-Tan cigar from his front pocket and stuck it in his mouth. He didn't smoke unless he was upset and never around his wife. Instead, he gnawed them down to a stub. The pickup bed was littered with turd-like remnants. That morning he was rebuffed by Barbara after waking up early with primitive urges. He'd been cross all day, smoking two cigars before lunchtime. Seeing his children enjoying their youth made him feel better.

Every once in a while, Mike smuggled one of his father's chewed cigars behind the white barn, lit up, and pretended to be a tough guy. Bill suspected as much, yet figured it was all part of growing up. Bill lit the cigar and watched his children take turns at the bar. With each success, they looked to him for approval. He clapped and removed the cigar with thumb and forefinger to make a comment.

"Looked like you were flyin' there."

More often than not, Jimmy hit the bar. Around their parents, Michael didn't pick on Jimmy as much anymore. "Next time, kid," he encouraged.

After a successful attempt, Jimmy joined his father on the tailgate and stared at the cigar. "Can I try?"

Bill narrowed his eyes at him. "It'll stunt your growth. I'd be tall as Wilt Chamberlain if I hadn't started."

"Really?"

"Yep." Then he added, "Don't tell your mama 'bout this. She thinks I just chew 'em."

"Okay."

So there it was—the first secret Bill kept from his beloved wife.

CHAPTER 8
LOFTUS

There were three kinds of farm kids in those days—rich ones who didn't do squat thanks to the hired help, middle-class kids with after-school chores, and children of poor subsistence farmers in survival mode, whose kids worked their asses off. The Koch family was firmly in the middle. Wealthy farmers owned lots of land and afforded Mexicans for nearly all hard labor needs. They also hired full-time workers, usually white. The Koch family had Loftus.

Loftus may have been in his early sixties. It was hard to tell. His teeth had finished rotting out ten years prior. His gaunt face was pastured with white stubble, and piercing brown eyes were trapped deep within their sockets. Every day he wore the same blue overalls tugged over a long-sleeved shirt. This uniform never changed, even if it was a hundred and twenty. It was noted that he rarely wore socks, which is why Barbara bought him two-dozen pairs every Christmas.

Karen was the first to report that Loftus didn't wear underwear. Her after-school chores included feeding the horse, Fern, as well as the dogs and cats. Out of pity, Bill had bought Fern from Jory Huckabee, one of the poorest farmers. Fern was eighteen and spent time grazing the pasture she shared with the Herefords and chewing on the wooden fence surrounding it. She was so tame that the children would sit on the top rail to click their tongues. Fern would mosey close enough for them to slip on and ride bareback. The horse didn't obey when spurred by bare feet. With reins, she'd move in the direction you wanted, but it was faster to walk. Fern seldom left the corral.

Michael was embarrassed by Fern. He wanted a real horse he could saddle up to pretend he was Rowdy Yates from Rawhide. Karen loved the old nag. Feeding her was easy enough. Karen kept a wheelbarrow in the white barn. A bale was busted up at the foot of the stack to gather, and Fern ate a bale a week. Sometimes her father or Loftus forgot to clip wires holding it together, and if Karen couldn't find wire cutters, she'd climb up and push one over the edge. The bale usually burst open when it hit.

One sticky afternoon she had almost arrived at the barn, freezing, when she heard a rustling of hay. Peeking around the entrance, she saw Loftus squatting in the hay they used as a landing pad for the rope vault. After wiping with a red hanky he carried in his overalls, he stood. She got an eyeful. The sight made her nauseous, and she backed away a good distance to wait. When Loftus emerged, she pretended to have just arrived.

"Hey, missy," Loftus greeted with toothless words that were sometimes hard to understand.

"Hey, Mr. Loftus."

"Need hay?"

"Yeah, I guess."

"Want me to git it for yuh?"

"That's okay. It's my job."

"Okay, missy." Slightly bent from arthritis, he made his way across the dirt road to the B-3 John Deere. He stopped to stuff a pinch of tobacco between his cheek and gum before climbing up.

"Damnit," Karen muttered when she saw that the bale she wanted was still wired. She climbed to the top of the stack and sat one bale to push another from the edge. It smacked the bottom and burst. She noticed the corner of a magazine sticking out from the bale she sat on. The disgust she felt for Loftus was replaced by images from the magazine as she thumbed the pages.

Her mother didn't look anything like the women she saw there. On the cusp of eleven, she didn't understand. *Why in the world would anybody wanna see this*? she wondered. A fold-out page depicted a man in a full tuxedo with a naked redhead fawning over him. Another showed a naked lady on her back with a martini balanced on her tummy, nibbling a green olive impaled by a toothpick. *Must belong to Loftus,* she guessed. *I'll tell Mike.*

When she did, Michael's face turned bright red. "I'll take a look."

"Want me to show you?"

"Naw, that's okay."

Before dark, Mike walked to the barn and returned an hour later.

"Find it?"

"Yeah."

"What yuh think?"

"Burned it."

"Why?"

He shrugged and turned red, knowing the magazine was safely tucked beneath two bales of hay in another area of the haybarn.

Mike was in charge of weeding, watering, and harvesting the family garden beyond the backyard fence. His mother grew tomatoes, carrots, cucumbers, and lettuce. Michael loved hunting for the hornworms that devastated tomatoes if they weren't controlled. They were intimidating—long, fat, with a diagonal white stripe on each body segment and a small black circle centered with a red dot that looked like an eye. The most remarkable detail was the long curved horn they carried on the back of the final segment. For Mike, they were the closest thing to the monsters he watched on Science Fiction Theater. The worms were formidable yet harmless. Father gave him a dime for every one he found.

When you smashed a hornworm, it squirted green guts in all directions. The possibilities for terrorism were endless. If Karen or Jimmy pissed him off, he used hornworms for revenge. He hid them in Jimmy's lunch box, laid them to rest beneath Sissy's bedsheets, and sneaked them into sock drawers. Results were satisfying. Even though he got into trouble for such pranks, it brought a furtive smile to his father's face. Mother warned, "He ever gets one near me, I'll castrate him."

Jimmy was tasked with washing his father's pickup and picking dog shit off the brown front lawn. For the latter, Jimmy used a toy yellow Tonka dump truck and skip-loader he'd gotten for Christmas. When the truck was full, he drove it to a trash barrel fashioned from a large oil barrel. Trash was burned every other day.

***

Lately, Mr. and Mrs. Koch had discussed the need for a bigger house or adding to the existing one. Karen needed her own space. They agreed, for the time being, Jimmy would move in with Mike, and Karen would use Jimmy's room. This caused quite a stir from Michael.

"No way! What's wrong with how it is?"

"Honey," explained Mother, "Boys should be with boys."

"Let 'im sleep in the washroom!"

"This isn't open for discussion."

"C'mon, Mike." His father put in. "Jimmy looks up to yuh."

"Jeez." Mike moped for the rest of the day.

Jimmy wasn't thrilled about the idea either. He lost his personal space, where he was left alone for hours to play with toys or to close his eyes and exercise his imagination. The tiny ten-by-ten room was his father's office until he came along. Now it belonged to Sis, and he'd be at the mercy of Mike. Karen gathered her things, and the rooms were quickly swapped out.

When it was finished, Jimmy sat on his bed and looked around. On Mike's side were posters of Sandy Koufax, Mickey Mantle, Sean Connery, and a calendar with a blonde in a bikini selling car air filters. He had a corkboard covered in pictures of Candy Schubert and newspaper clippings of his baseball exploits. There was a large, shared closet close to his bed with sliding doors. Beneath the bed, he kept his baseball glove. Jimmy thought if anything crept into the room at night, he'd use that to catch it.

CHAPTER 9
LADYSMITH

Jimmy's first night with Michael was memorable.

Without bidding goodnight, Mike turned off the bedroom light by the door. Jimmy was already tucked in. Mike slipped beneath his covers and lay silent for a minute. Faint light sifted in through a small window at the far end of the bedroom. His voice was cold and calculating when he finally spoke.

"Listen, Jimmy, somethin' I gotta tell yuh."

"Yeah?"

"The closet."

"What about it?"

"Remember the cyclops from Seventh Voyage of Sinbad?"

Jimmy didn't say anything, yet his head filled with images of the beast.

"There's one livin' in the closet. Only comes out nights if the door's left open. Have to make sure it always stays shut, got it?"

Jimmy was quiet.

"Got it?"

"Yeah."

"Closed," Mike repeated.

"Got it."

"Now go to sleep. Better not fucking snore."

"I don't snore."

"Better not."

Mike waited ten minutes. Then he slowly reached out his right hand until it came into contact with the closet door. It was too dark for Jimmy to see his brother's hand, but he could hear the door sliding open.

"The door!" Jimmy whispered loudly. "Mikey! The closet!"

Mike breathed loudly, feigning a deep sleep.

"Wake up! It's open!" Jimmy cried out.

"Huh, what? Go back to sleep."

"Closet's open!"

"Shit! Thought I told you—quick, hide under the covers. It can't see under you there!"

Jimmy did as he was bid. For many years after that, he slept with his head beneath the covers. On hot nights he nearly suffocated. Once in a while, he mustered the courage to peek out. As long as his brother was sleeping in the same room, the closet door was always open.

***

Smith & Wesson designed the LadySmith snub-nosed .38 for women. It's easily concealed. They are light, hammerless double-action wheel-guns that won't snag on clothing. A wife can fire without taking it out of her coat pocket or purse. Just point and pull the trigger. For fashion-minded ladies, it should be noted that LadySmith is beautiful to look at. Her finger-grooved handle is made of smooth wood. But don't be fooled by her loveliness. The stainless steel alloy .38 carries a five-shot cylinder with plenty of stopping power.

On April 2, 1956, the day before Jimmy was born, Andrew Koch went to the hardware store in Poplar and bought his wife a LadySmith. Lately, there'd been a spate of farm-equipment thefts, and it was reported in the local news that a knife-wielding man had come to the front door of the Grigsby family ranch house when the wife was alone. Andrew didn't know the Grigsbys, yet he felt empathy. He thought, *If she'd had a LadySmith....*

He presented a gift-wrapped box to his wife.

"What's this?" Gladys wondered.

"Just a little somethin'."

Beneath the box's lid was packing material, and beneath that was LadySmith.

"What in the world, Andrew?"

"Made 'specially for ladies.'"

Gladys wouldn't touch it. She shook her head violently. "Get that thing outta here!"

"But I—"

"Get it out!"

He'd never seen her so upset. No matter how he argued, she wouldn't be swayed, even when he embellished the Grigsby story with sordid details. "What if her kids hadn't been in school?"

"What if one of them found it?" Gladys rebutted.

Grandpa Koch was a pragmatist. Grandma was a pacifist. The brand-new gun stayed inside the box, buried beneath the packing material it came in. He was glad he hadn't wasted money on the shells for it. The hardware store was out of .38s. Andrew Koch banished LadySmith to a top shelf in the storage room, too embarrassed to return it. *Maybe she'll change 'er mind*, he reflected.

Jimmy found LadySmith by accident while his grandparents were watching Truth or Consequences. Rifling through his Grandpa's office desk out of curiosity, he found a steel ring with a dozen keys on it. He decided to see what they belonged to, pretending to be a spy looking for secret documents. A skeleton key locked the basement, which was always left open. Another was for a small kitchen cabinet with nothing in it. He tried others without luck. Then he went out to the storage room. Yes, the one that said Yale fit. There was a light switch chain in the middle of the room, and he yanked it once. Then he closed the door. The twenty-by-twenty room was made of concrete. He opened an old trunk, but there was nothing of interest for a young boy.

One shelf was lined with old-school textbooks and stacks of magazines. He found a box camera and peered through the flip-up lens. There was an Underwood typewriter, and when he tried using it, the keys jammed together. On a top shelf, he found a box that a pair of shoes might come in. He opened it. Beneath a packing of thin white paper sheets and wadded newspaper was LadySmith. His only previous experience with guns was his father's .410 shotgun. He let Jimmy shoot it a few times. The sound was deafening, and it made his shoulder sore.

"Gotta hold it tight and squeeze the trigger," Bill advised, replacing the shell with a fresh one and handing it over again. "Keep it pointed to the ground until you're ready to use it."

He shot it once more, and that was enough. His father laughed and chomped on his cigar.

Jimmy hefted LadySmith in his hand. It felt heavy, yet somehow comforting.

When his brother went off to college, Jimmy smuggled LadySmith into his room. *LadySmith* was engraved in cursive on the side. He hid it beneath his bed-frame during the day and under his pillow at night. Even without ammunition, he felt safer having it.

CHAPTER 10
KOCK 1967

Jimmy was eleven. Mr. Ganns still taught sixth-grade, though it was rumored this would be his last year. He kept a plywood paddle—shaped like an oversized ping-pong paddle—in the top drawer of his desk, its handle lovingly wrapped in bicycle tape. He called it the Whomper. Ganns only spanked boys.

Jimmy sat in the middle of the class and kept his mouth shut. He wore metal-framed glasses now, and for a time, he endured the ritual of being called four-eyes. The school desks were ancient, with tops that were lifted for storage. Graffiti covered every desk. There was an ink-well in the top-right corner. Beneath each desk was a century's worth of gum.

Clay Smith was well acquainted with the Whomper.

Clay Smith got it from both sides. Teachers didn't like him because he never paid attention in class. Kids didn't like him just because. Just because was a satisfactory response for most sixth-graders.

In reality, Clay Smith was a large, sweet, passive boy. He was tall, big-boned, and heavy as if predestined to fill a large hole somewhere down the road of life, perhaps as a professional wrestler. He had straight, unruly hair and an overbite which made it difficult to pronounce consonants like t, s, and ch. He wore black-framed glasses and showed up at school in the same clothes all week. His body gave off a strong odor. It's as if Clay was born with three strikes.

Woodland provided several housing projects for farm workers. Mostly Mexicans lived there. Clay was an exception. He lived in a ramshackle dwelling better suited to chickens. Jimmy knew the only reason Clay even bothered coming to school was because he qualified for a free lunch in the cafeteria. He ate everything in sight. The cafeteria workers were all Latina. They felt compassion for Clay. He always came back for seconds and thirds if there were any leftovers.

Whenever Ganns saw Clay nodding off in class, he'd call on him to answer a question. His usual response was, Huh? Even though Ganns expected no other response, it still angered him. Once every few weeks, Clay was ordered to the back room, where Ganns doled out punishment.

Before class one morning, a kid named Armando bet Jimmy a dollar he wouldn't chew a piece of gum stuck beneath a desk.

"Show me the dollar."

Armando held it out. "I get to choose the gum."

"Deal."

Armando went to the desk Clay Smith sat in.

"Hell no!" Jimmy protested.

"You made a deal."

Secretly he felt sorry for Clay. Jimmy was no stranger to bullying. He shuffled around on his feet. "All right, let's get it over with."

Five or six other boys gathered around to witness the rite of passage. With an effort, Armando freed a ball of fossilized gum from beneath the desk. There were over twenty to choose from. Jimmy popped it in his mouth.

"Gotta chew."

Saliva finally made the task possible. He chewed and showed it with his tongue, then spit it out. "Phew!"

Armando was laughing to beat the band. "What's it taste like?"

It didn't taste like anything. "Rat's ass. Gimme my dollar."

"Jimmy ate Smith's gum!"

For a minute, Jimmy was in the spotlight. Then he saw Clay standing at the entrance to the class, looking despondently at the tile floor. Suddenly Jimmy felt smaller than ever.

Ganns came over. His white hair made his face look redder than usual.

"What's goin' on?"

Armando and the others backed away, leaving Jimmy to stand alone.

"Nothin', Mr. Ganns."

"Did you just spit gum on the floor?"

"Was an accident. I sneezed, and it sorta shot out."

"Yeah?" Ganns could sniff out a lie for miles. "Now you can spend recess and lunch scraping gum off every desk in this room."

Jimmy clenched his teeth. The bell rang. He asked if he could get a drink of water.

"No. Sit down."

Clay went outside when Ganns confronted Jimmy and returned tardy.

"You're late, Clay. You can stay at recess and lunch to help Mr. Koch with the gum harvest."

Dolores Patchin sat at the desk behind Jimmy. She tapped his shoulder. "You're gonna get rabies, and they're gonna stick a big ol' needle in your stomach."

At lunchtime, Ganns sat at his desk and ate from a brown bag. Jimmy had brought his lunch from home too, but Clay had nothing. Ganns gave each a pair of safety scissors as a tool to remove the gum.

"Can I eat first, Mr. Ganns?"

"Five minutes."

Jimmy sat in his seat. Clay began working. Jimmy paused mid-bite on his bologna sandwich. He took a deep breath and tore it in half.

"Clay."

Clay didn't seem to hear.

"Clay!"

He looked up.

"Here." Jimmy held out the sandwich half.

Clay smiled and gratefully accepted. "Thanks."

"Yeah."

Ganns looked up briefly, then resumed his attack on a chicken drumstick.

Clay had wolfed his half. Jimmy fished inside his paper bag for an apple and two Hostess Ding Dongs.

"Here."

"You sure?"

"Yeah."

"Thanks."

A few minutes later, Ganns put them back to work. Jimmy was tall for his age, yet Clay dwarfed him. A few minutes later, Clay chuckled and motioned Jimmy closer, pointing to an inscription beneath a desk scrawled in permanent black marker. *FUCK YOU GANNS*! Jimmy smiled and gave Clay a thumb's up. The bond was complete. Clay wasn't what you'd call a bosom buddy—more a comrade in arms.

One cold November morning during recess, Jimmy participated in a familiar game. Water puddles were frozen over, and the boys liked breaking off chunks of ice, sneaking up on girls, and putting them down the back of their shirts or dresses. Watching them jiggle and dance was a cheap thrill. Since Jimmy had proven his bravery with the gum challenge, it was decided he'd be the best choice for a dare. The idea originated from Augusto Vasquez.

It had rained recently, and there were lots of puddles to choose from. You only had to step in one, clutch a piece of fractured ice, and search for a victim. Jimmy was pressured to put one down the front of Marcia Turman's dress. Marcia was the logical choice because she was the most developed of the sixth-grade girls. She liked showing off in V-neck shirts and plunging floral-print dresses. Ganns placed her at the front of the class. Marcia was a tough girl and wasn't shy about smacking boys when they got fresh.

At first, everything went as planned. Jimmy broke off a thick chunk of ice from a puddle near the bike racks. Boys watched from a safe distance as Jimmy meandered toward Marcia Turman, who was busy talking to friends. He walked as though he were a chicken crossing the road, concentrating on the other side. As he drew parallel to Marcia, he expertly deposited the ice down the front of her dress.

Marcia immediately lowered the straps to fish it out. Onlookers caught a glimpse of her breasts. Marcia tore out after him, but he escaped into the boy's bathroom, his glasses nearly slipping off on the way. The bell rang to return to class. She was waiting just outside the door.

"I'm gonna beat you, Kock, hear me? I gotta older brother and a mean goddamn uncle!"

"Get to class!" Jimmy shouted.

"They're gonna fuck you up!"

By the time Jimmy made it to class, he was two minutes late and a dollar short. Matthew Cloninger looked at Jimmy from across the way and shook his head gravely.

Ganns stood waiting around the corner with hands on his hips. His face was burgundy. Marcia was next to him, chewing gum rapidly. Although gum wasn't allowed in class, Ganns was making an exception. Clay was in the back row close to where they stood.

"Mr. Koch, you have an appointment." He pointed to the back of the room.

The back of the class was separated by bookshelves and storage cabinets. When somebody was whomped, the rest of the class could clearly hear it. Jimmy's body turned to jelly. His legs shook, and his eyes began tearing ahead of time. Through a blur of warm water, he saw Clay watching. His face was sympathetic. Jimmy walked past him on the way to the back.

Having heard Whomper results, Jimmy stared at the side door of the classroom next to the sink. *Freedom*, he thought. The side door led to the front of the school and was used only in an emergency or for fire drills. *This is an emergency*. Yet he figured it would go worse for him if he ran. Parents from both sides would be called in, and he'd probably have to endure more than one thumping. Marcia's uncle or big brother would catch him alone sometime. *Probably cut my nuts off*, thought Jimmy. His glasses began fogging up.

The classroom was quiet. He heard Ganns walking to his desk and sliding open the drawer where Whomper lived. Footsteps regressed, getting closer and closer.

Jimmy thought of Clay. When the Whomper came crashing down on Clay, he hardly made a sound, just a low *uhn*. Afterward, he returned to his seat and rested his head over folded arms. Ganns always left him alone for the rest of the day.

Ganns was there. *How many?* Jimmy wondered. The amount of blows depended on the severity of the crime. Ice down a dress, the subsequent revelation—*what will it cost?* Ganns had a white-knuckle grip on the Whomper's handle. *A lot*, Jimmy guessed.

There was a wooden chair back there. Ganns pointed, "Bend over and grab the back."

Jimmy did as he was told. He knew that soon after this was done, word would spread like wildfire. His sister would find out and use it against him. All because of a dare. A stupid goddamn—

The first whomp took Jimmy by surprise—as though he sat naked in a pile of red ants. It was followed by another. Jimmy's fogged-up glasses fell off onto the seat of the chair. He heard a sound coming from his throat—a chimpanzee screaming high in the trees. *Christ, my brother was right.* Another swat sealed Whomper's victory. Jimmy wailed and screamed for mercy. *I'll never sit again.* In the reflection of his glasses, he saw red-faced Ganns, his arm swinging back. Jimmy shut his eyes tightly, yet the next blow never came.

There was Clay with a hand clamped around Ganns's wrist. With his other, he twisted the Whomper out of his grasp, and with a swift motion, Clay brought the weapon down hard over his knee and broke it in half. He pointed the jagged handle at Ganns, who backed away. Then he tossed it aside disdainfully. For a brief moment, Clay locked eyes with Jimmy, and then he stormed through the back door, a stream of light flooding in before it closed behind him.

Ganns was a defeated man after that. Clay was a metaphor for malleability, shaping yourself into whatever you desired. Ganns took early retirement during the winter break and was replaced by Mrs. Shardik. On the first day of her reign, she earned the nickname, Sharkdick.

Mrs. Shardik must have been a beauty at one time, yet a car accident left her with prominent scarring on her face. The corner of her upper lip was damaged, so she always seemed to be smiling. She had thick black hair and a body that reminded Jimmy of Sophia Loren, a voluptuous Italian actress at the time. Despite scars, it was impossible not to notice her large, firm breasts staring when she faced you. They earned a nickname of their own—Bazookas. Whomper was replaced by the bazookas. She used them as a torture device, kneeling next to boys' desks to help them understand. And yes, the boys understood.

When she caught a boy staring at her bazookas, he was given detention and forced to write *I will not* about a quadrillion times, or worse, receive a lecture. She'd sit the offender directly in front of her and lean over to lecture him about his behavior. She insisted that perpetrators look her in the face, which was virtually impossible.

Clay returned to school after the break for a short time, long enough to be there when two ladies came to school to test hearing. It was determined that Clay was hearing impaired. They loaned him an amplifier and headphones for the classroom and suggested he sit closer to the front. Mrs. Shardik reluctantly complied. A few weeks later, Clay was gone. Nobody seemed to know where. The strange thing is everyone missed him. Clay was what hearts are made of. He taught more about social justice than any teacher ever did.

***

In 1967 Karen was finishing at Woodland. That year her teacher was Mr. Ryneman. He was handsome, and Jimmy overheard her gossip to friends about him. She was thirteen, and hormones were sabotaging her brain, changing her into an average student with delusions regarding Mr. Ryneman. During recess and lunch, she and her girlfriends hung around him. In class, they volunteered for menial tasks that needed doing.

One of Karen's eighth-grade friends was Norma. Her last name was Martin, thanks to a white stepfather, but her mother's maiden name was Ortiz. Norma was pretty. She had flirted with boys until Mr. Ryneman came along. She lived within walking distance of the school and arrived as early as possible.

The ending bell sent Karen and Jimmy to the orange bus, where Floyd was waiting to sing them all the way to Palm Tree Lane. Norma stayed behind, erased the chalkboards, and talked with Mr. Ryneman about how immature boys were and how she didn't want anything to do with them. He smiled and commented shortly as he graded papers.

***

"Any boy'd be lucky to have you." *Stop right there*, he thought.

"Think so?"

He stopped grading and looked up. "Know so." He turned back to his papers. *There's a line. Don't cross.*

"Why do you think that?" She moved, so she was looking closely over his shoulder, pressing against him.

Jesus! A war raged within. His heart raced in his throat and pounded elsewhere, reminding him of how powerful primitive urges were. *Married, first baby on the way. She's thirteen. Get up, go home. Sweet Christ....*

And he did. The next day he showed up ten minutes before class and left right after the final bell. He followed the routine for the rest of the term. The following school year, he accepted an English position at Meadowland High School. Norma was a freshman sitting in the front row, and by Christmas, Mr. Ryneman was a broken man. He lost his job and subsequently was registered as a sex offender.

***

Michael parlayed his baseball talent into an athletic scholarship to the University of Riverside. He'd caused a sensation in high school, winning twelve games his senior year and getting noticed by professional and college scouts. Riverside is the smoggiest city in California. In between innings, the shortstop had to breathe through wet towels to keep asthma attacks at bay.

Mike came home for Christmas and holidays. In the off-season, he grew his hair out long, sporting long sideburns and a wide mustachio. He introduced Jimmy to new music—Bob Dylan, Pink Floyd, The Rolling Stones, and Johnny Cash thrown in for variety. Candy Schubert tried to reconnect with him after high school, yet Mike wasn't interested. The relationship petered after their sophomore year in high school, yet she persisted in trying to reignite old flames. She took classes at Meadowland Junior College and didn't have a clue as to what she wanted out of life. Mike knew exactly what he wanted, and it didn't include her.

By now, you'd think big brother would've eased up on little brother. After all, he was studying biology, conducting bee research, and had friends with benefits in Riverside. The world was his oyster. Yet, it was as if breathing the hot, dry air of the central San Joaquin Valley had a dumbing effect on him.

One early spring break morning, Michael sneaked over to Jimmy as he slept. After lowering his underwear, he placed himself inches from Jimmy's nose and farted. Jimmy thought of LadySmith and was determined to find ammunition for her. For now, he resorted to his usual epitaph.

"Hate your guts, and I wish you were dead!"

Matthew Cloninger found three .38 shells in a metal pail, along with bolts, nuts, metal screws and nails, while rummaging around in his father's workshop for a bolt to fix his skateboard. They were dirty yet cleaned up reasonably well. Matthew knew about LadySmith, and gave them to Jimmy just before winter break with a warning: "Don't shoot your sister 'til I get a crack at her."

Matthew had a thing about Karen. Their families gathered for an annual Fourth of July celebration at the Cloninger farm. Matthew devoured her with his eyes yet was too nervous to talk to her. Even when he reached high school, he asked about her.

Jimmy slipped the three bee's into the hive as soon as he got home. He knew there wasn't a cyclops in the closet, yet his fears manifested in other ways.

Often he awoke at night sweating beneath the covers, listening to night sounds, and imagining footfalls just outside the window. Once a raccoon scratched at a mesh vent beneath the house. Jimmy pulled the hammer back and rested his finger on the trigger. The raccoon made a funny cat-like sound, and he relaxed. He thought about his brother, who was back at the university now. *Swear to God, next time he tries to fart in my face, i'll stick LadySmith up his ass and pull the trigger.*

After winter break, despite attempts to keep a low profile, kids persisted in calling him, Kock. Mrs. Shardik mispronounced his name when she called on him to read from Charlotte's Web.

"Mr. Kock, would you please continue?"

That opened Pandora's box.

"Kocks can't read," whispered Edmundo Garza.

"Yeah, they can," answered Leroy Hubble. "Got an eye, ain't they?"

The rest of the year, Jimmy endured an endless stream of Kock jokes. Shark-dick asks a question: Call on Kock! Kock knows! Shark-dick wants to know where Jimmy is: Kock's inside!

Whenever he looked around in class, someone was mouthing Kock. Matthew Cloninger got into the game by blurting Kock-uh-doodle doo! during a spelling test. Boys tortured girls by asking if they liked Kock.

Although he wasn't as tall as his brother, with the absence of Clay, Jimmy was the tallest in his class. When he pitched during baseball season, teammates called out, C'mon, Big Kock, blow it past him!

By the end of the school day, Jimmy's ears were ringing, and he felt a familiar twitch beneath his left eye. He lost his appetite and spent a lot of time after school reading in the white barn. Every month the bookmobile came to Woodville, and he checked out the maximum of three books. His love of reading was the one thing he inherited from his mother.

Barbara had an insatiable taste for historical romance. She devoured books that seemed to share the same cover—partially dressed white women in the arms of ardent lovers, fronting a southern mansion.

Jimmy devoured Edgar Rice Burroughs, Jules Verne, Robert E. Howard, and H.G. Wells—swashbuckling tales of heroes saving beautiful women, clashing with sorcerers, demons, and monsters. This got him thinking if fantasy heroes could vanquish evil with a sword or knife, so might he.

First chance he got, Jimmy returned LadySmith to his

grandfather's storeroom. The rest of the afternoon, he nosed around the red barn for something sharp, settling on a rusty two-foot machete with an orange handle. In a tool drawer, he found the sharpening stone. At the top of the haystack in the white barn, he honed the blade, removing rust and making it razor-sharp. *This's better,* he thought. *With a gun, you could make a mistake. Not with this.* He held up the blade and slashed at the air, then brought it down on a bale, severing baling wire. *Oops.*

The new weapon fit neatly beneath his bed under a wooden slat. That first night before clicking off the lights, he made sure the closet was wide open. He'd confront the enemy directly. If darkness took shape, he would battle, defeat it, and send it back into the shadows. He closed his eyes. Within a minute, he opened them a slit to scan the room. He closed them again, this time for over two minutes. Sweat trickled down his face. He opened just long enough to ensure there were no shapes darker than the night moving toward him. He closed again. *Don't open. Nothing there.* His grip tightened on the machete. The longer he kept his eyes shut, the more he became Conan, Tarzan, Captain Nemo, and Doc Savage, challenging intruders to infringe on his realm.

Sunlight streamed in through his window when he awakened. He felt more refreshed than he could remember. The machete was next to him. *Now*, he is determined. *I'll study boxing, karate, something like that. I'll only need these.* He lifted his hands to make fists.

That afternoon Jimmy used money he'd saved from doing chores to mail-order "Train Your Hands to Be Deadly Weapons." He found the advertisement in a Famous Monsters of Filmland magazine. He also sent for an alligator.

In the sixties, you could order an alligator or Caiman through the mail in California. Spider monkeys were also available, costing $29.95 plus tax, including the tiny cage they shipped in. Squirrel monkeys were $19.95. He settled on a sidekick that could help win the war against evil. An alligator.

By mid-February, it was clear he'd wasted five dollars on the Deadly Weapons guide. When it arrived, it was nothing more than five typed pages with crude cartoon demonstrations. The eye gouge, knife-hand thrust, kick to the groin—he practiced them over and over. With no one to spar with, he attacked hay bales, the walnut tree, and thin air.

CHAPTER 11
SYDNEY

Sydney arrived on a cold Saturday afternoon in a shoe box with holes in it. The box was cross-tied with heavy twine. The name, Sydney, was inspired by a story Jimmy read in Outdoor Magazine about a giant crocodile in Australia snagging swimmers. Incredibly, Sydney survived the rigor of mail delivery with gusto.

Bill usually picked up the mail every afternoon after 2:00. Lately, Jimmy had volunteered for the duty, which made his father suspicious. Then he remembered that school was out and no academic deficiency notices would be arriving for Jimmy to intercept. Mrs. Shardik had sent three that year for math, social studies, and citizenship. Citizenship meant behavior. In the comment section, she wrote: Jimmy has trouble focusing during class. She should have written: Jimmy can't stop ogling my Bazookas.

The afternoon of Sidney's arrival, Jimmy's father was meeting a loan officer at the Farmer's Credit Association in Meadowland and arrived home late. Jimmy and Karen rode bikes to their grandparents to make Jell-O chocolate instant pudding and drink Seven-up. He lost track of time because Science Fiction Theater was playing Attack of the Crab Monsters, one of his favorites. Ed watched with them, laughing when a fake-looking claw moved awkwardly toward a victim. "Uh huh-huh!"

Andrew was asleep in his favorite chair, and Gladys was out looking for something to add to her interesting things collection. More on that later.

Their mother was home, writing an order for more romance books. She read two or three hours every day, and the collection was usurping space previously reserved for *Reader's Digest* and the set of encyclopedias used for decoration. Barbara's novels had titles like *Wife by Arrangement*, *The Flame and the Flower*, and *Storm Fire*. Jimmy never paid them any attention until he fanned through *Valley of the Dolls*. That was the beginning of the dog-ear years. Jimmy stayed up late reading dog-eared pages, keeping Kleenex handy by his bed.

In addition to bodice-rippers, she hid other books in her underwear drawer—*Cindy's Desire*, *Maidenhead Tales*, *John's Seed*. On a whim that afternoon, she decided to brave the chill and walk to the mailbox at the entrance of Palm Tree Lane. The palms, planted by Bill's great-grandfather, were thirty feet tall, sticking up like enormous Q-tips. Everyone in the farming community knew the path as Palm Tree Lane, lending an ostentatious air to the farm. As she strolled, Barbara imagined a southern mansion looming in the background, magnolia's dripping with fragrant flowers, black folks singing in cotton fields, and a mint Julep awaiting journeys end. She fantasized about the men she read about—what they did with their women.

Nearing forty, Barbara found herself daydreaming often, wondering if something had been lost on the Palm Tree Lane of her life. She checked herself as she walked, trying to see what others did. She was trim and shapely. Her short dark hair was carefully dyed to cover gray streaks. She slowed her pace as she neared the mailbox. Without a sweater, her nipples revealed themselves through her cotton blouse with the top two buttons left undone.

In farm communities, you're acquainted with nearly everyone, even the mailman. He was thirty-one-year-old Delbert, who drove a '64 Studebaker Avanti. Every December twenty-third, Barbara placed a bottle of wine in the mailbox for him. Today he arrived at the same moment she did. The shoebox he delivered would have barely fit in the oblong metal mailbox. He idled and waited for her. His windows always rolled down.

"Hi, Delbert," she greeted him.

"Mrs. Koch, how 're you doin' this fine day?"

"A bit chilly," she said, noticing that Delbert's eyes tried unsuccessfully not to stray to the front of her blouse.

She handed him her purchase order in exchange for a new *Readers Digest*, assorted junk mail, and the mysterious box.

She grasped the box. "What in the world...?"

Del shook his head. "I've no idea. Has air holes, see?"

"Somethin' Jimmy ordered, no doubt." She handed it back to Del. "What you think's in there?"

Del tipped the box back and forth, resulting in a scurrying sound. He shrugged and handed it back. She studied Del, noticing his surly brown hair, boyishly handsome face, and straight teeth.

"Here." Del offered her a small jackknife. "Got my curiosity up."

Barbara kneeled with the box as Del peered down from the car. A gap in Barbara's white cotton blouse offered him a clear view. She wore red lipstick and had beautiful hazel eyes. He swallowed hard as she cut the string and lifted the lid.

Barbara screamed, dropped the lid, and scrambled backward on her hands and feet. "Oh my God, what *is* that?"

Del got out of the car, carefully straddling the box. He squatted and peered into the container. There was Sydney, all nine inches of him, wriggling excitedly with the winter sun beating down on his ridged back.

"It's a goddamn alligator," Del blurted. He offered Barbara a hand up.

She cautiously looked into the box. Sydney had settled. His head was raised, mouth open, as if saying Ahhh, for Dr. Parkinson.

"Jimmy," she murmured. "That little shit."

Del laughed. "Don't be too tough on 'im. Coulda been worse. Seen where you can order tarantulas, lizards, and whatnot."

"I'm *not* walkin' home with this thing."

"Hop in. I'll take yuh." Del put the lid on the box, re-tied the string, and set it on the back seat. Then he cleared the passenger seat of deliverables so she could sit next to him.

"Can't believe this. Wait 'til I get my hands—"

"Kids 're curious, Mrs. Koch. Had a pet gopher snake when I was a kid. Named him Petey. Lasted 'bout a week."

"What does this thing eat?" Barbara nodded toward the back. She was calmer now, enjoying Del's attention.

"Bit of meat, I'd guess. Raw hamburger, maybe some minnows or tadpoles. He probably won't last long. Read about folks flushin' 'em down toilets in New York City, and they grow up in the sewers."

"I read that too."

A few minutes later, he parked in front of the house.

"Let me take it in for yuh."

"I'd really appreciate that, Del." Barbara liked a man who took charge.

"He's too small to be dangerous."

"Just set it in the kitchen," she said.

"Got somethin' else to put him in?"

"I'll let Jimmy figure that out." *The toilet*, she thought.

"Gonna let him keep it?"

She heaved a heavy sigh and smiled. "We'll dig a moat around the house. That'll keep the Jehovah's Witnesses away."

Del laughed. "That'll do the trick all right."

"Jimmy and his sister are at their grandparents'." Her eyes

softened. "Bill's in Meadowland all afternoon. Can't stand the idea of bein' here alone with this thing."

Del felt a lump forming in his throat. "I can stay a while if you want."

"That'd be nice. I'll get you a beer."

***

Jimmy pulled up to the mailbox on his bike. *Empty*. He raced Karen down Palm Tree Lane and was surprised to win. The mailman passed by, going the other way, smiling and waving weakly. Without taking his hand off the handlebars, Jimmy tossed his head up and down to acknowledge him.

When they reached home, their mother was in the shower. Jimmy saw the shoebox on the kitchen counter and cautiously lifted the lid.

"Look, Sis! It finally came!"

"What?" She rushed over and looked into the box. "What the—?"

"It's Sidney."

Barbara came out, fluffing her wet hair with a towel. She was smiling to herself before she noticed the children. Her serene face flashed angrily. "You get that thing outta here right now."

"I'll put him in my room."

"No, you will not. It's not stayin' in the house, is that clear?"

"The washroom—"

"Not anywhere I can see it."

Jimmy put the top back on and carried it outside.

"Where yuh gonna put 'im?" Karen asked.

"Carport, I guess."

"Isn't it too cold?"

"He'll be all right in there long as the cats don't get 'im."

CHAPTER 12
THREE R's

Jimmy brought Sydney to school one day, thinking it would make him more popular. They had already forgotten about the gum challenge and the ice incident. Surprisingly, Mrs. Shardik was fine with having Sydney as a guest and showed no fear of the creature. Sydney looked up at her with a toothy grin.

Matthew whispered, "He's starin' at the bazookas."

Sharkdick didn't need a wooden paddle. She eviscerated bad behavior with menial tasks—filling pages with *I will not*, or making victims face the bazookas during lunch detention.

At Woodland Elementary, Jimmy was a minority. Woodland was a farm labor community populated primarily by Chicanos and Mexicans. The few white families surviving there were mostly poor. Mexican kids were usually nice, but Chicanos were different. You had to *earn* their respect. Many of them carried beef with gringos like Jimmy. He represented the privileged ruling class. Their job was making soft-shelled güero's miserable. Jimmy always had new clothes to start the school year, reminding Chicanos of the Grand Canyon separating their life from his.

Three particular Chicanos made life hell for Jimmy. He knew them as the three Rs, Raymond, Ricardo, and Refugio. Each day they showed up to school in T-shirts and Levi's, dark hair slicked back with gel. They pushed tacks into the heels of their battered shoes, so they aggressively clicked with each step on hard surfaces.

Summers, his father hired them to work in the fields. Seeing them on the ranch made his left eye twitch and his ears ring. To be fair, the boys had it rough. Each suffered from abusive stepfathers. During the school year, they were made to work Saturdays in the fields and never allowed to keep the money they earned. Legally you could obtain a work permit at fourteen, yet farmers needed workers and seldom asked for them. They paid cash to minors to avoid trouble.

When Jimmy brought Sydney, the three Rs lined up with the rest of the class to see him. Sharkdick demonstrated her valor by offering a minnow. Immediately it snapped, and the fish was gone. When it was Ricardo's turn, he teased the alligator with his finger, and Sydney snapped at it.

"Puta madre!" Ricardo jumped back. The entire class erupted into laughter. He pointed to Jimmy. "You gonna pay, white boy."

Mrs. Shardik hid a smile in her hand, and for a moment, she looked absolutely gorgeous.

The boys' bathroom was one of the only places you could do business without a teacher showing up. Dirty magazines were exchanged there. Cigarettes and alcohol were traded, along with juicy bits of gossip. The rumor mill worked at full capacity in the boys' room. That's where the three Rs cornered Jimmy.

Morning recess after the snapping incident, Refugio stood guard at the entrance, and the other two went in after Jimmy. Standing at a urinal, Jimmy heard the unmistakable clicking of tacks on the green tile floor. They stood back and waited for him to finish. Ricardo did the talking.

"Time to pay up, güero."

"For what?" Jimmy asked.

"Your fucking monstruo almost took my finger off."

"How's that my fault?"

Raymond stepped in front of Ricardo and shoved Jimmy hard. His head butted hard against the wall, and his glasses flew off and clacked to the dirty tile floor, sliding beneath a toilet stall. Raymond's knee went up, catching Jimmy squarely. He went down immediately, gasping for breath. Raymond stepped back to admire his work, and then they left. No one else came in. The recess-ending bell sounded. Jimmy managed to get to his feet. A large bump raised on the back of his head.

A toilet flushed, and an eighth grader named Bernie Sanchez came out holding Jimmy's glasses. He handed them to him, washed his hands, and left.

***

Jimmy sneaked off the school grounds and walked along the road toward the ranch five miles east. After forty minutes, a yellow station wagon pulled next to him. It was Floyd, the custodian. He leaned to roll down the passenger window.

"Thought I'd find you here. Hop in."

Jimmy shook his head.

"Fair 'nough. Mrs. Shardik says you had some kinda run-in."

Jimmy kept walking.

"Wanna talk about it?"

"Nope." Jimmy was already figuring ways to kill the three Rs.

"Listen, Jimmy. Them guys'll get what's comin', don't you worry. Need to tell Mr. Johnson what happened. Is it true you brought a crocodile? Like to see that."

"It's an alligator. I ain't goin' back."

"Know how yuh feel, son, but sometimes a guy's gotta."

Jimmy slowed to a stop. Without looking at Floyd, he got into the car. He wanted his alligator back. Along the way, he cursed the fact that he hadn't thought to fight back.

Johnson was sympathetic. Mild-mannered as he was, he also had gum stuck beneath his desk. He pursed his lips.

"Ricardo, Rogelio, and Raymond are suspended for two weeks." He knew the fathers of the boys would punish them more efficiently than he dared.

Johnson asked Jimmy questions, putting a few words in his mouth to make it more serious for his report.

"We have a statement from one witness. He says that after Ricardo and Ramon slammed you up against the wall and kicked you—"

"Just Ramon did that," Jimmy tried to set the record straight. Johnson nodded and took notes.

"Okay. Think that'll do it for now. Sorry this happened. You can go on back to class."

Jimmy headed for the exit, and Johnson's voice stopped him.

"Hey. Saw that alligator. Really somethin'. What's it eat?"

"Fingers," said Jimmy.

Mr. Johnson laughed. "Go on now."

***

Sydney lasted four weeks in the oval metal container he called home. It was the same place Jimmy had kept Go-go gopher years before. There was a bowl of water buried at ground level in there, and Jimmy set him in the sun every day. He put minnows in the water dish and watched Sydney gulp them.

Mother wouldn't allow Syd anywhere near her, so Jimmy kept it in a far corner of the carport.

"Can't be outside. It's too cold, and cats might get 'im." Jimmy said.

"That'd break my heart."

"C'mon, Mom. He's interesting, don't yuh think?"

She shook her head and turned her thoughts toward Del, her only connection to the alligator. Lately, Bill had made the mail pickup into clockwork. His work kept him too close for her to manage another special delivery from Del. *Yes, he delivered. Delivered so well. Patience,* she thought. *A shopping trip to Meadowland. A cheap hotel. A few hours together.*

One morning while having breakfast, a strange yowl issued from the carport. Jimmy darted out and was amazed to see Sydney clamped onto Louie's nose. Louie shook his head and pawed, but Sydney held fast. Desperate growls were followed by yowling as the cat twisted in circles.

"Get it off 'im!" cried Karen.

Bill stepped forward, but Barbara held him back. "Let Jimmy."

Jimmy cringed at the thought of prying Sydney's jaws open and fighting off the cat's whirlwind claws and teeth. He took a step forward and froze. The cat was bleeding.

Karen yelled, "Kill it!"

Bill shook his arm free and stepped forward. Jimmy stuffed his hands into his pockets and watched with slumped shoulders. The cat sidled away and hissed. "C'mon, cat. Just gonna…."

Father's hand shot out. He gripped the cat by the neck and squeezed Sydney's upper and lower jaw until it popped open long enough for the cat to escape. Bill dropped the alligator, and his tail lashed from side to side. Karen ran after Louie, but he'd found a hole in the mesh vent beneath the house and disappeared. Sydney was walking up the driveway. Jimmy put a foot out to stop him. Bill got a shovel from the back of his pickup and scooped him back into the container. Jimmy saw that his father had scratches on his hands.

"Here, kitty-kitty-kitty!" Karen pleaded for Louie to come out, and it was two days before he did. The puncture wounds weren't serious, yet the terror Sydney wrought was never forgotten. A few weeks later, Jimmy buried Syd beneath the walnut tree, and a few months later, Jimmy dug him up to see what he looked like. He also exhumed the yellow Indian for good measure.

Soon after, while walking home from school on Palm Tree Lane, Jimmy spotted a small tarantula. He coaxed it into his backpack, named it Harry, and stored him in a mason jar with holes punctured in the top. Harry lasted a few days.

***

Summer of 1969 was a time of change. Karen would be entering her junior year of high school. Michael was working on a BS in biology. Jimmy had a long way to go.

That summer, Michael returned home past midnight in early June. The temperature was a tolerable eighty-eight degrees. Michael coasted into the driveway in a red '65 Volkswagen van, adding to the hippie image he created in the off-season. He won accolades for his pitching that year and another deferment from the Vietnam war. He sneaked into the house carrying two paper sacks, leaving two bags full of clothes (one dirty) in the van. In one sack were a few simple gifts for the family—a paper red rose for his mother, a UC Riverside Highlanders baseball cap for his father and Jimmy, and a Frank Zappa poster for Karen, depicting the popular singer sitting on a toilet. It was labeled, Phi Zappa Crappa. In the other sack was a yellow plastic Wiffle-bat and three balls. The front door was unlocked for him.

Jimmy's grip on the machete tightened when he heard a noise at the front door, footsteps entering the house. Sleep-fogged, his brain didn't process that it was Mike. Fear was tempered by fortitude. He forced himself from beneath the covers and allowed his eyes to adjust.

He pictured the scene in his mind. *Rush at 'im screaming a warrior cry, slash 'til he's down, keep slashing 'til he's tiny pieces.* For a brief moment, he imagined his photo on the front page of the *Meadowland Recorder*. What would Marcia Turman think? Maybe she'd finally forget about the ice and give him a break. Rumor was she'd already done it with a high school kid.

The creak of the wood floors gave away the intruder's location. *In the kitchen, opening the fridge. In the living room, sitting on the sofa.*

Jimmy's hand rested on the doorknob. His machete hand ached. He heard a belch. *Could be Dad. Sometimes he checks irrigation at night, back in the kitchen.*

Creak-creak-creak. *Comin' toward the bedroom.* Jimmy let go of the doorknob and rushed back to bed, hiding beneath the covers with the machete gripped across his chest. The door opened, and Mike came in. He opened the closet to set the gifts inside, stripped down to his underwear, and crawled into bed. After letting out a series of staccato farts, he grew quiet. Jimmy listened until he heard the rhythmic cadence of his brother's breathing. Gritting his teeth, he forced himself to look. He squinted his eyes and saw the dark, motionless lump of his sleeping brother and the open closet.

At 3:36 AM, Jimmy fell asleep with the machete still resting on his chest.

The next morning Mike was up rather early. Pretending to sleep, Jimmy heard him dress and slip into the living room. He was greeted warmly by his parents and Karen.

"Hey, sleepy head." Jimmy heard his brother say.

"You look like Jesus," she said.

Mike's hair was long, and he sported a full beard. His parents asked him about school, and Mike yakked on about saving the Earth and how he had ideas about making farming eco-friendly. Since he was the first one in the family to attend college, Bill and Barbara hung on his every word, suffused with the wisdom of their very own Jesus.

Jimmy returned the machete beneath the bed, slipped into his clothes, put on his glasses, and joined. Mike narrowed his eyes yet managed a pleasant greeting. "How yuh doin', Jimmy?"

"Fine, I guess."

"I'll start breakfast," Barbara announced.

"Can I help?" Mike offered.

His mother's eyes flew open. "Wow, that's a first."

Father added, "Karen's right. You really *are* Jesus."

"You just relax, honey. I'll call you when it's ready."

"I'll get my clothes and jump in the shower then." Mike headed to the front door.

"If you've any dirty clothes, give 'em to me," Mother said.

"Thanks."

He got his clothes from the back of the van and returned to the bedroom.

Jimmy loitered as his brother chose clean clothes. Michael looked like a stranger, somehow taller and not as thin as he was.

"Here." He tossed the baseball cap to Jimmy.

"Thanks."

"Got somethin' else." He lifted the Wiffle bat. "Ever played?"

"Naw."

"We'll set up the field out front, use a garden hose for the home run line." He held up a ball. One side had holes, so you could make it curve and dip depending on the angle you threw it.

"Okay."

"How yuh been?"

"Good." Jimmy didn't know what else to say.

"How's school? Ol' Ganns still there?"

"Naw, he left."

"Got a girl?"

Jimmy shook his head. "You?"

Mike smiled. "Lots."

"Yeah? Candy's been callin' to see when you'd be home."

Mike shook his head. "Been there, done that. Rope still up?"

"Yeah. Me and Sammy Martinez play on it every once in a while when he comes over. He cleared nine feet."

Samuel Martinez lived on a ranch a mile east. His father managed it, and the house came rent-free. On weekends he'd walk over, and they'd play basketball or practice rope vault. Occasionally Sam would ask if Jimmy could come to his house, yet the gum beneath the table was stuck hard, and the answer was always no. Jimmy would have liked to have gone there. Sam had three beautiful sisters.

"Be sure you check the hay-pad. Remember what ol' Loftus likes to leave lyin' around."

Jimmy giggled at the memory. "Yeah."

Mike's new-found kindness invited him to share more, yet Jimmy held back. He wanted to tell Mike that his personal life sucked, that he was bullied, and was nothing but a Kock at school. He ached to say he was lonely, felt lost, insignificant, invisible—that there were times he thought of hanging himself with the rope in the barn—that he was afraid, afraid of everything. Afraid to live, afraid to die, afraid of girls, math quizzes, getting poked by rusty baling wire. *What can I do?* He wanted to ask his big brother. *How do I dig myself outta this hole? When will the fucking cyclops drop dead?*

Mike looked at Jimmy. He could tell his little brother was thinking. *Poor fucker*, he thought. "Hear Karen's gotta boyfriend."

Jimmy adjusted his glasses. "Jeff Mecker. He's a dick."

Mike laughed. "Why's that?"

"Comes over and tells me to get lost."

"Yeah, well, that's the way it works."

"I call 'im Pecker."

Mike laughed. "Come a time when you won't want anybody 'round when you're with a girl."

"Guess so, maybe."

"See yuh in a bit." He left for the shower room.

Jimmy put his new baseball cap on and waited in the living room. Dad was reading a Life Magazine. There was only one phone in the house, and Karen was on it with Pecker, talking in hushed tones. Mom was rustling around in the kitchen. He heard the shower running. Joe woofed a few times outside, and the male cat yowled in his search for a female. A sparrow struck the front window and veered away. A gathering of sweat trickled down Jimmy's forehead. He listened to life going on all around him.

Uncle Ed drove up. Jimmy's father put the magazine down and signed heavily. Ed visited when he was unsure about how to do something, and it was often that he didn't.

"What's he want?" Barbara looked cross.

Bill opened the door. Ed looked worried. He always wore a worried expression. Even when he laughed, his forehead refused to relax even for a moment.

"Hey, Bill. That Michael's van?"

"S'pose so. Got in late."

"Done real good this year. How many did he fan in that one game?"

"Sixteen against USC in a tournament."

"Jeez. Hey, was wonderin' you think I oughta water them prunes again before we pick?"

"Give it another week."

"Okay. Hi, Barbara!" he called past Bill's shoulder.

"Hey, Ed."

"Hey, Jimmy."

"Hey, Unkie."

"Hey, Karen."

"Unk." Karen put a finger in her ear. "It's just my uncle," she told Pecker.

"Tell Mike hey. The folks'll be happy to see 'im."

"Imagine he'll swing by later."

"Wonder if a guy could live in that thing?" Ed gestured to the red van.

"S'pose if he'd a mind to." Bill gave a little smile to his brother. "Okay, thanks."

Ed limped away.

CHAPTER 13
CONSCIOUS OBSERVATIONS

It was no picnic sharing Jimmy's mind, I can tell you. His free will was strong. Jimmy was at the edge of a drain, ready to swirl down, and I felt as powerless as a neutered Chihuahua. All I could do was offer a few suggestions to help him get on the right track.

There's more than meets the eye here on Earth—a deep-seeded essence that breaks the surface sometimes. When calamity strikes, there are those who stand as heroes. All humans are born with seeds, yet many choose not to water them.

Earth is filled with natural wonders rivaling anything in my world. The problem here is always ego. Ants have a more sophisticated social order. Humans are evolving into parasites, and Earth Mother is taking measures to rectify the situation.

I'm watching the sunset. The sun is glowing orange, softening into delicate pink as it hides behind distant mountains. Soon it'll be dark. What then?

CHAPTER 14
GRANDMA'S MUSEUM OF INTERESTING THINGS

Late the next afternoon, Mike, Karen, and Jimmy walked to visit Grandma, Grandpa, and Special Ed. Along the way, they met Loftus, who was servicing an old forklift. It was used to stack bins filled with prunes on a trailer to be taken to the dehydrator in Woodland. The Tule River Dryer was Woodland's only claim to fame. At one time, it processed more prunes than anywhere in the world.

"Mikey!" Loftus held his hand out.

"Hi, Mr. Loftus."

"Few weeks them prunes'll be ready. You gonna work?"

Mike shook his head. He'd labored a few seasons on summer vacation from high school with a high school buddy named Jason Milner. Machines had replaced most of the workforce. A tractor-like device known only as *the shaker* clamped onto trees much as Sydney had done to the cat. Attached to the catching frame were two canvases with handles that were drawn out and wrapped around the base of the tree. The shaker did its work. He and Milner gripped the laden canvases, leaning back as the canvas was retracted into the catching frame. A conveyer travelled the harvest into a waiting bin.

In between operations, Jason and Mike played a game. They faced off at twenty feet and took turns under-handing prunes toward each other's nut-sack. Scores were tallied for direct hits. Shooting BAs was also popular. You caught the other guy with his back to you, and when he turned, he was faced with a bare ass. They kept track of that too.

Jason was Mike's best friend because their fathers were. Jason's father was a double-vet—veterinarian and WW-2 vet. As a pilot, John Milner was shot down over Germany and imprisoned for two years. The first thing he wanted after being freed was chocolate pie. He ate so much that he never wanted it again for the rest of his life.

"Reckon we'll find Mexicans to do the job." Loftus spit a brown stream of tobacco onto the dirt below his feet. "I'm runnin' the shaker this year."

"Take it easy," Mike said.

"Yup. Nice to see yuh."

Mike thought, *Is Loftus a first or last name?* He'd only known him as Loftus. *Must be somethin' more to it.*

The three of them continued to the grandparents'. Along the way, Mike interrogated Karen.

"What's this I hear 'bout a boyfriend?"

She smiled shyly and shrugged.

"How long?"

"Nine months and three days."

"Jimmy calls him Pecker."

Karen shoved Jimmy. "You don't even know him, you little jerk."

"Next time, I'll call 'im Pecker to his face."

Mike laughed and changed the subject. "Alligator died?"

"Yep. He's under the walnut."

"Didn't know you could order shit like that. They belong in

nature, not a metal bin."

"Yeah." Jimmy knew not to argue. His brother was Jesus.

"Gonna cut your hair?" Karen asked.

"Before next baseball season."

"I think it's cool," Jimmy said.

"Smoke any grass?" Karen wanted to know.

Mike smiled. "Where you get such ideas?"

"Heard you threw a no-hitter," Jimmy enthused.

"Yep. Against UCLA—best team in the league."

Jimmy nodded. "Maybe we can play catch later."

"Yeah, sure. What's it like pitchin' with glasses on?"

Jimmy shrugged. "Don't make much difference."

"Still couldn't break a pane of glass with your fastball, eh?"

There it was—the first dig. Jimmy was surprised it had taken this long.

Uncle Ed was the first to greet the children. He was burning a pile of raked leaves. When they were close enough, he greeted them with an enormous rumbling fart.

"Don't stand too close to that fire, Unk," warned Mike.

"Unk rhymes with skunk," Jimmy observed.

"How you doin', boy? Yer dad says you done real good this year."

"All right, I guess."

"C'mon in, Grandpa and Grandma been waitin'."

Uncle Ed limped ahead, and Mike was greeted in the house with a handshake from Andrew and smothering hugs and kisses from Gladys. Andrew wanted to hear about Mike's studies, and Gladys went into the kitchen to get everyone a Seven-up. There were several things you could count on in her kitchen—Seven-up, instant pudding, and store-bought Mother's brand oatmeal cookies. The cookies were rock hard, and Jimmy often wondered if they'd be better served by skimming them across a lake.

Gladys was a terrible cook. Andrew was in charge of breakfast, cooking meat and mashed potatoes for supper. Lunch was usually a bologna or salami sandwich. Gladys could make salads heat up anything in a can, yet her culinary efforts were disastrous.

Uncle Ed loved eating out, yet there weren't many options. Woodland had Ken's Walkup, and nearby, Poplar boasted Leo's Burgers. During the weekday, he drove to eat lunch at one or the other.

After Mike finished filling Grandfather in, it was Grandma's turn. To say that Gladys was odd is an understatement. She was generous, loving, kind, inventive, artistic, and funny without even trying, and that balanced out the weirdness.

"C'mon." She gripped Mike by the elbow and led him into a large enclosed porch area. "Added some interesting new things to my collection."

They stopped at a large bookshelf. Normally you'd expect to see books there. Her shelves were stocked with mummified remains of animals she'd found dead around the property.

"I find them so interesting, don't you?" She picked up a toad that looked as if it had dried in the act of reaching to touch the sun. Next was a bat she'd found in the barn, lips drawn back into a sneer.

Mike sniggered during the show. "Grandma, you sure it's safe handlin' those things?"

"I soak 'em in Lysol and leave 'em to dry. Kills ants and other critters." She held up a mouse by the stiffened tail. "He was in the house, and your uncle got him. Threw a book at him."

"That's what cops say," Mike joked.

As if on cue, Ed stood in the doorway to the porch. When his mother wasn't looking, he rolled his eyes and circled his right ear with a forefinger. Jimmy clenched laughter behind his teeth. Gladys was odd, yet no more than the guy in Woodland who walked in circles talking to himself or the woman in Poplar who kept a hundred cats. At least there weren't cats in the collection. Karen wouldn't have stood for it.

Karen looked at Jimmy. "Oughta dig up Sydney for Grandma."

"See the lizards?" Gladys continued. "Got lots of those. Grandpa shot a red-tailed hawk, but—"

"That's illegal, Grandma!" Michael interrupted. "You're not supposed to kill raptors. They're protected by law." Mike was worked up.

"Oh, dear."

"We gotta go, Grandma—just came by to say hi. Be back soon."

"Do yuh have to go so soon? I can make somethin'."

"No thanks, Grandma, Got stuff to do."

"All right, sweetheart."

Before he could get away, she grabbed his face with both hands and kissed his cheeks. Jimmy and Karen managed to escape before she got to them.

As they headed back through the field, Jimmy asked, "Think Grandma's a ding-bat?"

"Could say that I guess."

"Got bat juice on your face."

Mike used his T-shirt to wipe where Grandma's hands had touched. "Christ. No wonder the sun hurts my eyes. I'm turnin' into a fuckin' vampire!"

"She held a gopher, too," Karen reminded him. "What's *that* make you?"

Mike stuck out his front teeth. "It's happening! It's happening!" He chased Karen around a prune tree.

"Get away, freak!"

"Jesus freak!" Jimmy amended.

They were all laughing now, conjuring new items for Grandmother's collection.

"What if she trapped one of Uncle Ed's farts in a Mason jar?" Jimmy asked.

"Some Loftus turds," Karen suggested.

"That would be interestin'," said Michael.

"What if one of us dies—" Jimmy began.

"That's sick!" Karen said. "Besides, the shelf isn't big 'nough."

Mike picked up a stick. "This's my most interestin' specimen—Jeff's pecker."

Karen chased him. "Hate you, hate you both!" Yet she was laughing so hard she had to stop.

CHAPTER 15
HELD TOGETHER WITH ELMERS

In 1969 George Lazenby tried his hand as James Bond and flopped spectacularly. Everyone preferred Sean Connery. Mike did a fair impersonation of Connery. After the family had been to the Meadowland Theater to see Lazenby's farce, he affected it.

On the way home, Barbara thought of something she needed in a small grocery store close by.

"Mikey, would you run in there for a gallon of milk and some eggs?" She fished in her purse and handed him a five.

"Oh, the things I do for England," he replied.

His father laughed. "Hey, that's pretty damn good."

Jimmy went with him. Walking the aisle toward the dairy case, they passed a condom display.

"Know what these're called?" Mike picked up a box.

"What?"

"Snugger Fit. Also known as *Jimmy's*. They're for teeny weenies."

Jimmy was crestfallen.

"It's okay, kid. There's pecker stretcher exercises you can do."

"Don't need 'em."

"From what I've seen—"

"Why're you lookin', fag?"

"I understand. It must be tough."

Mike found the milk and eggs. As he paid, Jimmy walked back to the car, heart racing. The ringing in his ears started. *LadySmith put a bullet in his head.*

When Mike joined, Jimmy was stuck in the middle of the back seat. As the youngest, he was relegated to the middle. Throughout his life, family drives had proved to be another source of torture. Casually Mike put his arm over the backrest, creeping his hand further until it touched the back of Jimmy's head.

"Stop."

"What?"

"I said stop it."

"I'm not doin' anything."

Bill twisted his head around. "What the hell?"

"Mike's botherin' me." His ears were ringing, and the eye-tic returned.

"Cut it out." Dad's imperative was only effective for a few minutes.

Soon, Mike had his hand in position again, forefinger positioned so that when Jimmy moved his head in that direction, it would enter his ear. When it did, Jimmy jerked away and glared at his brother.

Mike turned to look out the side window. "Jimmy, Jimmy, *little* Jimmy, banana-anna bow-bimmy."

"Shut up," he said in a low voice.

Karen folded her hands in her lap and stared out the window, thinking of Jeff—about what he wanted her to do with him.

"Little Jimmy."

"Better shut up," warned Jimmy.

His mother shot them a warning glance in the rear-view mirror yet said nothing. She was thinking of Del, wondering how she could manage another delivery.

Mike grew tired of the game and kept quiet the rest of the way.

The truce was held together with Elmer's glue. Jimmy knew the remainder of his summer would inch along at a snail's pace. He'd have no peace until Mike left for college.

When they got home, Mike wanted to play plastic baseball. Jimmy refused.

"C'mon, we need three people," said Karen.

"No." Jimmy walked away and headed for the white barn.

"Little Jimmy!" Mike yelled after him.

Jimmy lay on top of the haystack staring at the rafters. The sun contracted the metal roofing, causing it to crackle and pop like an enormous bowl of Rice Krispies. Pigeons cooed in each corner, and the hot, dry air was suffused with hopelessness. No breeze arrived to cool his thoughts—murderous thoughts that caused his eye to twitch and his eardrums to become sirens. He clenched his fists and imagined David slaying the giant.

CHAPTER 16
SAME-O-SAME-O

There's no God. Any ideas you may have to the contrary are self-indulgent pipedreams. Death doesn't get you seventy-two virgins, a condo in heaven, or reincarnated as a butterfly. The death toll related to Christians alone is fifty-six million. In the name of God, humans have subjugated by sword and gun, condoned genocide, ethnic cleansing, created countless wars, conquered and wiped out entire cultures and civilizations. Devotees won't agree. For them, God's will comes in handy for anything, from winning the lottery to knocking up a girlfriend. It's so much simpler that way. I wish it were true.

***

Jimmy didn't kill his brother. Perhaps you foreshadowed his demise as you were reading. It certainly would have been justified, unless, of course, you're a believer. The Bible says, "Thou shalt not kill." Does that apply to the aforementioned fifty-six million?

Every year over five million youth are bullied. A large percentage takes place in middle- school, yet it often carries into high school and beyond. Jimmy managed to make it to high school without murdering anyone, yet that doesn't mean he didn't think about it. He thought about it all the time. Whenever he heard his name bastardized into Kock, his thoughts revisited a deep realm inside his brain—an archive filled with scenarios and possibilities.

In eighth grade, Matthew Cloninger had a girlfriend named Lynn. He bragged to Jimmy about getting to third base. Matt also grew a nice pair of sideburns, which worked nearly as good as having a car to attract females. Lynn loved his sideburns. Matt made fun of Jimmy's attempts to grow a pair.

"Are those fuzzy caterpillars next to your ears?"

Lynn giggled and tugged Matt away. "C'mon, let's go, baby."

Matt added, "Dip 'em in milk and let a cat lick 'em off."

Lynn laughed harder. "There's an ol' stray that hangs out by the cafeteria."

Jimmy brought LadySmith to school the next day in his backpack. All day he waited for Matt to say something to piss him off. *Blast the three fuckin' R's and save one for* myself. Then he remembered he only had three rounds and was forced to modify the list. He'd shoot Matt and two of the three R's—Ramon, for sure. Then he'd barricade himself in the maintenance shack to slit his wrists with a pair of hedge clippers.

Fortunately, the day went smoothly. Matt Cloninger invited him to his birthday party. The three Rs were caught smoking and kicked out early in the morning. The eighth-grade teacher, Mr. Hale, smiled at Jimmy as he handed back an English exam with an 'A' posted on it. Jimmy usually did well in English. The accumulation of positive vibes brought a whimpering close to his murderous plans. After Floyd dropped him at Palm Tree Lane, Jimmy cut straight to his grandparents to return the weapon and had a Seven-up while he was there.

***

1970—high times for Republicans, and make no mistake, most farmers are Republicans. Tricky Dicky's president, Bonanza is still on the air, Apollo 13 had a problem, and eighteen-year-olds couldn't vote or drink, yet were forced to serve in Vietnam. Thirty percent of them were black. The federal government told these brave young men they were fighting for freedom, justice, and democracy...7,753 miles away.

Karen broke up with Pecker after he cheated on her. She listlessly attended Meadowland Junior College and started dating a nice conservative named David Lassiter. On Saturday evenings, he often came over to watch All in the Family. Funny thing about the show—it tackled serious social issues such as racism, war, homosexuality, bigotry, and misogyny. The main character, Archie Bunker, was always on the wrong side of the issue, which suited Bill and Barbara just fine. Instead of educating them, the show reinforced their twisted values, so the gum beneath the table was fossilized long before it was even noticed.

Jimmy liked the show too. He joined the menagerie before returning to his private Idaho—the room where a cyclops once lived.

He'd recently finished a book that Michael had left behind from high school, *Of Mice and Men*. When it was done, he sat the book on his bed, put hands over his face, and wept. Words echoed in his head.

"I thought you was mad at me, George."

"No," said George. "No, Lennie, I ain't mad. I never been mad, and I ain't now. That's a thing I want ya to know."

Jimmy was reminded of his father's relationship with Uncle Ed.

Michael had reread it as a requirement in high school, along with other required novels stacked in the closet. He'd sucked out the required information to spit back on exam day. Jimmy also read *Catcher in the Rye*, *Lord of the Flies*, a few works by Shakespeare, and *Huckleberry Finn*, all on his own. Classics spoke in a way pulp writers didn't. They told enduring tales, and the heroes were usually as miserable as he was.

A new high school had opened in Meadowland. Jimmy wasn't a Panther. He was a Marauder—a Monache Marauder, whatever the hell that was. The bus that delivered him forty-five minutes away was operated by a timid old man named Stinson. The three Rs sat in the back. Jimmy usually found a seat toward the front, yet there were times he was forced to sit further back. Matthew Cloninger didn't ride the bus. His father let him ride a Honda motorcycle to school even though Matt was only fourteen.

On the first day of school, Jimmy was forced to sit ten seats from the rear in front of a kid named Mike Gonzales. The first name made it even worse.

Next to Jimmy was petite Patrícia Rodriguez, who resembled a frightened sparrow. Jimmy couldn't remember what her voice sounded like. At Woodland, she'd been nearly mute for the eight years he'd known her. The lack of voice had made her appear smaller each day until, one day, he realized he hadn't noticed her for weeks. He turned in his desk until he found her. Patty was pretty, yet even that fact was diminished by her shyness.

Mike Gonzales wanted to impress the three Rs. As the bus lurched along, he flicked Jimmy's ears. When Jimmy leaned forward out of reach, Mike blew on him and whispered.

"Güero, eh güero. Where's your fuckin' alligator?"

Everyone knew about Sydney and the resultant drubbing he'd suffered at the hands of the three Rs. Bernie Sanchez had been the only witness, and his conscience made him go to Johnson. Jimmy was afraid of retaliation and had refused to say anything further about the incident.

"Güero, heard you took a shot to the nuts." Mike stabbed a finger into Jimmy's back.

Jimmy turned and glared at Mike. In his mind, he wreaked havoc—saw himself reaching for LadySmith in his backpack and unloading into Mike's stupid fucking brain. In the fantasy, LadySmith never ran out of stinging bees. He calmly pointed and fired. Three Bloody Rs, Mike, and the rest of his enemies, gaping holes where eyes used to be. Sirens were blaring, and his left eye was twitching.

All this time, Mr. Stinson merely glanced into the mirror and kept driving. *One more year and I'm out*, he thought. *They can murder each other for all I care.*

Reflexively Jimmy felt his backpack—only the hardness of pencils and the metal spine of a notebook there. Meanwhile, Mike was encouraged by the Three Rs. "Pinche gringo! Pendejo! Puta Madre. Hijo de la chingada! Gonna fuck you up!" they yelled.

Mike added, "Gonna pull a train on your sister, güero." Then he rhythmically pushed against Jimmy's seat-back. "Uhn, uhn, uhn, oh yeah baby, you like that?"

Patty jumped to her feet. She turned to face Mike with a look Jimmy had never seen. Her face trembled, and her dark brown eyes turned black with rage.

"Shut the fuck up, you stupid sonofabitch! I'm sick of you and your stupid goddamn lowlife buddies makin' everybody's life miserable. Shut the fuck up!" Patricia stood her ground. Mike narrowed his eyes, yet his weapons were neutralized. He could only think of one thing to say.

"Puta," he whispered.

Shit, thought Stinson. *Gonna have to pull over. I'm too old for this.* He downshifted. They were on a country road. In the distance, two students waited at the next stop by a rural mailbox. He set the brake and moved down the aisle to where Patty stood facing Mike.

"This ends now! Sit down, young lady. I don't wanna hear another peep, understand?"

Jimmy spoke up. "It's him. He won't stop bothering—"

"Don't give a damn whose fault it is. Stops here and now!" He stared menacingly at Jimmy.

Jimmy clamped his mouth shut. Mike sat with hands in his lap as if patiently waiting for a teacher to deliver lessons to his hungry mind—angelic in all respects.

Patricia sat down, trembling. Stinson returned to the driver's seat, glaring as he released the brake and ground through the gears.

"Mikey got schooled," jeered one of the three Rs.

"She your woman, Mike?"

"Thanks," Jimmy whispered to Patty.

"Shut up. That wasn't for you."

"Thanks anyway."

"Just shut up."

Jimmy nodded and stared at his backpack.

Patty stared out the window. She heard Mike whispering. "Puta. Puta. Puta."

Jimmy could've redeemed himself by turning around and throwing a punch or two, yet he didn't. Not even when Mike repeatedly kicked the seatback. His anger boiled, simmered, and joined the rest of the rage that was stored in an area of his brain reserved for catastrophic, last-resort action.

Fifteen minutes later, they arrived at Monache High. The drop-off area was behind campus, and they walked through large sliding gates to be on campus. The new school was dotted with flowered areas, while the buildings were Spanish style with red tile roofs and bull-nosed edges. It was beautifully designed, yet for Jimmy, it represented fear and anxiety—fear of the unknown, anxiety that high school would prolong his string of ugly, dripping failures one on top of the other. He'd have to empty the pan or else crawl so deep within himself he'd never escape. Off the bus, Patty quickly distanced herself from him.

Last off the bus, Mike joined the three Rs. They sauntered slowly toward campus. For them, the flowers and well-organized classrooms were in stark contrast to their homes. Preppy white boys wore bell bottoms and paisley shirts, and their hair was long. Girls wore hippy skirts. They drew peace symbols on their binders. Smiling white teachers tried acting hip, yet it all reminded Mike and the three Rs of a society that was setting them up for failure.

Half the faces at school were brown, yet the teachers were

mostly white. Brown faces cooked and served food in the cafeteria, swept floors, cut grass, and cleaned bathrooms. Disparities showcased a broken, inequitable system. And if the system was broken, so were the dreams of those oppressed by it.

The three Rs buzzed their hair and wore white T-shirts and black pants. They even walked differently. Chicanos were trapped between two slices of bread, one brown, the other white. Brown represented the Mexicans. Yet Mexicans didn't consider Chicanos Mexican anymore. Whites lumped Mexicans and Chicanos together and didn't like either, even though the entire country relied on them. Chicanos were forced to develop a subculture.

Spanglish developed as Chicanos lost the ability to speak pure Spanish. The process began with the second and third generations. First-generation immigrants kept Mexican traditions alive. Subsequent ones replaced pozole, enchiladas de mole, and tacos with hamburgers, French fries, and pizza.

Chicanos were evolving their style even before the Zoot-Suit era in the forties. Their aggressive behavior made many angry. Gum beneath new desks at the new school began accumulating on the first day. Few blacks lived in Meadowland, which made Chicanos a prime target for police. Prisons were filled with them. Most arrests resulted in the practice of cruising the streets using a marginalizing grid system, in which the poor neighborhoods where Chicanos lived were under constant surveillance. At any one time, there might be four patrol cars cruising the streets, and usually, three of them would be in the Chicano neighborhoods.

So much of what became of the three Rs resulted from this setup. They couldn't see a way out. If society expected them to be thugs, then that's what they'd be.

Jimmy was considered a rich kid. His mother bought him the latest styles. On that first day, he wore flared Levi's, a paisley shirt, and a thick belt with a large square buckle. His wire glasses were switched to black frames.

Children of farmers were bully targets unless they united together in groups of five or six. Mathew Cloninger was good at keeping a low profile. He was in college preparatory classes, thus minimizing contact with the outer fringe. Jimmy was an average student. His schedule placed him among enemies. On the first day of class, he sat at or close to the front in every class. Enemies kept to the back row.

Patricia Rodriguez was in his freshmen English class. Mrs. Hickman was the teacher, and she had a calming effect on the class. Mike Gonzales and Ricardo Garza sat in back. They placed their heads on the desktop to tune out. Jimmy sat behind Patty, who was in the very front.

Shirley Hickman loved creative writing. Her syllabus was sprinkled with poetry, short story writing, and novels. She encouraged students to find their inner voice and listen to it. Most of her students had never experienced the opportunity to connect themselves to English in a personal way. The norm was spitting answers on bubble sheets soon to be forgotten. Tests were run through a scantron machine for fast results. Students were thus impregnated with useless ethereal information. Mrs. Hickman's methods were different. She inspired something more.

Hickman gave an assignment on the first day. Write an original story. She explained the concept on the chalkboard and gave everyone a handout with step-by-step advice. She called the instructions suggestions, insisting she was more of an English diplomat rather than a teacher. She required those in her stead to be critical thinkers.

Patty raised her hand.

"It'll take a few weeks for me to memorize your names—forgive me, what's yours?"

"Patricia."

"What's your question, Patricia?"

"I don't know what to write about." She was wagging her pencil.

"Everyone has a story to tell. You may not realize it, but you've led an extraordinary life. There's a voice inside you. Listen to it. Dig deep."

Patty shook her head. Jimmy tapped her on the shoulder, and she stopped wagging the pencil.

"Write about what happened on the bus."

She didn't turn around or reply in any way. Her pencil began wagging again, and soon she was writing.

The Guys in the back heard bits and pieces of Mrs. Hickman's suggestions. Their inner voice was telling them who in class might buy a certain product they sold.

"Raise your hand if you need help," she reminded students as she strolled the room.

Patty stared at the blackboard and began scribbling again. Hickman moved toward the back to gently admonish Mike and Ricardo.

"How're you boys doing? Need help?"

"What're we supposed to do?" said Mike.

She explained everything again. Afterward, the two looked at her.

"So, what're we supposed to do?" Ricardo asked.

She simply said, "Everyone has a story to tell. Tell it."

"Ain't got no pencil," Ricardo said.

"Me too," echoed Mike.

"Here we go again," breathed Patty.

Jimmy thought of the cliché, *Can't change spots on a leopard.*

"I'll get you pencils. Do you need paper too?" Her voice carried a bit of an edge this time.

"I ain't comfortable writing about mi vida," Ricardo declared.

"I can't force you to do the assignment, only encourage you to try. I'll get you a pencil and paper."

"Naw, I think I got one." Ricardo fished a stubby pencil from his baggy pants, and Mike followed.

Mrs. Hickman started to leave.

"I got no papel," said Mike.

Her shoulders rose as she took a deep breath and thought, *A nice big glass of wine this evening.*

Jimmy knew what was more important than school for Mike and the three Rs. If you wanted weed, they could hook you up. Skunkweed, grass, pot, Mary Jane—in the seventies, over 10% of youth were trying it. LSD was also popular, yet heroin was considered a dangerous plague that only thrived in ghettos. Getting high was the new cool. This is not to say the three Rs were shot-callers. They were only mules delivering goods to paying customers.

Hearing the voices of enemies gave Jimmy an idea. He didn't write a title because Mrs. Hickman explained that titles should float to the surface when the story was done. He began: *I hated their guts and wished they were dead.*

CHAPTER 17
A FORCE AWAKENS

Jimmy's story chilled Mrs. Hickman to the bone. It consisted of six written pages. The handwriting was sloppy, yet she read it three times during her preparation period. The grammar, structure, and spelling were nearly perfect. Jimmy's impressive use of metaphor and symbolism reminded her of a much older writer. She wondered why he wasn't in her freshmen honors class. She picked it up again to read random passages.

Ramon twisted beneath the pitchfork, trying to push it out of him, but I tightened my grip on the handle and leaned all my weight against it. I watched his face, a mask of pain, the look of desperation in his eyes. Maybe he was wondering where he'd go from there, his faith conveniently returning after so many years avoiding the church. Blindly he reached out to God.

"Dios mío!"

I ignored him. Next would be Ricardo, then Mike and Refugio.

She turned to the last stapled page.

Each died differently. Screams are like fingerprints. Now it was finished, all but one loose end. Grandfather's .38 had five cylinders. I'd only need one.

Mrs. Shirley Hickman sat back in her chair. She glimpsed something deep inside Jimmy through his writing. *A warning. Something his mind is telling him to do. Yet his heart isn't in it.*

"My God," she said to an empty classroom.

That Friday after class, Mrs. Hickman asked Jimmy to stay after class during her prep period. She had returned the graded short stories except for Jimmy's. *Failed again*, he thought.

"I'll write a note for your next class," she reminded him just before the bell.

Jimmy nodded and looked at the clock.

The bell sounded, and the rest of the class emptied. Ricardo slapped Mike on the shoulder to wake him up, and they were the last out. Jimmy narrowed his eyes. Mrs. Hickman sat at her desk and motioned Jimmy to pull up a chair next to her. She held his story, pursing her lips as she stared at the title: Snapped!

"Interesting title," she nodded. "Did it float to the surface?"

"Yeah, I guess." Jimmy pushed his glasses up.

"Jimmy, I want to talk with you about your writing."

His heart was a tympani, and his skin prickled. *Went too far,* he thought. *Idiot!*

"Let me ask you something, Mr. Koch." Having pronounced his name correctly, she paused to gather her words carefully. "Has anyone ever told you you're a writer?"

He gave a short laugh and began to relax. Slowly he shook his head. "No, ma'am. Nobody's ever told me I'm much of anything."

Her eyes were saddened. "Well, I'm telling you. This story is deeply disturbing yet so well written. It grabbed my attention with the first sentence and didn't let go until the end. You have a real gift."

"Thanks." He turned away as her eyes bored into him, exposing secrets, defining who he was, seeing him.

She took a deep breath. "Having said that, I must ask—are you being bullied?"

Trapped. She knows. They'll make me see a shrink. Crazy ol'

Kock, they'll say. He pressed his lips together. "It's just a story."

She sighed, unconvinced. Then she added further surprise. "Jimmy, I'd like to move you into freshman honors English."

"Honors? I don't know. I mean…." Jimmy shook his head.

"You'd be a perfect fit, and we do a lot of creative writing in that class."

"Have to think about it."

"We're reading *Catcher in the Rye*. Ever heard of it?"

"Read it last summer."

Mrs. Hickman's eyes widened. "What else have you read?"

"Fantasy, science fiction. Steinbeck, Hemmingway. Shakespeare's pretty cool." He thought of other books—*Maidenhead Tales*, *Destiny's Desire*, stashed in his mother's underwear drawer—purloined, read, and returned.

Lately, his mother was mixing her interest in historical romance with James A. Michener's prolific drivel. Jimmy read a few yet found them formulaic. You could cut and paste any of his characters into the next novel. Alaska, Hawaii, Texas—same folks, different states of the Union, and nothing worth dog-earing.

"This year we're reading, *The Grapes of Wrath*."

He'd read that too. Jimmy made up his mind. "Okay, guess I'll give it a shot."

"Good. Do you have any other writings to show me?"

He shook his head. "I'll try to write some this weekend."

"Great. Plan on coming to seventh period on Monday. What do you have then?" She wrote notes on a piece of paper.

"History."

"Who's your counselor?"

"Mr. Norris."

"I'll talk with him."

"Thanks, Mrs. Hickman."

She wrote him a late pass.

Jimmy floated to his next class. In just a few moments, Mrs. Hickman had substantiated him and verified his existence. For the first time in memory, he felt truly happy.

CHAPTER 18
THE JOURNAL

In fact, Jimmy had been writing quite a bit, keeping a journal tucked beneath his mattress. He wrote himself as the protagonist in fantasies involving popular high school girls.

A few years back, he'd discovered the magazine his brother secreted beneath hay bales. Subsequently, much time was spent in the barn using Chapstick for something other than lip balm. The periodical was worn, and there was evidence that mice used tits and ass to line their nests. Still, there was enough left to keep him occupied. In reality, Jimmy hadn't even reached first base with a girl.

Jimmy wanted to impress Mrs. Hickman, to prove that she hadn't made a mistake. He needed something meaningful. Yet, meaning was something he purposely avoided. He'd tried for years to find reasons for Michael's behavior toward him and bullies at school. Rather than find meaning, he thought to kill it and ask questions later. Then it wouldn't hurt anymore. He'd meditate on his actions from a jail cell or the grave. If there was any meaning, he'd find it there.

Jimmy stared at the journal pages. He'd left off with senior cheerleader Cathy Riles telling him what she wanted. He fanned to a fresh page and let his mind wander. For Jimmy, ideas seemed to fall from the sky and into his head. After a few moments, foggy images floated in and materialized. He started with: *Christ Almighty, he hadn't seen it coming. War was a fairy tale about a faraway land with no happily ever after in sight.* This would be a story about his cousin Marty.

Jimmy found Marty's number in the Yellow Pages and called. A woman answered and asked what Jimmy's business was.

"I'm writing a story about a soldier in Vietnam."

"He doesn't like talking about that stuff," she explained.

"Can I just see how he's doin'? I haven't talked to him for a long time."

"Sure."

After a few moments of silence, Marty was on the line.

"Jimmy?"

"How yuh doin', Marty?"

"Jeez, been a long time. Last I saw you—hell, don't even remember when. What can I do for yuh?"

"I'm writin' a story 'bout a soldier in Vietnam."

"About me?"

"Someone like you."

Jimmy explained the need for first-hand information and how it would give the story more flavor.

"Jeez, I don't know, Jimmy. Been tryin' to get that shit outta my head."

In the background, Jimmy heard the woman. "Marty, just hang up. Already told him you wouldn't be interested."

Marty hesitated. "Maybe it'd be good for me."

"You'll have those nightmares again," she warned.

There was a long silence. Marty covered the mouthpiece with his hand. Jimmy was ready to apologize for the intrusion and let the notion go the way of the dodo. Then the hand was removed.

"Okay. What you wanna know, Jimmy?"

Jimmy asked questions he'd prepared and wrote furiously. Marty started by telling how he felt when he received the draft notice.

"Didn't look like nothin', just a piece of paper that said I had three weeks to get my affairs in order and report."

His voice quavered at times as he told his tale, and Jimmy realized he wouldn't have to fictionalize anything but the names. Marty talked about boot camp, then flying to Vietnam with a bunch of other scared kids to a place so foreign from Meadowland he couldn't wrap his head around it. Then came his first deployment. Things got more complicated from there. Occasionally there was silence, and the woman's voice could be heard again.

"Stop. You're gettin' upset."

Marty recalled his return to the US and secluding himself in his room on the ranch for three months. His parents didn't know what to do. Getting mental health services from the Veteran's Administration was nearly impossible. There wasn't a label for what ailed the returning vets. Government response was akin to, "Suck it up, soldier!" Mental illness wasn't considered a valid reason to suffer from prolonged depression, sleeplessness, and thoughts of suicide.

Marty confessed to writing a farewell letter to his parents, locking himself in his room, and putting the barrel of a .12 gauge shotgun into his mouth. He rested his big toe on the trigger yet couldn't bring himself to apply the final pressure. The thread separating sanity from inescapable darkness proved strong enough. He stumbled into the living room, where his mother was studying the TV guide. He sank to his knees and bawled like a child in her arms.

"She cried with me. Told her things I'd done over there, and she just stroked my hair, said it was all right, and that she loved me. Mom saved my life."

After that, he worked on the farm with his father, getting up early, having morning coffee, smelling fresh turned soil, and hearing the coo of mourning doves calling back and forth.

"That's what brought me back to reality."

After a time, he decided to get out on his own. He found a job at the Kmart in Meadowland, met a woman, and married. Eventually, he became manager.

"Come a long way since then, Jimmy. Do me a favor. Some asshole sends you a letter like that, burn it."

"I will."

"Promise me."

"I promise."

The following Monday, Jimmy gave Mr. Hickman his story before honors. She introduced him to the class. He didn't know any of them, but there were two cheerleaders he'd be happy to acquaint himself with.

They began discussing *Catcher in the Rye*, and the discussion questions on the blackboard were: What role do women play in the novel? Is love relevant? Do you think there are meaningful relationships in the book?

All questions were discussed in class. Jimmy had never been in a class where everyone was eager to participate. Some raised hands, others couldn't keep emotions in check, blurting opinions. A symbiotic relationship developed between literature and the critical thinking part of the brain. Jimmy smiled as he listened. Toward the end of class, Mrs. Hickman cornered him.

"Mr. Koch, you've been very quiet. What do you think of the relationships in the book?"

"Dysfunctional," he said. "Like my family."

Everyone laughed, and many nodded in agreement. Mrs. Hickman smiled and gave reading homework. When the bell rang, she asked to speak with Jimmy for a moment.

"What did you think?"

He pushed up his glasses. "Everybody seemed to be into it."

She lifted his story from the stack on her desk. "I'll give this back tomorrow. Interesting title. *Eighteen and Over.*"

"Floated to the top."

"I expect it did."

Jimmy left class with lifted spirits and wished other classes had the same effect. A few teachers tried to make class interesting, yet there were always students who stole learning time by being a pain in the ass.

The next day Mrs. Hickman handed his paper back and asked him to stay after class again.

"Jimmy, this story is publishable. Your style's fresh, exciting, heartbreaking, and uplifting at the same time. I can't get this image out of my head." She read, "Jerry was walking about twenty feet in front of me when we heard a loud click, followed by a deafening explosion. Jerry was turned into a warm red mist, and I was covered with his remains." Mrs. Hickman took a deep breath. "With your permission, I'll solicit this on your behalf."

"Solicit?" Jimmy asked.

"Find a publisher."

"Really?"

"Yes, really," she smiled, and then her face turned serious. "Jimmy, I'm not sure what your plans are after high school, but one thing's for sure, you're a writer."

By the end of the first semester, he'd completed three more short stories and a few poems. The One That Got Away was about the time Uncle Ed had an epileptic seizure during one of Michael's high school baseball games. A wild pitch forced his brother to hit the deck, triggering the episode. Strange and Interesting Things chronicled his grandmother's taste for collecting death to display on shelves. Students were always anxious to hear his work. Jimmy didn't like the sound of his own voice and dreaded reading in front of the class.

One afternoon, Mrs. Hickman handed him a letter from a

publishing magazine called Word House.

"This came today."

"What is it?"

"Rejection or acceptance—one or the other. Always prepare your heart for both." She sat at her desk to grade while students worked on essays.

Jimmy opened the letter.

Dear Mr. Koch,

On behalf of Word House, thank you for your submission of *Eighteen and Over.* We wish to include it in the May issue of *Word House Magazine*. If you accept the terms of the enclosed contract, please return it to us at your earliest convenience, and we will process your payment.

A hundred bucks. Jimmy stared at the figure. Then he looked up at Mrs. Hickman. She raised a questioning eyebrow. Jimmy handed her the letter. She smiled as she read.

"May I keep it for a few minutes?"

"Sure."

A short time later, she stood before the class. "I have something to read before you leave." She paused for effect, then read the letter.

The entire class clapped, and a few boys whistled. One said, Far out, man! A force awakened inside Jimmy—energy suffused with hope and purpose. He was no longer the invisible boy. *I'm a published author*. The thought made him giddy.

She glanced at the clock. "Jimmy, will you allow me to read your story to the class?"

Jimmy turned crimson and nodded.

Hearing someone else's voice reading his words was overwhelming. He felt a protective bubble forming around him. This classroom was a haven and a home.

CHAPTER 19
THE BUBBLE

Jimmy called his cousin to tell him the news. Marty was happy to hear it and requested a copy. A week later, Marty called to say how much he liked it.

"Made my wife cry."

Jimmy thought, *Marty, you've no idea what this has done for me.*

"Keep writin', you hear?"

"Promise."

Jimmy's parents were dumbfounded when he shared with them. His father read it, patted him on the back, and passed it to his mother.

"That's somethin', son. I'm real proud of yuh."

His mother's opinion was more measured. "A hundred dollars?" She handed the story back to Jimmy. "It's too personal."

Her words formed an oppressive cloud over his brow. Their relationship was always contentious. Michael was the apple of her eye, the ball-playing son with scouts dogging him, the son who would certainly sign a baseball contract. She doted on Karen, who was certain to marry and live happily ever after. Then she'd be left with Jimmy. Dust-devil thoughts swirled. *After Henry and Gladys are gone, Jimmy can live with Ed. He's definitely not staying here.*

Her words spread gesso over the new canvas he'd been preparing. That night he lay in bed thinking of the future. Mrs. Hickman's words, *You're a writer* were sullied by his mother's, *It's too personal.*

Mrs. Hickman upped the ante by giving *Eighteen and Over* to a female reporter for the Meadowland Recorder. She asked to interview him.

"I don't know what to talk about, Mrs. Hickman."

"Be yourself. She'll ask the questions. Listen, Jimmy, depending on how you face them, life's challenges make us stronger or weaker. By the way, Mr. Bierman asked if you'd consider taking journalism next year."

Jimmy's hair bristled with excitement. His mother's words slowly evaporated. The reporter came to school, and Jimmy was glad to be called out of math class. Mrs. Taylor, the librarian, let them use a reading room. He felt better there. Mrs. Taylor easily weighed over two hundred and fifty pounds, yet her sweet temperament overshadowed physical considerations. She was overjoyed to hear of Jimmy's accomplishment.

"You're our next William Faulkner," she said.

Sara Purcell carried a small black duffle bag. She was an attractive middle-aged woman with short brown hair, full red lips, and large sleepy eyes. Her perfume circled wagons around his head. After introductions, she sat in a chair close to Jimmy and crossed her legs. Her short skirt edged up well above her knees.

"Jimmy, how old were you when you took an interest in writing?"

"About twelve, I guess. Somewhere 'round there."

"What did you write about?"

Jimmy cleared his throat. He flashed on a fantasy he'd written about Candy Schubert cutting his brother's dick off and shoving it down his throat.

"Mostly made-up stuff. Now I'm readin' books like *East of Eden*, and I see I've a long way to go."

She wrote quickly on a steno-pad and looked up again. "How did you get the idea for *Eighteen and Over*?"

Jimmy explained how Mrs. Hickman inspired students to write. Then he talked about the phone conversation with Marty.

"Where do you get your ideas, Jimmy?"

"I don't know. They don't call ahead for an appointment, just sorta let themselves in."

"Wow, that's pretty cool, Jimmy. What are you writing now?"

"Been thinkin' about an alien who comes to Earth and lives inside a boy's head."

Sara's eyes flew open. "That sounds really interesting. What's the alien's purpose?"

"Helps the kid figure out what's right and wrong. Kinda like his conscience or somethin'."

"Marvelous. I think I have enough now. Can I get a photo?" She lifted a camera from out of the duffle bag. "Let's ask Mrs. Taylor if we can borrow her desk for a shot of you surrounded by books."

Tacky, thought Jimmy. Sara took several shots with a fancy camera.

"Story should be in Wednesday's paper, Thursday latest. Pleasure talking with you, Jimmy." She stood and offered her hand. "I wish you luck with your writing."

"Next Kurt Vonnegut," said Mrs. Taylor.

"Thanks."

Jimmy stayed in the library long enough to check out a William Faulkner and Kurt Vonnegut novel. He wanted to see if he fit any of Mrs. Taylor's comparisons.

By Wednesday evening, Jimmy was a local celebrity. Even Mike and the three Rs gave him a head-bob when he passed them in the hallway. Jimmy was invincible. He measured out the time when he'd qualify for a driver's license and decided to save his publishing windfall toward a used car. He already had eight hundred in savings from working summers. *If I work next summer, publish more stories. A car,* he thought. *Freedom.*

Luz Santiago sat next to Jimmy in math class. After being featured in the Recorder, she started talking with him. Luz was petite, cute, with a long waterfall of raven hair flowing down her back. She lived in Woodland and was a year ahead of him. Math class consisted mostly of worksheets. Mrs. Albright had one foot in the grave, and if anyone needed help, she was available at her desk. Luz and Jimmy talked softly and passed notes to while away the hour. She said her name meant light. She often ended sentences with *eh?*

"Read 'bout you in the paper, eh?"

"Yeah?"

"You're gonna be famous, eh?"

Jimmy laughed. "Don't know about that." He pushed up his glasses nervously.

After the bell, Jimmy walked Luz to her history class. By now, he stood six-foot-four, towering above five-foot Luz. As they passed classroom windows, he looked at their reflection.

"See you tomorrow, Jimmy."

"Hey, I was wondering...." He looked away to gather his nerve. "Got a phone number or somethin'? Could I call you sometime?"

"Sure, eh?" She scribbled it on a scrap of paper.

"Thanks. See yuh tomorrow."

He walked away with a lump in his throat the size of a golf ball. Nothing he'd written could compare to what was coursing through his body. That night he lay in bed thinking about the light. Her image shined down. He reached for a Kleenex on the nightstand and thought some more.

CHAPTER 20
THE BUBBLE BURSTS

High school students have short-term memories. The *What've you done for me lately?* attitude begins early on in the US. New stories Jimmy wrote were certainly good, yet lacked the impact of *Eighteen and Over*. He wrote about Ike, the three-legged dog, and the rise and fall of Sydney. They got a few laughs. He wrote about Loftus crapping in the hay barn, and they considered it too gross. A story about a teacher falling for a student was compared to *Lolita*. He hadn't read it, and when he did, Nabokov reminded him that, as a writer, he was a hack at best. He dared not write about LadySmith. Jimmy's sheen was worn. Now he was just another schmuck trying to make ends meet.

In late May, just before school let out for summer, Luz agreed to meet him at the river on a late Saturday morning. Jimmy rode his beat-up Schwinn, praying it wouldn't get a flat on the dirt road leading there. Luz was also on a bike. He arrived early and sat on the riverbank, feeling a familiar ache in his groin. He inhaled the familiar scent of weeds, dirt, scummy slow-moving water, and a nervous odor coming from his armpits.

He spied Luz in the distance, raising a small trail of dust. As she got closer, Jimmy stood and waved. She was smiling. Luz had asked him to bring some writing with him. He had his journal stashed in a nylon bag tied to the handlebars.

"Hi." Luz's bike didn't have a kickstand, so she laid it on the embankment.

"Hey, how are yuh?"

"Tired, eh? That's a long ride. Haven't exercised in a while."

"Least it's cooler than yesterday."

"Yeah."

"I brought water."

"Good." She pulled strands of long hair off her face.

"Haven't been here for ages," he said.

"Me either, eh? Used to come here with my brothers to swim."

"Water's nasty, but when you're a kid, you don't care."

"Yeah, kids do lots of stupid stuff, eh?" she agreed. "Did you bring a story?"

"One I wrote a while back."

"Let's see it, eh?"

Jimmy retrieved his journal and sat next to Luz on the bank. He read her *Eighteen and Over*. She liked it.

"Can I see?" She reached for the journal.

"Other stuff in there's terrible." He tried to take the journal back, but she moved it away from him. "What's this, eh? *Big Spread.*"

"Don't read that!" He made another grab. "It's trash."

She turned away to read, "As they kissed, his hands slipped beneath her shirt, finding the clasp—"

"Gimme that!" he laughed. "Just some shit I wrote when I was a kid."

She wagged a finger in his face. "He took a nipple into his mouth—"

"Awful."

"Kinda good, though."

Jimmy stopped trying for the journal. "Really?"

"Lotta experience, eh?"

It was a question with two possible answers—truth or a filthy lie. He decided to lie.

"Little bit."

"Who with, eh?"

His head was filled with row after row of cotton. The aching doubled its intensity.

"No one you'd know," he replied.

"Yeah?" She stepped close to him.

"Yeah."

This was the moment. He leaned over and touched her lips to his. She pressed against him, and he felt her tongue slip into his mouth. He knew what to do, had read about it dozens of times. He returned the action as they grew hungrier. The ache was delicious. He felt a trickling sensation.

They pressed their bodies together. Luz moaned and slipped a hand down his crotch. Jimmy's lower body suddenly jerked.

"Oh! You okay?" She looked at her hand and wiped it on her pants.

"Yeah, I just, you felt so good."

"Just with that?"

"Yeah."

She stepped back and saw effluent soaking through his Levi's.

"Bet that feels yucky."

"Naw." He tried to kiss her.

"That's a mess."

"It's okay." He drew her toward him.

"We better wait."

"Sure, all right." Jimmy changed the focus. "What about you?"

"Me what?"

"You know."

She nodded. "I've had boyfriends since seventh."

"Yeah?"

"Last one left for Mexico. He was a lot older."

"How much?"

"Ten years. Met him in the fields."

"That's illegal, yuh know."

"Yeah, but who has control over what the heart tells 'em to do, eh?"

"You're a writer too," Jimmy smiled.

"Think I gotta go. Long ride home."

Jimmy panicked. "Just got here."

Luz hedged. "Got protection?"

Jimmy shook his head."

She pushed up his glasses. "Sorry, Jimmy, no glove, no love."

"I'll pull out," he said, having read about men who did that.

She looked at his damp crotch and shook her head.

"I can do better."

"Another time maybe." She lifted her bike.

He kissed her, and his hand wandered beneath her shirt.

She pushed it away. "Like I said—"

"No glove, no love?"

"You got it."

Jimmy watched until she was a speck of dust. Then he hid inside a strand of bamboo to relieve the ache.

Later that day, Sam Martinez walked over to the ranch. He lived in a rent-free house on a grape farm a couple of miles away. Jimmy had known him since kindergarten. Sam liked coming over to throw a football, shoot baskets, or compete in rope vault. Jimmy's father erected a basket outside the fence in the front yard with a steel pole, plywood backboard, and a rim he'd purchased at Big Jim Maple's sporting goods store in Meadowland. It had no give to it. You had to swish it, or else the ball ricocheted, and they had to chase it down.

Sam had three beautiful sisters—Dolores, Connie, and Nina. Jimmy offered to swap his sister for any one of his.

"They don't date honkies," Sam teased.

"Why not?"

"Does your sister go out with Mexicans?"

Jimmy shrugged innocently.

"You know the answer to that."

It was true. He did.

Sam was handsome, funny, and unpretentious. He'd asked Jimmy to sleep over several times, yet Jimmy was never allowed. Occasionally he asked if Sam could, and his mother made a stab at political correctness.

"Jimmy, it's important to keep a certain distance between us and the workers."

"Sam doesn't work for us. Neither does his father. They grow grapes."

It was as if she hadn't heard. "Sam's a nice boy. You can play outside."

Monday arrived, and Luz wasn't in class. Jimmy called her house, but there was no answer. Tuesday, the same thing. On Wednesday, Jimmy stopped a girl he'd seen Luz hang around with.

"Seen Luz?"

"She moved."

"Moved?"

"Stepdad took 'em to Arizona."

"She comin' back?"

The girl shrugged. "He's got family there, I guess."

"Got a phone number or anything?"

"Nah, sorry."

Jimmy walked to his next class in a daze. So close, only to have the fish twist off the hook and swim away. He'd already asked Matthew for rubbers.

"Finally gettin' a piece?"

Jimmy knew Matt was more experienced. He'd had girlfriends since eighth grade and was currently with Susie, a freshman cheerleader. According to Matt, she did more than shake her pom-poms. He kept his wallet stocked with condoms. After school, Jimmy saw Matt and Susie sharing his motorcycle.

"Where you guys go?" Jimmy wanted to know for future reference.

"Shit, we've done it in old barns, prune orchards—yours a couple of nights ago—and at the airport."

The airport was a strip of overgrown tarmac that had once been used by crop dusters. Now it was a popular place to take girls.

"Did it on the bike," Matt finished.

"How'd that work out?"

"Voom-voom-voom!" He twisted the air.

Jimmy was bummed. He had a glove but no love. Friday was the last day of school, and in a few days, *Sonofabitchin' Mikey'll be home.*

Michael finished a BS in biology with an emphasis on environmental science. The war in Vietnam was winding down, yet the draft was still in effect. Mike put baseball dreams on hold to pursue a master's. That gave him another year of 2-S deferment. By then, he figured to be safe from becoming 1-A. Afterward, he'd pitch his way into the Hall of Fame. That was the plan.

CHAPTER 21
MAKING BUSINESS

Poor Jimmy, right? Just when things are starting to swing his way, shit hits the fan. Flaws are universal, and perfection is a myth. Disruptions to the time continuum are caused by too much curiosity. In my world, we're supposed to have all the answers, so we rarely ask questions. Curiosity kills more than cats.

You can't just go around forcing ideals on others without pushback. When I look at the mess you've made of the planet, it's clear a benevolent dictator might be needed—someone with a single-mindedness to cut through the bullshit and set things right. Then, when he gets too big for his pants, you can have him assassinated and find another one. Sound familiar?

At this point, I've gathered quite a bit of intel regarding the goings-on here. We're close to a turning point in Jimmy's life. You're probably anxious to know, does he sink or swim? What if he decides to float? Those are questions I can't ask. After all, I'm supposed to have all the answers.

***

In roughly 3,600 BC, glass was used in Mesopotamia. Scientists claim glass is neither solid nor liquid. It's amorphous. The universe is filled with fence-sitters.

Jimmy's heart was glass. For a brief moment, Mrs. Hickman had opened a door, yet it soon slammed shut. By the end of his freshman year, Jimmy's grade in Honors English dropped to a C. He managed the same in other classes—straight C's. Jimmy was officially average. Not that Mrs. Hickman hadn't tried.

"Jimmy, what's going on? The work you've turned in lately isn't what I've come to expect from you."

"Yes, ma'am. I'll try harder."

He remembered her look—sadness, disappointment. Like his mother's.

"I can't recommend you for Honors next year."

"I understand. Have a nice summer, Mrs. Hickman."

"You too Jimmy."

Other teachers didn't bat an eye. Average Jimmy was on the roster and took up a seat in class. That's about all they knew about him. He was a wasp snuggling inside its octagonal paper cell.

On the final day of class, Jimmy was in the boys' room pissing when he heard a familiar *click-click-click*. Joining him at the urinal was Refugio. Jimmy pushed harder as if trying to laser an inscription into the porcelain.

"Hey, güero," Refugio said.

"Hey," Jimmy answered, hoping that would finish the chat.

"Que hacen this summer, man?"

"Workin', I guess."

"Gonna work on your hacienda?" A note of bitterness was in his use of the word.

Jimmy shrugged. "Guess so."

"Wanna make some real bread?"

"Doin' what?" Jimmy stood at the sink.

Refugio joined him. "What you think?" He lifted a small baggy out of his pocket.

Jimmy raised his eyebrows.

"Beats hoein' cotton, don't it?"

Jimmy's emotions were spinning in a cheap blender. He was at an amorphous crossroad. One direction led nowhere. The other probably did too. He decided to hear Refugio out. *What difference does it make?*

"C'mon, man."

Refugio led him out to the student parking lot. The three Rs shared a '64 black Ford Galaxy. Officially it belonged to Ramon, but they all had access. He unlocked the passenger door for Jimmy. "Step into my officina, güero."

"Nice car."

Refugio slipped into the driver's seat and shut the door. "Roll down the fuckin' window. It's burnin' up in here."

Jimmy cranked the handle, and the window complained the whole way down.

"Why me?" he asked. "Last I remember, you didn't think too highly of me."

Refugio chuckled. "The good 'ol days, eh? Your gringo buddies want weed, but they don't trust us." He fished out the baggy and handed it to Jimmy.

"How's this work?"

"We give you product, you sell product, you get paid. Ain't rocket science."

"How much?"

"Ten percent."

"How much does it go for?"

"Forty an ounce. If you can get fifty, andale pues, more power to yuh. There's papers in the glove box. Roll a J for us."

Jimmy shook his head. "I never…."

"Pinches gringos." He grabbed the bag and reached over for the papers. "Use long papers." his fingers worked feverishly. "Take out stems and seeds, roll a cone 'cause it burns better than a straight roll. You can make a cardboard mouthpiece, but you don't got to." He licked the end papers and rolled it perfectly. He fished in his pocket and brought out a lighter. "Then fire it up." After taking a hit, he handed it to Jimmy.

Jimmy's first drag was followed by a coughing fit. Refugio shook his head and clapped him on the back.

Jimmy handed it back. His eyes burned.

"What you do on the hacienda all day? Fuck cows?"

"Chickens," Jimmy answered.

Refugio laughed and handed the joint back to Jimmy. "Take it slow and easy. Hold it long as you can."

It went easier. After a few more hits, his head was spinning. He saw the world from a different height, through a filter of pungent smoke. Refugio wrote down a number.

"Call me when you're set up. Tell your ol' man you got a job in town or some shit."

"Ain't gotta ride."

"We'll pick you up."

"Summer school starts the week after next. I'll tell 'em I gotta go."

"Whatever, man."

There was a tap on the rear window, and they jumped. It was Ramon and Ricardo.

"Need a lift home, güero ?" Refugio asked.

"Sure."

Ramon replaced Jimmy in the front seat, and Jimmy sat in the back with Ricardo.

"You in, Kock?" asked Ricardo.

Ramon burst out laughing. "You can't pull out once you're in."

Jimmy joined in the laughter. He was past caring what anybody called him. The effect of the weed burned a hole right through what was left of his ego. The rest of the way, the three Rs talked in Spanish, and Jimmy couldn't follow most of what they said.

During dinner that evening, Jimmy told his parents about summer school.

"Damn good idea," his father droned.

His mother followed with, "Straight C's. Why can't you be more like your brother?"

"Gotta try harder, son. Shits fire."

"Is there a bus?" Mom wanted to know.

"Gotta friend with a car. He'll stop at the end of the lane."

"Good. When's it starting?"

"Monday. Week after next."

"Mikey'll be here next week sometime," Mother said as an afterthought.

"Yep," sighed his father.

"Could you pass the green beans?" Karen asked.

Lately, Jimmy hadn't seen much of Karen. She was taking dental assistant classes at Meadowland Junior College and still dating David Lassiter. Yet the only studying she did was in the back of his Ford Mustang Boss 302, though how they managed would be the envy of any contortionist.

Seven days later, Ramon picked Jimmy up at 7:00 AM at the end of Palm Tree Lane. The other two Rs were busy in Woodland.

"Where we headin'?"

Ramon took a drag on a cigarette and sent a plume of smoke through the side window. "Remember when I caught you in the nuts?"

Jimmy swallowed. "Kinda hard to forget."

Ramon smiled. "You didn't rat."

"You wanted me 'cause I ain't a rat?"

He shook his head. "Nah. Luz Santiago."

"What's she got to do with it?"

"Her brother Frankie got the business goin' in Woodland. Don't ever mess with him. Mean motherfucker. Jack you up good."

"Luz?"

"She liked you, man. Hell, she liked a *lot* of us."

Jimmy stared out the windshield. The town of Poplar loomed like a cold sore.

"You'll see plenty of action this summer. Young pussy—bust some piñatas. Girls like bad boys, ese."

Ese was Chicano slang for dude, and Jimmy heard it a lot around them. It sounded like an English assignment.

They entered Poplar, population 2,411. Why someone would choose to live there was anybody's guess. Jimmy used to play Babe Ruth baseball there. Teams were named after local company sponsors. His team was Nelson Pipe. The coach was a co-owner named Burt, and he knew nothing about baseball. He penciled in players to take the field and watched the ensuing chaos from the safety of the bench.

The ramshackle park had one caveat—lights. The dimness of the lights gave rise to the field's nickname, Candlelit Park. Jimmy's fastball seemed to travel at the speed of light when he pitched night games there. In his former quest to be like Mike, he did well until he was asked to pitch a day game. Then his fastball became a beach ball.

Jimmy had a refined, smooth delivery. His mechanics were unparalleled thanks to Floyd, who'd taken a few late afternoons to work with him as a favor to his father. Floyd was instrumental in refining Michael's mechanics, taming the flamethrower's right arm into something more akin to an acetylene torch. In the end, Jimmy came up with a decent curveball capable of inducing ground balls and weak pop-ups.

"Snap it off right at the release point," Floyd said, "and follow through."

Jimmy practiced with his father once or twice a week. Bill

squatted behind a makeshift plate. He built a backstop out of wood and chicken wire. Jimmy toed the rubber on a hill of red dirt that Bill erected to major-league specifications. Jimmy pitched carefully. If he bounced too many curveballs, his father lost patience and quit.

There they were—the lights. Baseball drew good crowds because there wasn't much else to do in town. No bowling alleys, parks, movie theaters, or fancy restaurants. Just dope. People brought lawn chairs because there was limited seating in the rickety bleachers behind home plate.

The umpire was a local celebrity by the name of Hayden Hood. Hayden was in his late fifties, short, heavy, and had four remaining teeth. He sported a perpetual gray stubble on his face. He made up for physical shortcomings by uttering hilarious remarks during the game. Sometimes he'd sneak a flask out of his back pocket to take a swig between innings.

The lack of teeth made Hayden's remarks a target for impersonation. Strikes became *srrri-i-ike*, and balls morphed into *bow*. What he said between pitches made the games even more interesting. If a batter backed away from a pitch, "Don't be a pussy. Get in there and swing, boy!"

Jimmy remembered a night game against Exxon. His catcher was a hefty Portuguese kid, Arsenio Nunez, nicknamed Arson. His talent in baseball hardly warranted the moniker. Jimmy bounced a curveball into his nuts. Arsenio wasn't wearing a cup, so he immediately dropped to his hands and knees.

Hayden laid into him. "Why ain't you wearin' no cup?" He reached into his back pocket and offered the flask. "Take a shwig. Put hair on your balls."

Burt's only advice was, "Walk it off, kid."

Arsenio made it back to his feet, and the bleachers scattered with applause along with jeers: Rang your bell! Busted the family jewels!

Hayden took a swig and returned the flask to his back pocket. "Don't lishun to them ashholes. Ain't a nut-shack between 'em."

Arsenio tenuously settled into a crouch.

"Gonna play next year?" Ramon asked.

"Naw, figure not."

"Brother's some kinda hotshot, ain't he?"

"Guess so."

They passed Candlelit Park. "Seen him put a kid in the hospital."

"Oh yeah, some fucker named Randal somethin'. Cracked his battin' helmet."

"Clocked him good."

"Parents raised hell, and they wouldn't let Mike pitch no more that season."

"Threw BBs."

Ramon turned down a street that looked like every other one in Poplar and cruised to a decrepit house. There were half-a-dozen jalopies parked there.

"Lemme do the talkin'. Keep your mouth shut." He reached over, took a nylon bag out of the glove compartment, and stuffed it down the front of his pants. Then he checked his mirrors and looked up and down the street before getting out.

Jimmy thought about LadySmith and wished she was there. A mangy looking mutt with dreadlocks barked and nipped at their ankles as they made their way to the front door.

"Pinche perro!" Ramon kicked, and it scampered away, only to dart in again.

There were free newspapers moldering on the dry lawn scattered with beer cans. A rectangular cavity showed where a doorbell had been. Loud Mexican music blared from inside. Ramon banged at the door, waited, and banged louder.

He motioned for them to step back, so they were visible from a window. The music was turned off, and a menacing face peered through tattered curtains. A moment later, the door opened a crack, and a chain was undone. Blocking the entrance was a cigarette-smoking Chicano wearing a wife-beater and a pair of black trousers. His hair was slicked back and tamed with gel. He had a net over it.

"Hey, Flaco," Ramon greeted him.

Mexican nicknames are very accurate. They described physical attributes and personality traits. Flaco's face was skullish. He wore a tattoo on his forearm that said, Nuestra Familia and kept the cigarette in his mouth when he talked.

Flaco barely acknowledged Ramon with an upward nod. He stepped aside to let them in and closed the door. The small living area was suffused with smoke, lit by two floor lamps. Windows were covered in a variety of dark-colored curtains. There were five pieces of furniture in the room—a threadbare loveseat, ravaged sofa, and three grey steel chairs. On each end of the sofa, two men sat cross-legged, facing each other and counting money. In between was a small stack of bills and a pack of cigarettes.

On the loveseat sat a man with a brown-skinned girl. Jimmy couldn't guess how old she was—fifteen or thirty. Her shoulder-length hair was in need of washing. She wasn't bad looking, yet the tightness around her mouth, narrowed eyes, blue mascara, and false eyelashes spoke volumes about the way her life was going so far. She wore a halter top that revealed half her diminutive breasts.

The man with her had an angry face covered in patchy black hair. If it's true that each person grips the mallet and positions the chisel to carve out their lives, then he and his associates were dreadful sculptors.

You're a writer, whispered Jimmy's Yin. *You're a goddamn fool*, his Yang corrected. *Jesus Christ*, summarized the thought.

"This the güero?" He glared at Jimmy. The girl bit a fingernail and picked at it. He snapped at her. "Gimme a beer."

Without a word, she got up and went into the kitchen. The living area saw through to the kitchen, separated by a blue vinyl breakfast counter.

"Yeah," Ramon said.

Jimmy kept his hands in his pockets. Flaco shuffled into the kitchen. He came up behind the girl and cupped a breast.

"You smell," the girl complained. "Get away."

"Orale, baby, don't do me like that."

"Take a shower." She shoved him back and opened the refrigerator. "No beer."

"Go get some," said the man on the loveseat.

"Gimme some money."

"Earn it," Flaco said.

The man on the loveseat laughed. "Gotta earn it before you burn it."

"Shit." She shuffled into a bedroom, followed by Flaco. He didn't bother shutting the door.

"León." Love-seat man stuck a thumb into his chest. "Means lion, güero. Means I'll tear you into tiny pieces if you fuck me over. Entiendes Mendez?"

Jimmy nodded.

León switched to Ramon. "Told him how it works?"

"Yeah."

His mouth curved down, and he returned his attention to Jimmy. "Start with an ounce. Bring back forty, keep five. Then you get two ounces, keep ten. Work your way up. Got it?"

Jimmy nodded. Various sounds from the bedroom were floating down the hallway.

"Lemme hear you say it."

"Yeah, I got it."

The man nodded slowly. "Get busted. That's on you." He made his right hand into a finger gun. "This's what happens to rats."

"Turn around," Flaco commanded from the bedroom, followed by a rhythmic slapping of flesh against flesh.

"Don't pull my hair, asshole!" the girl protested.

León watched Jimmy's face and his mouth lifted on one side. "Chucho, give the güero an ounce."

One of the guys on the sofa got up and went into the bedroom.

"Get the fuck out!" said Flaco.

Chucho returned, shaking his head, carrying a small baggy.

"Hurry *up*," said the girl.

Slap, slap, slap, followed by, *slapslapslapslapslap* and a finishing growl.

Chucho handed the bag to León. Leon, Chucho, Flaco. Jimmy memorized their names. The other man on the couch was nameless.

Flaco came out of the bedroom, pulling his wife-beater down. León looked up at Jimmy.

"Stay in there," he yelled toward the bedroom. "You still got business!"

"You talkin' to me?" said the girl.

"You heard."

"What about the beer?"

"I said stay there!" He nodded his head to Jimmy. "Go hit that shit, güero."

"Fringe benefits," Chucho nodded.

***

After returning home, Jimmy showered as his mother prepared the evening meal. She hardly acknowledged him, and he was glad. A myriad of aromas wafted from his body—weed, cigarette smoke, and sex. Jimmy was the flip side of a 45 nobody listened to.

After cleaning up, he took his reeking clothes into the back laundry room. Then he skirted around the house to sit on the front doorstep. Despite the walnut tree's size, it seldom grew nuts. *How disappointing to be a Christmas tree without ornaments.* He reflected on his day after receiving the ounce of weed from León. He sold it within fifteen minutes to a white guy at Murray Park in Meadowland. Risking jail or worse, he pocketed five bucks. *Tomorrow,* he thought, *two ounces, ten bucks.* He calculated how much he'd have to sell to equal a day's pay on the farm. *Ten ounces.*

After waiting a lifetime, he'd gotten laid. He reflected on how disappointing it'd been. His experience with Chapstick in the hay barn was more gratifying. Ramon said her name was Mirella. Life choices take us to our ends, yet sometimes there's little or no choice. Mirella was sinking in the silt of a stagnant lake just like him. Despite the filth of the room, stains on the bare mattress, and the smell of stale body fluids hanging in the air, he'd been able to perform the deed.

"Saddle up, cowboy."

Jimmy fell over, taking off his Levi's. She sighed impatiently and raised her knees. Jimmy crawled between, and she placed him. Despite the lack of ambience, he pushed inside, his eyes rolled up into his skull, and he spurted immediately.

"Christ, what a mess," she complained.

Jimmy watched as she grabbed a roll of paper towels and wiped the fluorescent river flowing from her gaping entrance.

From the doorstep, he reimagined the scene under better conditions. Mirella was freshly bathed, encouraging with kind words, kissing him passionately as they wrestled in each other's arms. The daydream was shattered by the boom of an aerosol can exploding in the steel drum trash barrel.

That night Jimmy closed his eyes, and it seemed a moment later, his mother shook him awake. She encapsulated everything she had to say to him within a run-on sentence.

"Get up, you'll be late for school. I made a peanut butter sandwich you can eat on the way. Your brother called and said he'll be here tonight, so get home right after school and don't forget you have a dentist appointment Friday, but it's walkin' distance from the school, so I'll ask Michael to pick you up afterward."

"Okay." The simplicity of his reply was sufficient.

CHAPTER 22
BACK TO SCHOOL

Ricardo was driving the Ford Galaxy. He was quieter than Refugio and Ramon. Jimmy told him his brother was picking him up after summer school that Friday.

"You can let me off at the high school. I'll hang out there."

"Mmm," grunted Ricardo. "Heard you got paid by Mirella."

Jimmy didn't reply. He pursed his lips, nodded, and looked out the side window.

"First time's free. Next time it's five bucks."

"Five bucks?" His profit for selling an ounce.

"That shit's nasty." Ricardo made a face.

They stopped at the Poplar house. Every town has a distribution house. Flaco was the only one there. He gave Jimmy four ounces, and Ricky got fifteen. They headed to Meadowland. Ricardo stopped the car in front of Monache High School.

Jimmy raised his eyebrows. "Really?"

"Find your güero friends." He handed Jimmy smaller bags. "Nickel and dimes. Make 'em pay double."

Jimmy did as he was asked. He divvied up the product into smaller parcels and placed them in his school backpack. His heart raced even though he realized it was unlikely anyone would question his presence on campus. The school district employed two aged security guards for summer school. In the seventies, AR-15s, Glock 17s, and school massacres weren't in vogue. Thanks to the NRA and the conservative far-right, students will soon be wearing Kevlar to school.

"Two o'clock across the street at the little park," Ricardo said. Then he broke into a spontaneous song. "My name is Poncho, I live on a rancho, I make my five dollars a day. I go see my Lucy, she give me some poosy, and takes my five dollars away."

Jimmy chuckled and got out. Ricardo screeched the tires as he pulled away. *What the fuck've I gotten myself into?* Jimmy wondered. Yet there was something about the three Rs. Now that he was earning their respect, they treated him as an equal. It felt good. It felt right.

That morning Jimmy slipped onto the school grounds to blend in with the students. The trick was finding buyers. He didn't know many of the summer students. Meadowland and Monache High School combined for the summer program. Five hundred students roamed the hallways to make up for failed classes during the regular school year or to get a jump-start on graduating earlier. They represented malleable clientele seeking escape from the drudgery of programmed academics.

Jimmy went into one of the boy's restrooms, a common marketplace. He smelled smoke and knew he'd hit the mark. He stood at a urinal to piss. The kid finishing a cigarette stood in front of an open stall. He was short, white, and skinny. His brown hair was tied into a ponytail. Jimmy made an offhand remark.

"Care for somethin' a little stronger?"

"What you got, man?" the boy asked.

Jimmy fished into his backpack for a nickel bag.

"I only got five bucks," the kid said.

"That'll do."

Two other white kids came in, and they all knew each other.

"Hey man, got any bread?" the skinny kid asked.

"For what?"

"How much?"

They took out wallets and collected twelve bucks between them.

"Find Teddy. He's flush."

Jimmy was getting nervous. "Listen, man, get it together and meet at the park after school." Another student came in.

They agreed. If it worked out that they could be trusted, Jimmy thought they could provide other clients for him.

"Right on. Lay some skin!" said one.

Jimmy reached his hand out. "Listen. Don't have to tell yuh to keep your traps shut, right?"

"It's cool, man. We ain't rats," answered another.

"Bring exact change," Jimmy added. "I ain't no grocery store."

At 12:45, Jimmy was encircled by eight white kids. Nervously he distributed took cash and stuffed it in his pocket until he ran out.

"Send one guy tomorrow," he said.

This was met with, Right on, far out, let's get stoned.

Ricardo pulled up and saw the gathering as it dispersed. "Pinche gringo," he muttered.

Ricky kept the car parked and looked at Jimmy when he got in. "That shit ain't cool, man. Might as well paint a fuckin' sign on your back!"

"I know—"

"What the fuck do you know?"

"Won't happen again. I'm gonna need a lot more dope."

"Shit."

Jimmy handed Ricardo the money, and he counted out a hundred and sixty dollars and relaxed.

"You can fuck Mirella four times." He pointed to his right temple. "I gotta head for math."

***

Michael arrived on Wednesday afternoon. He'd changed from being an off-season hippy to a clean-cut conservative WASP. He greeted Jimmy with a smile. Mother gave him a long hug, and his father offered a customary handshake.

"You look great," Bill said. "Never cared for the Jesus look. Sit down. Let's catch up."

Karen wasn't there. Jimmy listened to his brother summarize the latest events in his life. Bill questioned the wisdom of Mike turning down a baseball contract with the Twins to stay in school.

"Risky ain't it? What if they don't want yuh when you're done with school?"

"Can't play baseball for the rest of my life. But I got some news. Drum roll." Mike used the coffee table. "I signed with the Twins, and they agreed to pay for my masters. I can study in the offseason."

"You mean…?"

"Yeah, Dad."

"I'll be goddamned!" He pumped Michael's arm. "Fantastic!"

"We're so proud." Mother dabbed her eyes with the sleeve of her blouse.

"Congratulations," Jimmy said.

"Thanks. Where's Sis? Hear she's marryin' that Lassiter guy."

"Made it official two weeks ago. Movin' to Sacramento. He's gettin' a masters in accounting."

"How they gonna live?"

"We said we'd help out, and so did his folks. They're real nice," said Bill.

"And Karen found a dentist to work for. It's just for a year," added Barbara.

"I got a twenty-five thousand dollar signing bonus. I'll help."

"She'll be home this evening. Has a late class."

"When they gettin' married? Gotta fly to Elizabethton, Tennessee in a few weeks for Rookie League."

"Soon, I imagine." Mother's smile tightened, and she looked away.

"Yep," his father's voice dropped several octaves.

"She's pregnant?" Mike's eyes were wide.

Barbara nodded weakly. It was news to Jimmy too. He shifted on his feet.

"Jesus." Mike shook his head. "Helluva way to start a life."

"Yep," his father repeated.

That night Michael muttered in the darkness. "Believe it? Sonofabitch knocked 'er up.'"

Jimmy didn't have anything to say. He thought, *Least now, I'm not the biggest screwup in the family.*

It was Thursday, and Jimmy managed a clean escape. He was ready to make some easy money. *Buy a car next year.* He was given ten ounces. After school, one buyer showed—the same kid he'd run into the first day. His name was Ryan. He collected the cash and distributed to his friends.

Jimmy made over four hundred dollars. He thought of Mirella and set aside five for when they returned to Poplar for the money drop. *It'll go better this time,* he thought. He hoped she was fresh.

When they arrived, Mirella wasn't there. León saw him looking around and guessed.

"Bitches come and go, güero. Keep rakin' it in, and you can fuck my sister."

After being dropped at the head of the Palm Tree Lane, Jimmy walked taller. He'd scored over fifty bucks. There was only one tense moment when a police cruiser parked nearby but never got out of the car. Jimmy took out a tattered copy of *East of Eden* and pretended to read.

As he neared the house, he saw his brother jogging on the dirt road next to the white barn. He went inside the barn and came out a few minutes later. *Checkin' on the magazine*, thought Jimmy. Mike saw Jimmy walking and jogged toward him. Then he walked to cool down.

"Jimbo, how's it goin', man?"

He didn't like being called Jimbo. "Okay."

"What's school like?"

"All right, I guess."

"You're gonna be Uncle Jim."

Jimmy shrugged.

"Backpack looks light."

"Don't have books for summer school."

"Hmm. What you takin'?"

"History."

"Gotta plan?"

"For what?" Jimmy was getting irritated.

"Your life."

Jimmy knew his mother would put Mikey up to this. Dad was too passive for much in the way of fatherly advice, so it fell to Mike.

They still consider me the family fuckup? "Haven't thought on it."

"Good time to start. Shit, when I was your age...." Mike went on about how he'd wisely chosen his path to success.

Whoop-de-do, motherfucker. "Look, Mike, I see what you're tryin' to do. Don't worry, okay?"

"Straight C's? Hell, I couldn't do that if I tried."

"I get it, Mike."

"Listen, you and me haven't always seen eye-to-eye, but I want you to know...."

Here it comes! Jimmy's fists were balled up now. He wanted LadySmith tucked behind his lower spine. He felt Mike's arm hook around his shoulders.

"I care about you, man."

Jimmy's lips quivered with anger. He took a few quick steps to leave the arm behind.

CHAPTER 23
BROTHERHOOD

Barbara spat another run-on sentence. "Don't forget you've a dentist appointment today. Mikey'll pick you up after, so don't wander off."

"Yeah, Mom." He scooted through the door.

As he walked down the lane, he scratched his crotch, which had started itching that morning. Ramon was driving, and Ricardo was in the front passenger seat. He twisted around to say something and saw Jimmy scratching.

"What's up?"

Jimmy shrugged. Ricky laughed and shook his head.

"Mirella. Flaco got crabs too."

"How you get rid of 'em?"

"What's that shit Flaco used?" he asked Ramon.

"DDT," he said.

"Got some in the barn," Jimmy said. "Put it on ant mounds. Wipes 'em out quick."

"Get a nice Catholic girl," Ricardo suggested. "I got one in Woodland. Maria Elena. Her pinche ol' man hates my guts."

"Popped 'er cherry yet?" Ramon asked.

"Airport, two weeks ago, Right where the güero's sittin'."

Jimmy smiled and scratched. He didn't look forward to enduring an itchy day ending with Michael. *What a drag.*

They turned down the familiar street toward Poplar house.

"Fuck!" Ramon pulled over.

"Shit, man!" Ricardo said.

Jimmy's heart sank. The street was lined with cop cars, lights flashing. Two cruisers blocked the way in and out for half a block.

"Chill," Ramon said. He calmly flipped a U-turn and returned to the main road.

"Motherfucker." Ricardo said.

"What now?" Asked Jimmy.

"Lay low. Head back to Woodland and tell Frankie if he don't already know."

Jimmy turned white. Dizziness consumed him. He was supposed to be in Meadowland that afternoon. In the midst of panic, he thought, *I really am a fuck up.* He remembered Mrs. Hickman lecturing about romance versus reality when they read *The Lord of the Flies.* He knew exactly what she meant.

They were lost in their own thoughts on the drive toward Woodland. Jimmy got an idea.

"Hey, drop me here."

It was Matthew Cloninger's ranch. He wasn't in summer school, so he'd be there.

Ramon stopped. His eyes were stony. "Listen, güero, don't forget the fuckin' rules."

"Yeah."

"We'll find another gig."

Jimmy nodded. Ricardo fired up a blunt and stared at his watch. "Later, man."

Matt's mother greeted Jimmy warmly at the door and told him what part of the ranch her son was working. He thanked her and walked toward a plume of diesel smoke in the distance, climbing into the sky from a Ford 3000.

Jimmy waited at the end of a row. Matt smiled and spit a brown stream of tobacco on the right fender. He turned off the motor.

"What's up?"

"Got summer school."

"Beats this." He gestured at the wheel of the Ford.

"Any beer?"

"Naw, ol' man's careful 'bout where he stashes it now."

"Hey man, I need a favor." Jimmy cut to the chase.

"Yeah? More Trojans?"

Jimmy smiled. "Naw. Need a ride to Meadowland."

"Miss the bus?"

"Somethin' came up."

"Why not go home?"

"Kinda complicated."

"How's that?"

"Truth is, I ain't been in school."

"Now I get the picture. What you doin' when you ain't there?"

"Sellin' pot."

Matt smiled and slapped his knee. "You're the man! Got any?"

"Nah. My connection got busted."

"No shit. You all right?"

"Hope so."

"How'd you get in?"

"Long story. Can you get me there?"

"Hang out 'til lunch? I'll sneak you there." Matt chuckled. "Jimmy, the dope fiend. Far out. Hook me up."

Jimmy changed the subject. "Still bangin' that beaver?"

"Balls deep, man."

Matt's work was a close walk to the river, so Jimmy hung out there until lunchtime. The smell of death hung in the air. He didn't want to know what it was, but the odor drove him further down the riverbank. He found a Smith's Market shopping cart. Transients sometimes stole them to store belongings. One homeless guy who lived on the river was nicknamed Mush-mouth because you couldn't understand a word he said.

Goddamn, thought Jimmy. *Life's like this ol' river. Full of weeds, cockleburs, and dry sand. You could walk it forever, and nothin'll change.* Jimmy wasn't wearing a watch. He stared at the sun and figured it to be about ten. Thoughts showered him.

What you gonna do with your life, shit for brains? Oughta put that rope in the barn to good use. He remembered a country song... *hang me from the highest tree, woman would you weep for me?* His crotch itched, and he imagined the tiny lice laying eggs on shafts of fine hair, multiplying, setting up house. He recalled his initiation into manhood with Mirella. *Lasted fifteen seconds*, he thought. *How many other disappointments are waitin'? When Karen's baby comes, I'll be the uncle who never got his shit together. Goddamn me all to hell.*

Jimmy glared at the sun. Almost time. He started the journey back.

Matt took Jimmy to Meadowland on his motorcycle. When they got there, his hair was twisted into odd shapes. He thanked his friend and entered the dentist's office.

The dental assistant cleaned his teeth before Dr. Wilkes came in to do an exam. He found a cavity and asked if Jimmy wanted it taken care of right then.

"Yeah, why not," he said.

Wilkes numbed him with Novocain and drilled. The smell of burning tooth was worse than the dull ache of the drill. A filling was placed, and Jimmy was free to go. He couldn't feel the right side of his face. Mike put down the Sports Illustrated he was reading, nodded to Jimmy, and they went to the red Volkswagen van. The engine struggled to keep the speed limit. Finally, about halfway home, Mike talked.

"Remember the time Dad took me deep-sea fishin', and I caught that little shark?"

"Yeah."

"We buried it, and a few years later, I got the idea of diggin' it up so I could make a necklace or somethin' out of the teeth. Dug around for hours. Never did find it."

"Hmm."

"Guess sometimes the past needs to stay buried."

Despite filters he'd installed to protect from Mike's sermons, this one got in. Jimmy swirled the words around in his brain. He looked at his brother.

"Know what you mean."

Mike nodded solemnly. "I wasn't any kinda brother to yuh. Sorry for it. Wanna try and make it up."

Jimmy had fallen for this a million times. The shoe would drop any second now, and he'd feel miserable again. *Don't listen.*

"You got quiet all of the sudden," Mike laughed. "Scare yuh?"

"Nah."

He changed the topic. "How was school?"

"Okay."

"Got cavities?"

"One. Still can't feel my face."

"Wanna play catch when we get back?"

"Okay."

At the turnoff to Poplar, Mike said, "Gotta cravin' for a burger. Want one?"

Hell no! Jimmy's thoughts screamed. He was starving, yet the idea of returning to the belly of the beast made him nauseous. Before he could answer, Mike made the turn.

The burger joint was called Leo's. When it first opened, he offered four burgers for a dollar. Jimmy remembered his father taking him there for lunch one day after buying pipe fittings from the hardware store. They shared a good laugh when they got the burgers. His father took a bite, lifted the edge of a bun, and said, "Hello, any meat in there?"

Leo was in his late fifties, gruff but friendly. He had a weathered face like you see on old westerns. He knew Jimmy by name from his Babe Ruth days, coming there after a game with Uncle Ed. His uncle loved watching him play even though he wasn't near as good as Michael. He took Jimmy to his games and treated him to a milkshake afterward. There was a small place inside with two tables where they could eat, or they could sit outside beneath an awning at one of the picnic benches.

Jimmy went inside to the ordering window with his brother. Out of the corner of his eye, he saw Mirella sucking soda from a straw. She smiled. "Hey there."

Jimmy tried to smile back, but his lips were still numb, and his crotch was itching more than ever.

"Hey!" she said loudly.

Jimmy lifted his hand and waved. Mike looked at her, then at Jimmy, as if a new secret was revealed. Mirella smirked.

"Order'll be out in a jiffy," Leo said. "Four bucks twenty-three cents."

Mike paid, and Mirella motioned Jimmy over.

"Go on," said Mike. "I'll wait in the van."

Despite the itching, his traitorous hardness pulsated. He sat across from her.

"How yuh been?"

"Haven't seen yuh," Jimmy said.

"Ain't gonna. Hear what happened?"

"Saw this morning."

"León got busted. Can't say I'm torn up about it. What *you* doin'?"

Jimmy shrugged. "Layin' low."

"Don't worry. They're dirt-bags, but they ain't snitches."

"Yeah?"

"Pigs don't give a shit about you."

Jimmy started to relax, like a leg cramp easing up. "Sure?"

"Yep."

"I'm out now anyway."

"Good."

"What've you been up to?"

"Cuttin' hair. Gonna open my own place someday, but not in this shit-hole."

Jimmy nodded. "I'm thinkin' of college."

"Schoolboy," she teased.

"Order's up!" shouted Leo.

"Who's that you're with?"

"Brother."

"Kinda cute."

From the van, Mike saw that the order was ready and returned to the window.

"Take your time," he said to Jimmy, "I'll wait in the van."

"Or you can join us right here," Mirella suggested.

Mike smiled and sat with Jimmy.

"Brothers, eh?"

"Yeah. Forgot the sodas." He pointed to Mirella's drink. "What's your poison?"

"Coke," she said, veiling her eyes.

Mike got up for the drinks.

"He's cute. How tall is he?"

"Six six."

"Jeez."

Mike brought the drinks over.

"Thanks, you're sweet."

"Welcome."

"Gotta use the head," Jimmy announced, standing up and walking to a small door marked, Cowboys and Cowgirls.

Mirella didn't waste time. She reached into her handbag and used a receipt to write her phone and address. Then she shoved it over.

"What's this?"

"Whatever you make of it," she replied.

"How old 're you?"

"Old 'nough. What's your name?"

"Mike."

"Mirella." She held out her hand, and Mike took it.

"How you know Jimmy?"

"That's his name?"

"You didn't know his name?"

"Didn't know yours either. Now I do."

"Point taken."

"Why don't you call me later? Might just let you buy me another Coke."

"Yeah?"

"Yeah."

Jimmy returned. Mike stood. "Time to head out, little brother."

"Nice to meet you, Mike. See yuh, Jimmy."

"Yeah." Jimmy wanted to scratch so bad it made his eyes tear.

Mike somehow had managed to thaw a layer of the ice covering his heart. Jimmy had never understood what was at the root. *Maybe I oughta ask Karen.* Yet it seemed unlikely she'd have an answer other than recalling the pact she'd made with Mike when Jimmy was born. *You and me gotta stick together...us against him, understand?*

Mike fired up the van and was smiling as he checked the rearview mirror. He didn't mention the girl.

"Jimmy, when I go pro, I'll get yuh into the games for free."

"That'd be nice."

Mike smiled and patted Jimmy's knee.

As soon as they got home, Jimmy sneaked into the red barn and searched the steel cupboards where his father kept pesticides, herbicides, insecticides, and other suicides. He found a small sack with DDT written on it. After pulling down his pants, he grabbed a handful to sprinkle in his pubic hair and dusted his ass for good measure. It was odorless and felt like the powder he sometimes used to cure athlete's foot.

That evening Jimmy showered, and the itching stopped. After dinner, Mike said he was driving to meet up with friends in Meadowland. He returned after 2:00 in the morning. The next day he looked tired but content. Jimmy put two and two together.

By God, now we really are brothers, he mused.

CHAPTER 24
BROKEN DREAM

Me again—Jimmy's consciousness. By now, you're trying to guess how this game's gonna end. Will ignorance get control and turn him into one of those goddamn Trump supporters? Can goodwill ride to the rescue on a white stallion of Truth? It's good to wonder. Wonder is a main ingredient separating humans from primitive counterparts that rely on instinct and rudimentary cognitive tools. If you continue this chronicle, it means that your sense of wonder is alive and well. Let's celebrate!

Sometimes the best way to write a story is to let it simmer on the back burner a while after the first draft is finished. That's why it's taken sixty-five years for this to happen.

***

How could Jimmy continue the summer school ruse? He pondered the domino effect of the previous week.

Water under the bridge, he thought. *Hell, after what I've been through, facing angry parents is a stroll in the park.*

That next morning, Michael woke up feeling invincible and announced he would break the rope vault record.

Jimmy shook his head. "Don't yuh think you're a little old for that?"

"C'mon, man."

"Okay."

Karen reluctantly tagged along. Her relationship with Michael was on shaky ground. She mostly kept to herself. Mike was still angry that she'd let herself fall into a common trap. He'd learned to be responsible, find his own way. Why hadn't she? Mother was busy making preparations for a quickie wedding in Three-rivers, a mountain community in the Sierras not far from Visalia. She rented a small catering service for an outdoor wedding. Tents would be erected, food laid out, and a minister would mumble the oath of fidelity.

After helping pad the landing area with hay, checking for Loftus turds, and recovering it with the grey canvas, Karen sat on a hay bale as the two brothers took turns raising the bar. Jimmy beat his old record with ease.

Michael felt a tinge of guilt when he thought of talking Karen into a turn. Perhaps she'd land badly and jar the baby loose. She'd be free, not trapped into marriage. Guilty thoughts dispersed into the vapid fumes of heated air surrounding them. It was 10:45 a.m., yet the temperature was ninety-eight.

Michael faced the bar, raised to eleven feet six inches. In order to clear such a height, he'd have to generate extraordinary momentum on the outward run, then turn it into the energy needed to pull himself up and over the bar.

Jimmy heard a rustling in the haystack above them. Orphan Annie peered over the edge and mewed.

"Bet she has kittens," Karen remarked.

"We'll check later," said Mike.

He took a deep breath and sprinted toward the barn opening, swinging higher than ever. At the pinnacle, the rope snapped, and Michael smack-landed on his right arm in the dirt roadway. Screams of agony and disbelief filled the superheated air. Jimmy and Karen rushed over and saw bone pressing against the skin of his elbow.

"Oh fuck God, no God no, Oh fucking Christ!" Mike screamed and rolled beneath the sun.

Jimmy sprinted toward the house. Michael's voice filled the air with an irreverent homage to his Lord and Master. As he ran, Jimmy began sobbing for his brother, and a bizarre thought entered his mind. *The cyclops. Mike was right all along.*

Doctor Parkinson was in his final year of practice. For nearly thirty-five years, he'd delivered Kochs, stitched them up, examined and vaccinated them, and watched them grow. His heart ached to see Michael's arm.

Bill and Barbara stood by, putting on brave faces to support Michael. Jimmy and Karen were in the waiting room.

Parkinson made an incision at the break to reset it. Michael was awake during the procedure, and a nurse held his left hand and talked with him.

"Hear that you're starting a master's. What're you studying?"

"Biology." Michael felt pressure and heard a grinding sound as bones reunited.

"Interesting."

Doctor Parkinson stitched the arm up and wrapped a splint around it. "In a few weeks, we'll fit you for a cast."

"Will I pitch?"

Parkinson's mouth bent down at the corners, and Mike had his answer.

"Doc. Will I?"

"It's a serious break, Mike. It'll take at least twelve weeks for the bone to heal, longer before you can put stress on it."

***

Jimmy was glancing through a Highlights Magazine when the inner door opened, and Mike came out with Mom and Dad. His lips trembled, and tears flowed down his cheeks. Jimmy set the magazine down and stood. Mike's eyes shot daggers at his little brother.

"Rope vault. Great idea, Jimmy."

Jimmy's mouth fell open. His parents' expressions were a mixture of sadness and disappointment. Karen hadn't known whose idea it was, yet she was now convinced it was Jimmy's.

"But I…," was all that escaped from his mouth.

"Let's go home," said Bill.

"Have to stop at the pharmacy," reminded Barbara.

"Sit in front, Mike. More room."

CHAPTER 25
KNOCK-KNOCK

Jimmy distanced himself from Michael. For whatever reason, he was made a scapegoat. He wasn't there when Michael called Twin's management to lie about being in a car accident. They'd be less sympathetic if the end of a promising career was attributed to a rope vault. In reality, they didn't give a shit. Prospects were a dime-a-dozen, and most of them were fresh out of high school. Mike's replacement would be younger and better. He got to keep what was left of the signing bonus. Luckily, his undergraduate academic success opened another door, and he received a full post-graduate scholarship. A week later, Bill drove Michael to the University of Riverside, where he began summer coursework on his masters.

Jimmy's summer school dilemma resolved itself within the chaos of events. During breakfast on Monday morning, his mother and father hardly noticed he was there and never questioned why he wasn't at school. Once again, he was invisible.

When prune harvest time arrived, Jimmy drove the catching frame. From dawn 'til dusk beneath the relentless sun, he centered the awkward-looking contraption next to a tree. Two Mexicans drew out the canvases. The catching frame had a black rubberized canvas angled to direct prunes into a conveyer. Loftus clamped onto the trunk with the shaker and pulled a lever. Prunes sounded like thunder when they hit the canvases. The shaker backed away, the canvases were returned, and a conveyer spilled prunes into a bin residing on a fork behind Jimmy. There was a powerful blower at the exit, which separated leaves and small sticks from prunes. When the bin was full, he dropped it off and replaced it with an empty.

The shaking caused an explosion of dust. Strange creatures were ejected by the force. Baby birds often accompanied prunes on the conveyor. Occasionally a confused bat darted out. Once, a weasel was catapulted into a canvas man. A flurry of foul Spanish erupted, and everyone was still laughing about it at the end of the day.

Breaks were taken at 10:00, 12:00 (lunch) and 3:00. They often worked until dark. Jimmy tried to understand what the others said in Spanish. He brought bag lunches into the fields and ate fast so he could snooze for fifteen minutes beneath a tree afterward. The other men did the same. Loftus never mingled with the Mexicans. The only difference between them was language and skin tone. His upbringing was steeped in double standards and intolerance. Racism was worn like a badge of honor by many poor whites.

Jimmy was paid five hundred dollars for the four-week harvest. Added to what he'd saved through the years, he had enough to put down on a used car. In the meantime, he qualified for a driving permit. Michael's van was still parked in front of the house. The keys were on a bed-stand next to the closet. It would be a long time before he'd be able to use a stick shift.

During the second week of his sophomore year, Jimmy's parents took a well-deserved vacation to Morro Bay, a three hour journey west. For them, it was a million miles from the ranch. There was nothing to do there, which was the whole point. The cold Pacific ocean smelled of kelp and fresh hope.

His mother insisted that Jimmy stay in town with Grandma

Dobbs. Jimmy argued that farm animals needed feeding and that Loftus and Ed would need help while his father was gone. Finally, it was agreed he could stay with Grandpa and Grandma Koch. Mother rolled her eyes, knowing Jimmy would be unsupervised. Jimmy was happy not to be marooned with the Mud Dauber.

They left on a Friday morning and promised to return the following Tuesday or Wednesday evening. That morning at school, Luz walked into science class late. She was back from Arizona. She handed Mr. Funderburk an add-slip. When she saw Jimmy, she smiled and lifted her head at him.

After the bell, they walked to her next class.

"Glad you're back."

"Mom split from that asshole she was with, eh?"

"Good."

"Heard about what happened."

Jimmy nodded. "Helluva summer."

"Knew you were down for it. Quite a change, eh?"

"Two years in the joint would've been a change."

"Ramon said you did good."

Before he could respond, a former client stopped them.

"Hey man—"

Jimmy put a hand up. "Can't help yuh, man."

"Know anybody?"

He shook his head again and resumed walking. He'd been repeating the same thing for the past few weeks.

"If I was still in business, I'd be rich."

"Or in the slammer."

Jimmy changed the subject. "Hey, listen, what're you doin' after school?"

"Got a license?"

"Sort of," he hedged.

"Can you drive me home?"

"Took the bus, but my folks're on vacation, so I got my dad's pickup or my brother's van."

"Van?"

"Red one."

"Pick me up at 7:00." She took out a piece of paper and wrote a new address and phone number. "I'll say we're going to the library to study."

"She'll buy it?"

"She buys whatever I sell."

"How's Frankie?"

"Doin' time."

"Yeah, sorry to hear."

"Not me."

"All right then. 7:00."

Ricardo, Ramon, and Refugio hadn't returned to school. He hadn't seen them since the bust, although he'd talked with Ramon on the phone a few times. They found another gig.

"Pigs got Leon, Flacco, Chucho, and some other fuckers. Gave 'em a fuckin' year, believe that shit?"

"What you doin'?" he asked.

"Frankie's locked up, so we're keepin' the business goin'. Interested?"

"Naw, thanks."

"Schoolboy, eh?"

"Guess so."

"Change your mind, lemme know, bato."

"Yeah."

On the bus ride home, Jimmy achingly recalled his river rendezvous with Luz. Mike Gonzales was riding too, yet avoided contact with Jimmy. The three Rs had put the word out—you mess with

Jimmy, you mess with us.

That evening he ate dinner with his grandparents and Uncle Ed. His parents called at six sharp to check in as they did every evening. You would've thought they were in Timbuktu. Jimmy showered, dressed, and made an excuse to walk to the ranch.

"I'll take yuh," offered Ed.

"Nah, thanks, Unkie, need the exercise."

Jimmy walked leisurely across the field to his house. It was still over ninety, and he didn't want to appear at Luz's, sweating like a pig. When he arrived home, he splashed cologne his brother left behind, making sure to put a dab where he hoped to gain special attention tonight.

Fifteen minutes to seven, Jimmy sat in the van. He'd never driven it. There was a flatbed truck with a stick he'd used. He figured the van was easier. Jimmy decided on the van rather than his father's automatic F-100 pickup. Maybe they'd go to the abandoned airport. The inside of a van was better than the back of a pickup.

It started right up and relaxed into the familiar Volkswagen purr. Then he remembered Luz's words before she left him with a case of blueballs on the river bank. *No glove, no love.* The condoms Matthew'd given him were in his wallet. *In my room.* He shut off the engine and went to retrieve it. The phone was ringing. He ignored it, stuffed the wallet into his front pocket, and returned to the van. He turned the key. The engine made a whirring sound followed by *tick-tick-tick.* He tried again repeatedly. It was ten 'til 7:00.

"Fuck shit sonofabitch!" He pounded the steering wheel.

He rushed to his father's pickup. The doors were locked. He returned to the house and searched for the keys. *Dad doesn't trust me. The flatbed?* He didn't find those keys either.

"Goddamnit, give me a fuckin' break," was the only prayer he could think of. Finally, he plopped on the worn couch to phone Luz. Her mother answered in Spanish.

"Luz, por favor," he said, and in a moment, she was on the phone.

"Hey Luz, van won't start. Any way you can get here?"

"That's okay. See you Monday."

"Fucker started once, then it wouldn't."

"See you Monday," she repeated.

"Okay."

She hung up. Anger stirred in the cauldron of his chest. "Sonofabitch!"

The phone rang again. *Might be Luz.* "Hello?"

"Who's this?" A female voice.

"Jimmy."

"It's Mirella. Mike there?"

"No."

"When'll he be back?"

"Winter break."

"Oh yeah, I forgot."

"How're you doin'?"

"Gotta number?"

"Naw. He uses a pay phone. Want me to give 'im a message?"

"It's personal."

Jimmy's throat tightened. *Personal?* "Does he have your number?"

"Lemme give it to you."

Jimmy found a pencil stub and a Parade Magazine to write on. His heart wrestled with his brain. *None of your business.* He grit his teeth. *None of your goddamn business!* Then he made it his.

"You pregnant or what?"

Dead silence on the other line. Finally, in a deadpan voice, "Yeah."

"How you know it's Mike's?"

"I know."

Jimmy suddenly felt protective of Mike. Having his baseball aspirations shattered and, on top of that, knockin' up a girl like Mirella, it was too much.

"What's the plan?"

"Just need to talk to him."

There was another long silence.

"Gonna keep it?"

"Thousand dollars to get rid of it."

Jimmy's heart sank. Might as well be a million. His brother's baseball bonus was spent. He'd helped Karen, bought his mother an electric dryer, and a pickup-bed toolbox for his father. The rest was for living expenses in Riverside.

"Christ," breathed Jimmy.

"Yeah."

A fleeting memory elbowed its way into his thoughts—flashing images of Mirella laying on the filthy bed, spreading, sharing effluents with several others she'd serviced that day. *Don't you dare!* he warned. *Don't even think about it.*

Male teenage brains are governed by two principles, eating and fucking. There's no angel battling a devil, good pitted against evil. Dopamine is released, and it's clear what has to happen.

"Listen, Mirella, I have the money. Come over, and I'll give it to yuh."

"You got a thousand bucks?"

"Been savin'."

"Where you live? I'll borrow my sister's car."

He gave her the address and described Palm Tree Lane.

"This's private. Come alone."

"Be there soon as I can."

"All right."

He met Mirella in the driveway.

"Got it?"

Jimmy nodded. "In the house."

Mirella's lips thinned. "Lemme guess."

"Only fair," he said.

She got out of the car, slammed the door, and followed him into the house. "Where you want it?"

Jimmy pointed toward his room and showed her to his bed.

Without hesitation, she kicked off her tennis shoes and peeled her pants and underwear off at the same time, leaving socks and a T-shirt on. Jimmy stepped out of his pants as she centered herself on the bed. There was a slight swell to her tummy. Despite her detachment, Jimmy performed twice without stopping.

Afterward, Mirella used the bathroom. He heard her mutter, "Fuckin' mess."

Jimmy handed her an envelope packed with small bills.

Without a farewell, thank you, or adios, Mirella left. Jimmy found his father's whiskey stash, drank half a tumbler, replaced the missing portion with water, and stepped into the shower. He soaped repeatedly, guilt and shame swirling down the drain. That night he stared at the wet spot on his top sheet. *Soon it'll be perfectly dry, just like hope.*

CHAPTER 26
CONFESSION

"Let's be friends." That's how Luz put it when Jimmy called her the next day to apologize and make another appointment. A week later, she hooked up with Ezekiel (nicknamed EZ). He saw them holding hands, enjoying lingering kisses between classes. Jimmy couldn't think of Luz as a friend. His only motive was adding a notch in his belt, and when the mission was scrapped, so was the relationship. *What's wrong with me?* he wondered.

During winter break, Mikey returned home. Karen came too, packing a baby girl named Charlotte—Charlotte Lassiter. Her husband, David, wore thick glasses from studying debits and credits. Nearly finished with his accounting masters, they planned to stay in Sacramento. He had a job lined up at the firm he interned with.

Sacramento, thought Jimmy. He'd often heard the saying, Sacramento is the right armpit of California, and Bakersfield is the left. *What's that make Meadowland?* he wondered.

Karen foisted the baby into his arms. "Here's Uncle Jim," she cooed. Charlotte spit up every time he held her, creating cherished memories for the parents to share when they ran out of things to talk about in his company. Jimmy remembered his father taking a photo of him sitting on the toilet wearing an oversized felt cowboy hat. He was four. It was an endless source of embarrassment, especially when the family album was passed around for friends and relatives.

Mike's arm was still two shades lighter than his other. The cast was off, and he was under orders to go easy on it. He still blamed Jimmy for his fragmented dreams. One night as Mike prepared for bed, he searched for his misplaced wallet.

"Seen my wallet?"

"No."

"You sure? Had it right here." He pointed to a chair next to his bed. Then he spotted it on the floor. "Never mind, here it is."

Something inside Jimmy snapped. He stalked over to his brother, jabbed him in the chest, and pointed to his face.

"Think I'd steal your wallet, asshole? Remember Mirella, the girl you were fucking last summer? Why don't you give 'er a jingle and ask who paid for her goddamn abortion."

Blood drained from Mike's face. "Wha—?"

"She was lookin' for yuh. I took care of it."

Michael was dumbstruck. Jimmy walked away, stripped to his underwear, and got into bed. Mike stared blankly into the open closet.

"Get the light, would yuh?"

Mike flipped the switch and got into bed. Night sounds were muted by the pounding in his ears.

"You did that for me?" His voice was husky.

"Asshole," Jimmy added into the blackness.

"Thanks."

"Fuck you."

The next morning Mike asked Jimmy to go out to the red van. Mike fished the keys from his pocket and handed them to Jimmy. "Yours."

"You'll be drivin' soon enough. You'll need it."

"I'll find something in Riverside. Cars 're cheap there. I still got some little left for a downpayment."

Jimmy smiled and got in. He tried again to start it.

"Been sittin' too long."

"Yeah. You sure 'bout this?"

Mike nodded. "Never been so sure of anything, little brother. Ever see that girl anymore?"

"Naw."

"Good. Best to stay clear o' girls like that."

Jimmy had a different perspective. He was acquainted with both sides of the coin. Sure, Mirella wasn't educated, so what? She used her body to get attention first, then earn a living. So what? *Girls like that. What the hell did he know about girls like that?*

***

Oh, blessed oblivion. The remainder of the year was relatively uneventful. Jimmy got a license, drove to school, improved his grades, and was allowed back into Honors English. He hung out more with Matthew Cloninger, who'd broken up with Susie. They attended every Clint Eastwood and Bond movie and confessed their souls with pints of liquor that could double as paint remover.

How important it is to have someone you can tell everything to. Each had secret lives, and it was a relief to unburden on each other.

"Thought Susie was pregnant last month. Hell, I ain't even eighteen. What the fuck am I doin'?" Matt shook his head.

Jimmy talked about the Michael investment. Matt was in awe of Jimmy's sacrifice.

"Coulda been me just as easy," Jimmy noted.

Matt chuckled, "DDT for crabs. We pulled some shit in our time."

"Yep."

"Know where we can score some grass?" Matt changed the topic.

"Best stick to booze." He changed the subject. "Ever need the van, lemme know."

That's how friendships are supposed to run. You talk about everything and nothing, stringing together unrelated themes, trying to fit a dozen paintings into one frame because nobody knows how long we'll be on Earth.

By Jimmy's junior year, his big brother was working for an oil company writing environmental impact studies—a fancy way to say he covered their asses. He met a woman named Lisa. They married and bought a house in San Luis Obispo. Rarely did they visit the ranch. Karen and David now lived in Fresno with their daughter. They were only an hour from the ranch. American culture encourages estrangement. Baby birds leave the nest. Disembodied voices on the phone occasionally reminded Bill and Barbara that they still had a daughter and a granddaughter.

Jimmy's parents were civil to one another, yet Jimmy saw years taking their toll. Father immersed himself in the land, and Mother kept things running smoothly within. She read romances, and he built Joe a new doghouse every year until the unfortunate mutt had a terrible accident. In his youth, Joe could jump effortlessly into the back of the pickup. When age caught up, he struggled, so Bill had to give him a final boost to help him over the side. Most times, he'd lower the tailgate, and Joe was able to make it in.

One afternoon the tailgate was up. Joe tried to jump out by himself and hooked his testicles on the corner of the tailgate. Momentum placed him on the ground without his balls. Bill took him to Dr. Milner. Doc shook his head and suggested that Joe be put down.

"He lost a lot of blood. Think it's best if you let 'im go, Bill."

Bill pursed his lips. Joe was laying on his side, panting. Milner had injected him with a painkiller. "All right."

"Wanna stay 'til the end?"

"Naw. Best be goin'."

"Sorry. Ol' Joe had a damn good life."

"Yep."

Bill walked slowly out to his pickup. He sat for a moment, turned on the engine, and turned it off again. Then he hid his face in his large hands and wept.

Joe had listened to everything on Bill's mind without passing judgment. His passing was a sign that permanence is an illusion. *We're all flowers on the vine*, he thought.

Bill's parents were getting on in years. Often, his father didn't know where he was. His mother was still as dingy as ever, changing colors on vinyl furniture with spray paint. The dachshund, Gretchen, and the cats disappeared without a trace. Everything was changing, and he was powerless to stop it.

"Coyotes," Bill guessed.

"Poor Gretchen," Barbara remarked, looking up from a novel.

Undoubtedly she reminisced about Delbert, the mailman. He'd brought more than an alligator into her life. Together they'd written a short historical romance. Lasting less than a half-hour, embellished memories sustained her now that her sex drive had shriveled to an occasional warm breeze.

As for Bill, he had a secret.

Farming offers the advantages of solitude, independence, and opportunity. Bill often hired small Mexican crews to work in his orchard and fields. He wasn't a vegetable farmer, so he didn't need many. Yet there was some hoeing, pruning, and gleaning to be done. Gleaning was after the harvest. A small crew was hired to collect prunes left hanging after harvest.

Bill had noticed Magdalena when she joined a gleaning crew the summer after Jimmy turned twelve. He often worked alongside crews to show he wasn't above placing himself in their shoes. They worked quietly when he was there. When he left, conversations picked up, someone began singing, and the slings and arrows of gossip caused fits of giggles. Whatever their personal circumstances, Mexicans seemed happy.

Bill was knocking prune clusters to the ground with a long wooden pole—the same ones commandeered for rope vault. He peered into the tree and struck a laden branch. Magdalena Flores gathered them with a white bucket. When the bucket was full, she emptied it into a bin close by. Bill appraised her with his peripheral vision. She was a tiny woman with medium-length black hair. Her eyes were large and luminous. When she caught him looking, she gave a small smile. This evolved into short mixed-language conversations.

"Can I call yuh Maggie?" he asked.

"Claro que si, that what people say me."

"Where you from, Maggie?"

"Guanajuato."

"Never been to Mexico."

"You like," she gushed. "Is beautiful. Guanajuato es muy Famoso for los momia's…how-you-say, mummies?"

"Mummies," Bill repeated.

"Si. Day put dead peoples in tunnels," she pointed to the ground, "Make dem mummies."

"Saw that on Ripley's Believe it or Not."

"Guanajuato very famous for dis."

"Famous for beautiful women, too."

Even in the heat of midday, Maggie blushed. It occurred to Bill that his father and mother had been looking for someone to help clean their house. In addition to being a terrible cook, Gladys was no hand at housework. She needed that time freed up to collect specimens for her menagerie of interesting things. *Match made in heaven*, thought Bill.

The elder Koch family welcomed Magdalena Flores, and she

proved invaluable. Uncle Ed flirted shamelessly and bragged to Bill that they were a couple. Bill smiled yet inwardly cringed. He wanted to know more about Magdalena and questioned her bit by bit whenever he saw her. She drove a beat-to-hell Chevy pickup, taking her two small children to Woodland Grammar School before coming to work.

Bill increased visits to his parents' house three-fold. He always managed to find Maggie. One early afternoon he found her in the basement. It hadn't been cleaned in ages, and Maggie took the initiative to tackle the job.

"How you like it here?"

"You parents very nice me. Tank yous so much for deh opportunidad."

"How're your kids?"

"Day good, gracias a dios. Learn deh English rapido."

"Husband?"

"He gardener when he can." She shrugged, and Bill translated that he was a deadbeat.

"I've a confession," Bill said.

She put down the broom she was using to face him. "Si?"

"I like you. I like you a lot."

Magdalena Flores smiled and looked away coyly. "Si?"

"Yeah."

"We married."

"Yeah." He pulled her into his arms, and the first kiss caused his knees to wobble.

She pulled away breathlessly. "We can no—"

He interrupted her with another kiss. She pulled away again yet resumed a moment later without additional protests.

Bill's hand slipped up her shirt.

"No here," she gasped.

"I know a place." He kissed her again. "Come with me."

Bill grabbed a set of keys from his father's office desk. Maggie followed him to the storage room attached to the garage. One bulb lit the room. Their enthusiasm was safely muffled by thick concrete walls. The door was locked, and neither of them was missed for the next fifteen minutes.

CHAPTER 27
JIMMY'S FIFTEEN MINUTES

One afternoon Jimmy sat on the front step and listened to a small breeze rustling through the leaves of the walnut tree. The base of the tree held memories. Somewhere was a yellow plastic Indian buried in a blue canoe, Sidney's remains, and perhaps the fangs of a Harry, the tarantula.

Jimmy wondered. *Does anything we do make much difference?* He doubted it.

***

Andy Warhol said, "In the future, everyone will be world-famous for 15 minutes." Mike famously struck out twenty-two hitters in a nine-inning high school game his junior year. Karen cleared eight feet three inches in the rope vault. Bill was renowned for building doghouses with a shingled roof that could be lifted off for easy cleaning. Barbara was legendary for her peanut butter cookies.

There were moments I managed to add logic and profundity into Jimmy's conscious thoughts. It came in handy at times.

My collective colleagues know what they're doing. Too much input would prove disastrous, causing a Butterfly Effect. My involvement was understandably restricted. Data was stored, studied, and analyzed. Every world we visit is a classroom, each person a book awaiting review on the cosmic Amazon. Occasionally I was permitted to make edits. Ego is so powerful that trying to tame it is paramount to riding a wild bull. An iron will is nearly impenetrable.

So far, I've kept most opinions to myself, yet the time has come to think louder. The human population has suffered a pandemic. Vaccinations help it to ease up until it mutates and reappears as a variant. Yet, life resumes in one form or another. My question to mankind is, What then?

When this mini-series is over, Netflix will premiere another. Corona will only be remembered as cheap, pissy Mexican beer. Pandemics, war, racism, natural disasters—you'll pick up the remote and change channels. Man has developed an adversarial relationship with nature, fighting for the heavyweight championship without earning a title shot. It's the fifteenth round, yet no one goes the distance.

In 2016 you chose a president with a Malignant Narcissism Personality Disorder to lead the USA. His base—society's cockroaches, racists, bigots, gun-toting idiots, and mostly white. That was the beginning of the final round. In the meantime, Mother Earth has busied herself with spring cleaning.

Sheltering in place saved thousands of lives from respiratory illnesses. Factories shut down. The drop in carbon emissions was dramatic. Remarkable how quickly Earth mends given half a chance. In Venice, you could see the bottom of the canals, shoals of tiny fish, crabs, and flourishing plant life reestablishing. Swans were returning. Earth tried to tidy up the mess you've made.

COVID-19 offered an unprecedented opportunity for rethinking how to make Earth sustainable for future generations. It's clear Earth doesn't rely on humans in any way, shape, or form. You are bolt-cutters to the food chain. Earth is socially distancing herself from humans.

This represents the core of what's wrong with Jimmy's nation: Jamestown, Virginia, 1619. First slaves were brought to North America by Portuguese traders. May 25, George Floyd is murdered by police officer Derick Chauvin as three other officers stood by watching. In between, more of the same. Seems the past hasn't taught you anything. Black people don't want your thoughts and prayers. They need justice. Democracy, the grand experiment, was dead on arrival. You built your house of straw. George Floyd's words, "I can't breathe," apply to the entire world, suffocating beneath the weight of intolerance.

The war being waged is within. You are the enemy. Truth pounds on the door, and you respond by adding deadbolts. The battlefield is reflected in the mirror. If you're satisfied with the status quo, be prepared for the consequences.

For those who believe God will save you at the end…farewell and adieu to you fair Spanish ladies.

***

High school senior year—for many, graduation represents a pinnacle in life. You'll attend each five-year reunion to relive the good ol' days. James Irwin Koch was a senior, and this I *can* say—he'll never attend one.

In his senior year, Jimmy got an A in English and PE and C's in everything else. He was dubbed, Average Jim by his parents. Michael's success could easily be measured by a series of luxury cars, homes, resort vacations, and stock market growth. By placing patches on the leaking oil industry, he was able to live a good life. He had a son named Neil, who broke his parents' hearts by refusing to do much of anything besides play video games and learn guitar.

Karen was successful by default. Having migrated to Bakersfield, she was a housemother with another bun in the oven. She supported her husband's battle to protect wealthy oil clients from the digestive juices of taxation. He was good at it and soon opened his own accounting firm.

If money, power, and prestige are gauges for success, what else could Jimmy be but a total failure? Yet there was one bright spot.

Her name was Mary Mancha. She was very pretty. Thick black hair fell in a straight even line to the middle of her back. Mary stood five-one and was full-figured with a backside that turned heads. She was humble, lived in Woodland, didn't own a car, and gratefully accepted a ride home one afternoon from Jimmy.

Mary represented the first generation born in California, and she still carried an accent. Mexican traditions, morals, and her Catholic belief were intact. Her parents took pains to know Jimmy before Mary was allowed to date him. The relationship developed slowly through the first months of their senior year. Her lingering goodnight kisses left him rubber-knee'd.

Mary's father was Jorge, and her mother was Rosalba. He worked for a local rancher, and she took sewing projects, sold tamales, and occasionally cleaned houses. Mary had two younger brothers. Luciano was nine, and Rafael was eleven. Every Mexican child gets a nickname or a shortened version of the first, so they were Luci and Rafa. Jimmy brought them a football, a couple of worn baseball gloves, and donated a pair of old cleats that fit the oldest.

For the first time, Jimmy had someone other than Matthew to talk to about anything. He was invited to family celebrations, weddings, and quinceañeras. They only held hands in front of the parents, who always asked where they were going and when they would return.

After three months, Jimmy decided it was time to round third and head for home.

The van had bench seating behind the driver. The third row was removed by the original owner. Michael had laid down a quilted foam pad, making the red minivan into a bedroom on wheels. In the glove compartment beneath the owner's manual, Jimmy kept condoms.

On December twentieth, 1974, Christmas vacation was in full swing. Air outside was cold and dry. In the morning, frost looked like a dusting of snow. Tonight he'd take Mary to the abandoned airport.

"Where you childrens go?" Jorge asked in broken English.

"Visalia to Christmas shop," Jimmy said.

"Okay." He looked at his watch. "It 6:30. Be back a la *once*."

"Yes, sir."

Jorge gave him a pat on the back. "Take care my little girl."

"Will do."

"Why you don't eat something?" said Rosalba. "Pozole warm you."

"We'll grab a burger."

"Ay-yi-yi los hamburguesas y pizzas…."

"Bring us one back!" chorused Luci and Rafa.

The father pointed, "Go set the table. You have pozole with mucho Chile to burn away those funny ideas in your cabeza."

Jimmy winked at them and gave a thumbs-up. Thanks to Mary, Jimmy felt a sense of true family.

On avenue 168, Jimmy turned in the opposite direction from Visalia.

"Where're we going?" She raised her eyebrows.

"We have an appointment with the stars."

"Is that right? Can't we see them from Visalia?"

"Too much ambient light. Learned that in science."

She nodded. "I see."

It was a ten minute drive. They were alone. Broken pavement surrounded an old storage shed, home to pigeons, mice, opossums, feral cats, and an occasional transient. Weeds had reclaimed the landing strip, pushing up from the fissured blacktop.

It was a moonless night. Jimmy parked behind the metal shed. Not far away, the river banks loomed, resembling a primordial snake. Cold and darkness dampen the acoustics of the heart. A moment after turning off his engine, he turned to Mary. The look on her face warned Jimmy that the best laid plans of mice and men often lead to naught.

"Somethin' wrong?"

"Jimmy, I know what you want. My father wanted the same thing, and my mother was fifteen when I was born."

"I have condoms."

"I love you, but I'm not ready."

Jimmy sighed heavily. She leaned over, and he met her halfway. The touch of her lips reminded him. *She's worth the wait.*

"Visalia?" she suggested.

"Yeah."

Jimmy turned on the headlights. Less than twenty feet away, a full-grown mountain lion was caught in the glare. It crouched, bewildered for a moment, then sprinted into the night.

"Jesus Christ!" Jimmy shouted.

Mary gasped.

"Did you see that?" Jimmy laughed.

"He was so beautiful!"

"That was really somethin!'"

"Yes!"

"Seen coyotes, but never anything like that."

"Spiritual."

"Yeah, guess it kinda was."

Mary snuggled in next to Jimmy. "I love you, Jimmy."

"Love you, baby."

In Visalia, they visited the new Sequoia Mall, crowded with Christmas shoppers. In the parking lot were trees for sale. Santa Claus greeted shoppers at the main entrance, and he was also found in other stores—Sears, JCPenney, Hickory Farms, See's Candy, Orange Julius. Jimmy bought an assorted smoked sausage basket for his mother and boxes of chocolate for his father, Karen, and Michael.

They window shopped at a jewelry store, and Mary squeezed his hand. He wondered if he'd go the whole nine yards with her. *Feels like it.*

The indoor theater was playing, The Man with the Golden Gun. Jimmy didn't like Roger Moore as much as Sean Connery. Moore was campy. Yet the poster was cool. They smuggled in a bag of peanut M&M's to share.

Afterward, they strolled to the van, holding hands. In the parking lot, they met Sam Martinez. He rarely saw Sam at school anymore.

"Hey, honky." Sam said. He had a girl on his arm too.

"How you doin', Sam?"

"Can't complain. Took an after school job at Thrifty's."

"How is it?"

"Beats workin' the vineyards."

Jimmy turned to Mary. "Sam used to come over so I could dominate him in basketball."

"You're trippin'. Still got that rope up?"

Jimmy explained the accident that ended his brother's promising baseball career.

"Sorry to hear that, man."

Then they said farewells and promised to get together soon.

"Sam used to come over a lot." He opened the van door for Mary. She faced him. "Why'd you stop?"

He shrugged. "Don't know. Just one of those things, I guess."

"Hope it doesn't happen to us."

"Not a chance." Jimmy kissed her.

"I keep thinking about the mountain lion," Mary said.

"Yeah, that was far out."

"Strange to be here after that."

"You're really somethin', know that?" He kissed her again, took a deep breath, and let out a mist of heated air.

"I'm really hungry, I know *that*."

"Let's go to Mearle's."

Open until midnight, Mearle's Drive-in was an icon even in 1974. It served the best hamburgers, milkshakes, and fries in town. Circular in design, booths lined the inside perimeter, or you could order from your car. An open kitchen allowed customers to watch the entire operation. On cold nights, most diners went inside. Waitresses in short pink dresses were friendly and efficient. There were a dozen other diners there when Jimmy and Mary arrived.

"Please, I'd like onion rings and a chocolate malt," Mary decided.

"And you, young man?" The waitress was cute, shifting on her legs and chewing gum.

"Same."

"Chocolate malt?"

"Yeah."

"Good choice." She smiled, did a pirouette, and left to place the order.

"Quit staring at her." Mary's voice startled him.

"Was just...." He lifted placating hands.

A smile made it to the corner of her lips. She lifted her hands and made claws. "You're like that mountain lion."

Jimmy laughed. "Gotta admit, I'd eat you up."

"Someday, I'll let you."

Lifting an eyebrow. "It's still early."

"Not according to my father."

"Your dad won't kill us if we're a bit late."

"You're bad."

"That's good."

Mary narrowed her eyes, yet Jimmy could tell she was thinking about it.

It happened so fast. A man rushed into the diner wearing a blue ski mask and a green Army surplus jacket. He stood at the cash register and pulled out a revolver. The waitress that had served them was ringing up an elderly man. The thief snatched the man's wallet. "I'll take that." The other waitress dropped two orders of onion rings.

He tossed the cashier a paper bag and gestured toward the cash register. "Empty it!" He grabbed the old man by the shirt and made him sit in a booth. Waving the gun, he yelled, "Put your valuables on the table!" He glanced back at the waitress. "Hurry up, bitch!"

The cook took a step forward, and the robber aimed at him. The cook stopped. The bag of money was handed over, and he stuffed it into his jacket. Then he stopped at each table.

"The watch, asshole!" He pointed at a wife's finger. "The ring!" Three young male friends had eleven dollars between them. "What the fuck?" He delivered a short punch to the jaw of the closest. On to Jimmy and Mary's booth. He rested the muzzle against her head. "Empty the purse, bitch!"

Jimmy's ears were filled with static noises, and his lower left eyelid jumped with each tic. Something roused—a primitive force—the mountain lion living inside. His glasses flew off as he grabbed the hand holding the gun, stood, shifted his weight, and slammed it into the table. Then he stabbed two fingers into the intruder's eyes. The weapon was released. Jimmy swept the man off his feet and followed with the full force of a knee to his chest.

The scumbag was wheezing, "Sonofa—I'll fuckin'—"

Jimmy's right hand smashed into the man's mouth. He reached up. "Hand me the gun."

Mary gave it to him. Jimmy pressed it against the man's throat and cocked it. The cashier called the police.

"How's that feel, asshole? Like it?" Jimmy didn't recognize his own voice.

Mary's voice was a distant roar. "No, Jimmy! The police are coming!" The rush of adrenalin muted his hearing.

"Let's see what you look like, punk," Jimmy jerked off the man's ski mask.

Wide-eyed, unshaven, a prominent scar dividing one eyebrow.

"Move, and I'll blow your ugly face off."

Minutes later, policemen arrived. They pointed revolvers at Jimmy and screamed for him to put the gun down.

"It's the other guy!" chorused the other diners.

Jimmy set the gun down, and an officer took his place, handcuffing the perpetrator, patting him down, and helping him to stand. He was marched, bloody-faced, to a police cruiser. A news team arrived.

Jimmy suddenly felt tired, as if he could curl up in a booth and fall asleep. His hearing returned. Everyone was talking about him.

Mary was in his arms. "Oh my God, Jimmy…," sobbing in his shirt. "Are you all right?"

"Yeah."

The officer handed Jimmy his glasses. "Yours?"

"Yeah."

"That took guts, kid, but listen," reprimanded the officer, "material shit can be replaced. You can't."

Jimmy nodded. The officer took Jimmy's statement. A female reporter looked over the officer's shoulder and took notes in shorthand. The camera focused on him. The reporter introduced Jimmy and asked more questions.

"Jimmy Koch, a senior at Monache High School in Meadowland, was enjoying a peaceful meal with his girlfriend, Mary. Things didn't go as planned…." She went on to describe the incident.

"Jimmy, where'd you learn to fight like Bruce Lee?"

Jimmy shrugged, "Couldn't tell yuh. I just reacted."

The reporter ended with a note of finality. "Tonight, one man is a hero, and another is behind bars."

Jimmy turned to an officer. "Can we go?"

The serving waitress put up a hand. "Can you hang on a second?

Mearle's comin', and he wants to thank you."

Jimmy and Mary waited. He pointed at the floor. "Onion rings gettin' cold."

She elbowed him playfully, then kissed him lightly on the lips. "My hero."

After the drama of dropping Mary off at home, the ensuing hugs and praises, Jimmy sneaked home without waking anyone and crawled into bed. The phone immediately rang, and his father soon stood in Jimmy's doorway.

"Son, you okay? We just heard."

"Fine, Dad."

His mother flipped on the light and stood in a pink robe. "Thank God! What's this world coming to?"

"They say you gave that guy what he had comin'."

"Got lucky, that's all. I'm really tired. Can we talk about it in the morning?"

"I'll fix waffles—your favorite."

"Okay."

The phone rang again. "I'll take it off the hook so you can sleep. See yuh in the morning."

"We love you, Jimmy."

He hadn't heard those words from his mother for a long time.

The story was featured in the Fresno Bee, Visalia Times Delta, and the Meadowland Recorder. It even took up two inches in the *L.A. Sunday Times*. Mearle gifted Jimmy free meals for a year, knowing that the human body has a limited capacity for hamburgers, milkshakes, and French fries. The next morning friends and family called. It felt good.

"Rope vault training came in handy," Michael said.

Karen put little Charlotte on the phone. "Say hi to Uncle Jimmy," The child did as she was told.

Uncle Ed, Andrew, and Gladys came over. Jimmy hadn't seen Uncle Ed smile that big since Michael threw a shutout and hit two homers against Hanford High School.

"Seen yuh on TV. Dang, that was somethin' else what you did. Real proud of yuh."

Hearing his uncle say that somehow meant more than any of the others. The words came from the deepest well of his heart. Simple words are powerful when they spring from there. His grandmother hugged him, and his Grandfather squeezed his hand. Jimmy's mother secluded in her bedroom, unable to shrug off years of self-indulgent contempt.

Reporters called to see if anything else could be squeezed from the event. The robber was a heroin addict named Bowie Morgan from Poplar. He had a record as long as Jimmy's arm.

After the excitement died down, Jimmy showered, dressed, and drove to Mary's. Rosalba and Jorge greeted him with genuine hugs, and the mother peppered both his cheeks with kisses. Mimicking Bruce Lee, Mary's brothers pretended to attack Jimmy. *Wha-poo-ah!*

"Basta!" Mary pushed the boys away. She kissed Jimmy in front of her parents, and he turned red.

Rosalba patted him on the shoulder, "You one of the family. I still no believe dat monstruo hold a gun to my baby's cabeza." Rosalba began weeping. Mary held her.

Jorge went to a cabinet filled with knick-knacks from various fiestas. He found two shot glasses with baptism dates printed on them and cleaned them with the bottom of his shirt. Then he opened a cupboard and took out a nearly full bottle of tequila. He poured two glasses and handed one to Jimmy.

"You save my little girl. God bless you." He raised his glass, "Salud."

They downed the shots in one gulp.

"Merry Christmas," Jimmy blurted, and they all laughed.

"Mmm?" Jorge lifted the bottle toward Jimmy's glass.

"Jorge. It not even lunch, and he—"

"He is a man!" Jorge cut her off. "Jimmy is a man." He poured two more. "Salud!"

"Ay-yi-yi," sighed Rosalba.

"Can we have some?" the boys asked.

"I'll give you a shot," Jorge raised the back of his hand mockingly, and the boys backed away.

What a difference, Jimmy mused. The only time he'd brought Mary to his house for supper, his parents buttoned down the hatches. Conversation was stilted as if stolen from an instruction manual on *How to Make a Guest Uncomfortable*. Absently Jimmy ran his fingers beneath the table and felt it—a wad of gum placed there decades before.

"What're you going to do after high school, Mary?" Barbara asked politely.

"I was thinking to study nursing."

Bill chimed, "Great profession. Always have a job."

Mary smiled. Jimmy added, "She could be a doctor. I keep tellin' her. She's the smartest girl at school."

Barbara looked wistfully at her son. "Hope it rubs off."

Mary saw what was happening. Jimmy had warned her. "I think he'll be a writer."

The look on his mother's face froze Jimmy's heart. She made a show of enthusiasm, yet disappointment dripped from her face like print from a wet newspaper.

"That's a nice dream, but he'll need a real job."

Mary reached beneath the dining table and took Jimmy's hand. In those moments, he loved her more than ever.

Jimmy's fifteen minutes of fame extended into the first few months of school after winter break. The glassed-in bulletin board in the front office carried the article from the Meadowland Recorder. He was greeted by teachers, administrators, and students with respect and awe. Even the best student/athlete, Marcus Wilson, chatted with him. Marcus was one of only three black students at Monache, yet his exploits were represented on seventeen yearbook pages.

Jimmy was on three. Pages 112, 113, and 114 of the 1974 Monache Yearbook. The headline read, *Crook VS Marauder.* Jimmy's senior photo depicted him with shoulder-length brown hair, crooked eyeteeth, and long sideburns. He'd swapped the black-frame glasses for a pair of John Lennon knockoffs.

"What's up, bruthuh? They slapped palms. "Man of the hour."

"Don't know about all that."

Marcus appraised Mary. "Party this Saturday at Jerry Berkfalk's. Lemme give you the address." He wrote the information on a slip of paper. "His folks 're outta town. Bring this pretty lady with you."

Jimmy looked at Mary. "What you think?"

"Sure," she said. *Don't be square*, she warned herself.

Saturday evening, Jimmy picked Mary up, and they drove to Jerry Berkfalk's house in the suburbs of a Meadowland community called El Rancho Estates. Homes were scattered hundreds of yards apart in each direction. Jerry's parents were perceptibly well off. When they arrived at 9:00, cars were parked like a Pick Up Sticks game.

Mary was wearing a flowery Mexican blouse that pulled down over the shoulders and a short red skirt. Her face didn't need makeup. It was mocha smooth, highlighted with red lipstick. Kids loitered, swigging beer in the front yard. The boom-boom-boom of dance music inside shook leaves on the trees outside. Several guests nodded and grunted greetings as they entered the house. Marcus Wilson spotted them right away and zoomed over, trading skin with Jimmy.

"C'mon m'man, got everything you need." He led them into a large kitchen and opened a refrigerator filled with beer. On the counters were bottles of liquor. "What'll yuh have?"

Jimmy grabbed two beers, but Mary surprised him.

"Tequila." she pointed to a half-empty bottle.

"Good choice. I'll join yuh." He opened a cupboard, but there were no glasses left. He found paper ones in a bottom cupboard and poured.

"Salud," Marcus touched rims with Jimmy and Mary. "Cheers to men who are big, cheers to those who're small, cheers to men who think they're big but really aren't at all!"

Mary giggled. Jimmy laughed, yet something about the toast didn't sit right. It reminded him of locker-room bravado. The words, *little Jimmy,* came to mind. Mary drained her shot and lifted her cup for another.

"Dang girl, put me to shame." Marcus was impressed.

She arched her eyebrows and smiled.

"Slow down, baby," warned Jimmy.

"I want to dance."

What's gotten into her? he wondered.

The music was deafening. Marcus yelled into Jimmy's ear. "Jerry put me in charge of security. Gotta cruise 'round, make sure nobody's stealin' shit or fuckin' in the parents' bed, know what I mean?" He excused himself and disappeared. Jimmy nursed his beer. He was responsible for bringing Mary safely home. Sofas and chairs were moved back, and a throng was dancing in the large living room.

Jimmy was a terrible dancer but gave it his best. Mary literally danced circles around him. When salsa played, she paired with a Chicano who knew how. Her hips undulated suggestively as she shook her upper body from side to side. Jimmy wasn't jealous, yet he was out of his league. After every dance, another boy cut in. Jimmy went for another beer. Sam Martinez was in the kitchen with the same girl he'd accompanied in Visalia.

"Honky."

They bumped fists. "Sam, what's shakin'?"

"No more tequila. What's wrong with these pendejo's?" Sam complained.

"Mary killed it off."

"No shit?"

Sam's girl said nothing yet was obviously ready to move on. She stared passed them into the crowded dance floor.

"Where's your girl?" Sam asked.

"Out there." Jimmy nodded toward the throng.

"Vamanos."

"All right." Jimmy finished his beer and set it on the kitchen counter.

He spotted Mary right away. Midnight at the Oasis was playing, and Mary was slow-dancing with Marcus. Her eyes were closed. She was smiling. Marcus whispered something into her ear, and she laughed. Jimmy felt the first pangs of jealousy. He felt stupid, standing there alone, watching them.

Marcus spotted Jimmy, pulled away from Mary, and nodded toward him. Mary waved, and they kept dancing 'til the end of the song. Then they both walked over to him.

"Kept her warm for yuh," Marcus joked.

"Thanks."

Mary hugged Jimmy. "Having fun?"

"Yeah."

"I'm glad we came. I want another shot."

"Tequila's gone."

"That's okay. I'll have something else."

Jerry Berkfalk was there now. He was upset. "Marcus, gotta end this thing pretty soon. Gettin' outta control."

"Chill. I'll make sure nobody's streakin' in the street."

The two of them left together. Mary and Jimmy returned to the kitchen. She found a warm beer. They toured the house, trying doors, exploring. All four bedrooms were locked. Sounds of lovemaking emanating from each.

"Somebody's havin' a good time," Jimmy said.

Mary pulled him away, and they strolled into the back yard. Couples were kissing, a few guys were huddled in a circle sharing a joint, and there was a small swimming pool with two drunks beating chests and daring others to join.

"Must be freezing," Mary said.

"They're feelin' no pain."

A short time later, Jimmy coaxed Mary away from the party.

"We should find Marcus and say goodbye."

"He's probably in one of those bedrooms."

"Really?"

"That guy's a player."

"What's that?"

"A player's a guy that knows how to get what he wants from women."

She smiled coyly. "What do you think he wants?"

"Same as me, I'm guessin'."

Mary felt as if she were floating. All her life was measured by responsibilities. She was the first in her family to graduate high school. She would be the first to graduate college—an example for her little brothers to follow. Tonight she felt alive. Her only responsibility was to have fun, to think of herself for a change.

"Jimmy, you think that lion is still out there?" She slurred slightly and swayed.

Jimmy laughed. Mary was obviously two sheets to the wind. He knew he'd catch hell if he brought her home that way.

"Darn good chance."

"You want to be a player?"

Dopamine flooded Jimmy's brain, and it seemed his entire blood supply was diverted South. "Sure."

Mary reached for his hand. "Wish there was more tequila."

Thirty-five minutes later, they were parked at the same spot they'd seen the mountain lion. When he turned off the motor, it was nearly one in the morning. They pulled the privacy curtains. His brother Michael had installed a clever curtain rod to separate the front seat from the rear area. Once in the back, they were closed off from the world. He opened the slider, and they slipped into the back.

"Close your eyes," Mary said as the slider sealed them in.

"Okay." Jimmy pretended, cheating as she reached back to free her bra and pulled the Mexican blouse over her head. *Jesus Christ,* he thought. Her perfectly formed breasts were topped by large nipples. She slipped out of her short skirt and set it aside, leaving the underwear on. *Oh my God.* He closed his eyes to gain control. She leaned back on her elbows.

"Okay, you can open now."

"Jesus, you're beautiful." Without another word, Jimmy hurried out of his clothes and faced her.

Mary was still feeling the effects of the alcohol. "You going to play me now?"

"Yeah." Jimmy crawled forward. "Yeah, I am."

Mary raised her knees.

Encapsulated within the safety of the minivan, Jimmy slipped his fingers beneath the elastic of her panties. She lifted, and he pulled them off. Again for a moment, he shut his eyes to think of something else. *Rope vault. Uncle Ed. LadySmith.* Resting on his elbows above her, they kissed. Her lips quivered, and his hips moved. *Rubbers. In the glove compartment. Too late.* Jimmy found her. He pushed. Mary flinched, shivered, and slowly accepted him.

He didn't last long. As they lay side-by-side, Jimmy gazed into her eyes.

"Want it to be like this forever."

"My player."

"Let's get married."

Mary lifted a leg over him. "Let's play again."

Jimmy smelled her shampoo and tasted the salt from her nipples. They practiced takeoffs and landings at the abandoned airport until 3:30 in the morning.

CHAPTER 28
GOING, GOING...

Jimmy got an earful from Mary's mother, who was waiting up for them. She was told that they were going to a school dance.

"You know what time is it?"

"Sorry, Madre. We were dancing, having fun, and didn't notice the time."

"Dancing? You think me like a pendeja?"

"No, Madre."

Jimmy tried to look as innocent as possible. Rosalba glanced at him and refocused on her daughter. Her thoughts were piercing. *I was fourteen when I had you. Life has been a struggle.*

"Mrs. Mancha, I'm sorry. It's my fault. Honestly, after the dance, we went to Lake Success with Sam Martinez and his girlfriend. We were laughing and talking, and it's my fault. I didn't even look at my watch."

Rosalba glanced at Jimmy again. Her eyes softened a little, and the corners of her mouth loosened up.

"Say goodnight and go bed, hija. If your father he finds out, he will no let you out of this house."

Jimmy was crestfallen. Rosalba gave a wan smile and heaved a great sigh.

"Don't worry, Jimmy. Jorge, he sleep como muerte."

Yet the worrying began immediately. Once the rush of dopamine had leveled off, the thought occurred. *No glove, no love.* He'd spilled inside of Mary several times without a condom. *What if she's pregnant?* He tried to remember when she'd last complained of cramps. He couldn't remember. *Chill,* he thought. *What're the chances?*

Two weeks later, there was no evidence that Mary's cycle had begun. His fear faded when they found opportunities to make love. What an elixir she was! When sex is combined with deep emotional attachment, Nirvana is created. It's easy to be obsessed under those conditions. Innocence is lost as comfort levels increase—when you've seen each other unclothed numerous times, you can say what you like and how you like it. Emboldened by the sanctity of the van, they did it almost anywhere.

They purchased a copy of David Reuben's, *Everything You Wanted to Know about Sex but Were Afraid to Ask* and hid it beneath the van's mattress. They enjoyed stripping down to their underwear, facing each other, and reading from it until desire forced them to try a new suggestion. Born with Latin rhythm, Mary proved skillful. Each session was a new dance to master. The power of her orgasms was intimidating. Mary's voice deepened, her whole body shivered, and her utterances were otherworldly.

As for Jimmy, he ensured each investigation was accompanied by latex. When he ran out, she purred in his ear. "Pull out."

Sometimes on the road, she'd take him into her mouth. More than once, he parked off the highway to finish, or they were late to first period because she needed him. He learned how to give her oral pleasure, and she enjoyed it immensely.

After three weeks, Jimmy was twisted inside, expecting two fatal words, *I'm pregnant.* There had been no signs of bleeding. Either she'd just finished her period before the first time together, or she wasn't going to have one—bad news.

What now? Jimmy obsessed as if the outcome was inevitable. The school year was ending, and so was life. Eighteen, a bun in the oven. He'd have to join Sam at Thrifty's for minimum wage, ashamed to work on the ranch. The stress of not knowing wore him down. They no longer held hands. He no longer opened doors for her. By the third week, they'd copulated so often that it became routine. Gentleman Jimmy was gone with the wind. Often on the drive home from school, there were extended periods of silence. One afternoon, Mary interrupted a long one.

"I started."

Jimmy was overcome with relief. He pulled over, reached for her hand, and heaved a sigh. The angels of his better nature returned. Thoughts flooded his mind. *Always have condoms. No more chances. Maybe she can get on the pill.* "Love you, baby."

There was another silence. She was looking out the side window. As a flock of starlings whirred by, she said, "You will never guess who asked me out."

"Who?" A lump formed in his throat.

"I was surprised," she said softly. "He knows we're together."

"Who?" Jimmy repeated. He was uncomfortably hard. Jealousy forms strange partnerships with libido.

"Marcus Wilson."

"Marcus?"

"Yeah."

"What'd you tell 'im?"

More silence. In between, a scenario played out in his head even before the words escaped her mouth.

"What if we took a break?"

It felt as if a chip of obsidian entered Jimmy's heart. His face grew pale. He stared straight ahead. The two-lane highway was cracked. On one side was an open field recently disked. A small trail of dust followed a coyote loping diagonally across it—running, always running. They were a mile before the airport. He wanted to take her there, make her forget what she'd just said. Wanted to have her, possess her completely, take vows of fidelity, and grow old together. These thoughts converged together in a split second.

"What?" he answered.

"Just thought, you know, might be good for us to—"

"Fuck other people?" he finished.

"No!" She looked away. "I knew you'd be like this. We've got our whole lives—"

"And you wanna fuck Marcus before you're stuck with me?" he finished.

"Take me home."

Jimmy gunned the engine and spit gravel as he pulled back onto the highway. The coyote was long gone. He swallowed, and it felt like a stone was lodged in his throat.

"Lemme know when he's finished," he managed to say. "He doesn't stay with anybody very long."

Tears rolled down Mary's face. *Smaller, smaller, smaller, and now we're almost gone*, she thought. *In the blink of an eye.*

As they came to the airport, Jimmy's eyes teared up. He willed them not to spill. There it was, the metal shack where they'd seen the mountain lion and shared their bodies for the first time, where Pandora's box was opened. He rolled down his window, hoping to cool the resentment, guilt, and anger. They were silent the rest of the way. She got out with her backpack and didn't turn back.

"Don't pick me up tomorrow," she said.

He watched her enter the house and disappear behind the peeling brown wooden door—going, going, gone.

Jimmy drove to the white barn and pulled inside. The frayed ends of the rope hung from the metal pulley. He looked at his hands. *So many splinters*. The cross-brace loomed above. He got out of the van, climbed to the top of the haystack, and looked down. *I did whatever Mikey said.*

"So what do I do now, asshole?"

A pigeon responded by taking off from a nest and whirring above him before returning and cooing.

Sitting on a bale, he noticed a triangle of paper sticking out. Lifting the edge of the bale, he found the magazine he'd hidden a lifetime ago. Thumbing through, he shook his head that such images could inspire a rush of hormones. The girl on the front—eyes vacant, smile forced. He dropped it and closed his eyes. "She'll be back," he mumbled.

A silent rush of tears collected on his chin and dripped onto the cover girl, who cupped her ponderous breasts, lifting them toward the camera, tongue reaching out to a nipple. The metal roof of the barn clicked and popped.

"Goddamn!" Jimmy sobbed. The strength of the emotion flattened him like a steamroller, doused his heart with liquid nitrogen, and celebrated his demise by giving him a spontaneous hard-on. *Vietnam*, he thought. *I'll fucking volunteer*.

The final three weeks of school were agonizing. He went to a recruiter and told him his wish.

"Vietnam's almost finished," he said. "Don't worry, somethin' else'll pop up, always does."

Jimmy didn't want another war. He wanted *this* one. Wade into the fray, M-16 blazing, die a hero or a fool. He promised the recruiter he'd think about it.

He saw Wilson and Mary walking, holding hands, stopping to kiss. He stalked from a safe distance. Once he spied them kissing so passionately, she pushed him away with a smile to enter math class. Jimmy didn't hate Wilson. He'd only exercised home-field advantage when she returned his interest. Can't blame the guy. Jimmy knew if he started a row with Marcus, he'd get clobbered. *What's the point?* he wondered. The gum beneath the table was there, and he hated that it was. He would never be like his parents, who wore ascendency like a comfortable pair of sneakers. *Wilson's black. My ex is Mexican. I'm the cake left out in the rain.*

Jimmy picked up his 1974 Monache Marauder Yearbook that day. Page 112, Crook VS Marauder. Him with Mary. He thumbed through to Mary's senior picture, her in the choir, a proud member of the Latin club—all taken before emptiness filled his heart. He was ready to die for her. *LadySmith*, he thought.

That evening at the dinner table, his mother asked, "Signed up for junior college?" It was a veiled question implying something deeper. What she meant was, Time to leave the nest, come home for Thanksgiving and Christmas. Hasta la vista!

Jimmy lost fifteen pounds in the final weeks of school. He pushed aside his mother's offerings, and she didn't notice until one morning as he stared at an untouched plate of eggs, bacon, and hash browns.

"You okay? You look thin."

"Girl trouble?" His father guessed, taking a final bite of toast.

Jimmy was silent.

"Somethin' happen between you and Mary?" Mother looked back from the sink as she cleared dishes.

"Yeah."

His parents took turns spouting clichés, scraping scabs off of fresh wounds. Lots of fish in the pond. Time heals. This'll make you stronger. She wasn't the right one. Someday you'll find Miss Right.

"Gonna work the catchin' frame this year?" His father changed the subject.

"May as well." Jimmy got up from the table and left through the front door.

Entering the van, he smelled the musk of fusion past and decided to walk instead. He made it to Palm Tree Lane and cut across the orchard to his grandparents.

***

Green prunes hung in heavy bunches. In a month, when the sugar levels tested high enough, the harvest would begin. A screech sounded from above—Jimmy shaded his eyes to watch a red-tailed hawk circling. Through the trees ahead, he spied Grandfather's red barn. Nearly every barn in the valley was red or white, in various stages of disrepair. This one had an open loft and a wooden ladder bolted to a wall to get to it. Up there was an unfinished rowboat Jimmy's father had begun when he was ten. The bow was complete, and the rest was a ribbed skeleton. The floor of the attic was littered with vacant mud-dauber nests, ancient straw, and not much else. At one end was a large double door that swung outward. Years earlier, his brother had pissed on him from there as he walked below.

Jimmy sneaked into the house through the side door, which led directly into the office. Uncle Ed's pickup was gone—one less thing to worry about. The television was blaring because his grandfather was hard of hearing. He imagined Grandmother sitting with him, dutifully enduring a gameshow, perhaps wondering if she should paint the television blue. He quickly found the key and stuffed it into his pocket.

The storage room smelled like a century of memory. He opened a steamer trunk filled with old photos, postcards, a harmonica, a Shriner's hat, ancient documents, and a worn brown baseball glove, circa 1920s. Jimmy had perused the trunk when he was younger, always expecting to find something new, yet he was always disappointed. There was a striped goose-down pillow there. He lifted it out and closed the trunk.

The storage room walls were lined with shelves. Textbooks from another era were there, along with stacks of *National Geographic*, *Life*, and *Look* magazines. A box camera was waiting patiently for another opportunity. There was a 1903 Springfield 30–06 rifle in a zippered case, used during World War One. Ammunition was no longer available. He held a branding iron tipped with the slash Bar K.

Everything signified change. *Things always change.* For a moment, he forgot where he was, lost in the surroundings of the past. His grandfather was also lost, as often occurs to eighty-eight-year-old's. Uncle Ed once said he heard a noise outside his bedroom window in the middle of the night. His father was in the back yard naked.

"What're you doin' out here, Papa?" Ed asked.

"Takin' a leak."

"Why here?"

"Feels better."

"C'mon, Papa, let's get you back inside."

More than one night, Andrew called Jimmy's father to say he was dying.

"Better get over here, William. Ain't got long."

Bill sat with him the rest of the night, listening to his father reminisce about the good ol' days as Gladys fussed, bringing tea, fixing toast, and calling Dr. Parkinson, who assured her that Andrew wasn't going to die.

"Gladys, we've talked before. Andrew's got Alzheimer's, and it's not going to get any better. Need to think about getting a caregiver or placing him somewhere he can get the care he needs," the doctor explained patiently. "I'm retired. You have another doctor."

"We have Magdalena. She could stay in the spare room. He likes her."

"Gladys, call your doctor. Andrew'll be fine."

Gladys hung up. *Of course, Magdalena won't leave her family to live here.* She knew it. Parkinson's honesty caused a crying jag which lasted for hours.

At such times, Bill wished his wife was more empathetic.

Woman's been spiteful ever since the alligator thing, he fumed. *Like a switch got flipped.* He recalled the experimental role-playing phase while the kids were in school. *Some were kinda fun, but others, where I played a goddamned mailman, that was just plain silly.*

Jimmy found what he was searching for. She was beautiful as ever. Checking the cylinder, he saw three bees hunkered down in cells, ready to sting. He removed all but one, dropped the others into the box, and covered them with wadded newspaper packing. He'd held the LadySmith many times. Her weight was familiar in his hand. *Take me away.*

Times like this, the only weapon a conscience has is fighting negatives with positives. I tried flooding his mind with good memories, yet there were too few to string together, and Mary provided most. *Think, think, think! Can't let his iron-will triumph!*

Jimmy held up the musty striped pillow. It looked as if coffee had been spilled over it. He carefully left the storage room with LadySmith and the pillow. The barn opening looked like a toothless mouth. He thought of Loftus. The roof of the barn was made of wood. Yellow moss covered the remaining shingles. The barn was starting to lean, and it was only a matter of time before it collapsed. Heat rose like a dry flame licking at his forehead. It didn't make him sweat as much as it threatened to mummify.

The barn was ten degrees cooler inside. It creaked and cracked. In winter, it swayed. Wind soon would give its final kiss. Jimmy stopped at the opening for a deep breath. He tried to feel something. *Nothing.* Peggy Lee's voice—*is that all there is to life?* His parents loved that song. Jimmy climbed the ladder leading up to the loft.

Filthy, he thought. He sat on the bow of his father's unfinished rowboat. *Like a coffin.* He faced a wall covered in cobwebs and dauber nests. *Dobbs never gave me the time of day.* Dauber was a good nickname—dried mud surrounding a past she would never leave behind.

Feel something, for Christ's sake!

"You're a writer, Jimmy." Mrs. Hickman's voice was clear as a bell.

LadySmith trembled as he stared into the barrel. One dark eye looked back. *What if we took a break?* An image formed in his head of Mary and Wilson rutting on a worn mattress.

Jimmy lowered himself inside the ribcage of the rowboat. His thumb found the trigger. He opened his mouth and closed his eyes. He tasted the metal of the barrel. The closet in the bedroom was opening. The cyclops emerged on hoofed feet, a large horn protruding from its forehead. It turned its head and found him with one all-seeing eye. His thumb added pressure. Mikey, the three Rs, Mary, his folks. *Beat down 'til I was nothin'. Mary. Christ help me, Mary! Nothing written. No closing chapter. Just the final act.* His hands trembled. Gasping sobs escaped, and he nearly choked on the barrel. *Do it…do it!*

"Hey, Jimmy!"

A distant voice that the howling in his ear couldn't filter out completely.

"You up there?"

Special Ed, always happy, ignorance is bliss….

"Hey."

Jimmy screamed into the mouthpiece and squeezed the trigger.

***

End of story, right? Death is a part of the give and take. If that's what you think, you're a pragmatist. Others are idealists, praying for a happy ending, something you can sleep on. That's the great thing about writing books. You get to play God until the hammer falls.

***

The sound of the hammer striking the primer was deafening. In a way, small sounds are when you're immersed so completely in the moment that sound is everything. Orgasm, a woodpecker playing castanets in a lonely forest, the beating of your heart after a bad dream—moments of pure truth captured and confessed into sound. Life and eternity spreading out before you like jewels on an endless beach.

Jimmy's final thought was an understanding of sound, a language beyond words.

"What you doin' up here, boy?"

Jimmy opened his eyes. He was laying in the rowboat, and his uncle was staring down. *Heaven or hell*? He debated.

"Seen you when I pulled up."

"Hey, Unk," Jimmy said. The words squeaked from his mouth.

"What you got there?"

Jimmy lifted LadySmith off his chest. She weighed a hundred pounds.

Ed reached to help Jimmy up. "I remember when your grandpa bought that thing. Grandma didn't want nothin' to do with it. Where'd you find it?"

"Storeroom."

"Lemme see."

Jimmy handed it over. "Careful, it's loaded."

He swung the cylinder out. "Shit's fire." Ed looked at Jimmy. He closed it up and put LadySmith in his pocket. "Let's go get us a beer."

His uncle's words were perfectly timed. Pulled away from death's door, adrenalin still rushed through Jimmy's body. It felt as if he'd already guzzled a six-pack of Hamm's, the beer refreshing. Jimmy said they should return LadySmith to her home first.

"Smells like cat piss in here," Ed remarked when they entered the storeroom. "Ain't been in here for years."

They drove to the only market in Woodland, where Jack and LaRue worked the front, and Zeke was still the butcher.

Questions zig-zagged through Jimmy's mind. *Why didn't she fire*? A strange feeling of elation suffused his body. He didn't want to die anymore. *For a girl*! Now that he'd shopped for death and walked away without paying, anything was possible.

After they parked, Ed asked, "What kind yuh want?"

"Don't matter, Unkie. Whatever you think."

"I'll see what they got. How old 're you?"

"Eighteen."

He nodded, "Close enough." Before closing the door, he let out a long, ragged fart, followed by, "Uh huh-huh!"

While Ed was making the purchase, Jimmy stared out the windows. Woodland was a labor-camp town built to house a poor, neglected, disenfranchised segment of the population. Old man Soto, the town drunk, walked unsteadily into Jack's. Thunderbird wine was his preference. Green bottle, red label, Thunderbird was fortified rot-gut made especially for alcoholics. A few years back, Jimmy had seen him on the sidewalk next to the Shell station as his father filled the pickup. Soto carried a paper bag twisted at the top. He stopped in his tracks and pissed his pants before staggering along.

"Let that be a lesson, son," his father said. "Too mucha anything ain't good."

As he gazed out the window, his happiness flourished. Thoughts carried him into the realm of faith. Speaking aloud, he asked, "Why was that bullet a dud? Somebody pullin' strings? Is there a reason I'm still here?"

Jimmy could see Ed through the glass front door of the store. He was holding a paper sack and jawing with Jack. Another pickup pulled in—Matthew Cloninger, driving his father's Chevy. Jimmy rolled down his window.

"How's it hangin'?" Matt asked.

"Low to the ground."

"Good to hear. Goin' to MC next year?" MC was Meadowland Junior College, more like an extension of high school. Most kids went for a year or less and got regular jobs working at Thrifty's, Foster's Freeze, gas stations, Kmart, and the like. They grew into full adulthood and stayed in Meadowland, attending five-year high school reunions. Some high school girls would soon be single moms, and a few of the boys would do time. Yet they all started the first day at MC with a dream of something better.

"Figured to give it a shot."

"College girls, man." Matthew was slated to represent the new generation of Cloninger farmers. "Hell," he added, "got the rest of my life to farm, figured a year or two to dip my wick won't hurt nothin'."

"Logical."

"Sorry to hear 'bout you and Mary."

"I'm over it."

"Except for the good stuff, I imagine."

"Yep."

"Went to the prom with Georgia Mikkelsen."

"Yeah?"

"Took her to the Oak-pit Barbecue, brought flowers, whole nine-yards. Didn't get shit."

"Bad investment," Jimmy said.

"No shit. Saw Wilson and your ex."

"Yep," Jimmy droned. He wanted to return where he'd been before Matt pulled up. The feeling was starting to wither.

"Took Georgia up to Lake Success. Told her we was gonna watch submarine races. She said, They got submarines in there for real? Anyway, guess who was parked next to us?"

"Wilson."

"Yep. Drives that ol' '69 Buick Electra, fuckin' love boat. Steamed them windows up, and God almighty, what a racket. She sounded like a banshee. Didn't inspire ol' Georgia none."

Jimmy nodded. Uncle Ed finally came out.

"Hey, Ed," Matt greeted.

"Hey." He got into the pickup and handed the bag to Jimmy. "Coors."

Jimmy reached in and handed one out to Matt.

"Thanks, man."

"One less for you," said Ed. "Let's go while they're still cold."

"See yuh, Matt."

"Later, Jim."

Jimmy and Ed parked next to an irrigation canal bordering the property. No matter how you opened canned beer back then, you were stuck with an aluminum pull tab. As a result, they were everywhere. Jimmy put his tabs into the sack, along with the empties. His uncle tossed empties out the window. After each long guzzle, he let out a sasquatch belch, each longer and louder than the last. Sometimes he followed with a fart or else harmonized them.

"Christ, Unk, you could power a small town."

Ed burped through his nose and rubbed it. "Uh-huh-huh!"

There followed a few minutes of peace, a contrail tracing its finger in the sky. The air was hazy and hot. Another pickup was stirring dust half-mile away.

"Thanks, Unk."

"Knew sumpin' was eatin' yuh."

Jimmy nodded, took a large gulp, and let out the mother of all belches.

"Gawd dang, boy! Been savin' that up?"

Michael's sensibility forced Jimmy out of the pickup to collect his uncle's castaways.

"Can't leave evidence," Jimmy said.

"Your dad'd tear me a new asshole if he found out."

"Kinda fucked up—can't vote, can't drink, but I can get my ass blown off in 'nam."

"Seen Marty at Kmart the other day. Hardly knew him. Gotta big belly now."

"He's lucky to be alive."

"Walter Cronkite says it's gonna be over soon."

"Hope so."

"Where you want me to drop yuh? I gotta get back to work."

"My place."

"All right."

***

Jimmy sat on the front steps gazing at the ancient walnut. White bark was cracked in places, exposing darker wood. He wondered if rings would reveal how old it was. *Older than the Indian*, he nodded. A crow was perched at the top, twisting its head this way and that, one eye on Jimmy.

"Haw-haw!" It cried.

"Jokes on me," answered Jimmy.

***

Where do we go from here? Could end nicely here. But that's not how life is. Marriage, divorce, kids, gettin' hired and fired—embarrassing, exasperating, soul-crushing moments followed by hope, elation, and mitigation.

1978. Jimmy turned twenty-one on a Monday. *Stayin' Alive* was a hit. *Close Encounters of the Third Kind* played in movie theaters around the world. Jim Jones told nine hundred members of the People's Temple to drink Kool-Aid in Guyana, and they did. Son of Sam was convicted of murder, Garfield made his debut, and Jimmy (Carter) was president.

Jimmy was a year at MC. He enrolled in creative writing with a professor who hadn't published a damn thing in his life. He learned about non-verbal cues in Communications One and took a weight-lifting class. Jimmy discovered he was naturally strong, and it filled him with irony. *Hell*, he thought, *Could've kicked all their asses*, recalling the bullies he grew up with.

Mary Mancha was there. Her tenure with Marcus Wilson lasted two weeks after high school. He was offered a full athletic scholarship to UCLA. She enrolled in the nursing program and dressed in a white uniform for classes. He couldn't stop his heart from accelerating when he saw her. She smiled and waved sometimes, yet pride wouldn't allow him to take it any further.

Jimmy was hired by Franey Floor Service. Pay wasn't bad, and he learned how to lay carpet, linoleum, and tile. He rented a small studio apartment in Meadowland. At first, he was lonely, but then he met a few friends to hang out with. He earned enough to pay for gas, rent, food, and not much else. Yet he was independent, and you can't put a price tag on that. He knew a few girls—the kind that needed a few drinks, some attention, and kind words before they'd allow him inside. That was okay too.

Jimmy's parents built a new house after he moved out. They chose land at the beginnings of Palm Tree Lane and put up a lovely three bedroom Mediterranean style home, renting the old ranch house to Magdalena and her family. Bill was happy with the arrangement. Over nine (cautious) years together, he liked her close by. Her husband, Rodolfo, was often unemployed, and his relationship with Maggie was conflicted. Bill hired him to do yard work once a week. This gave Barbara more time to read. On hot days, Barbara kept Rodolfo hydrated with sun tea. Often she was seen gazing out the kitchen window down the palm tree lane. Perhaps she saw herself walking to the mailbox. Delbert was a fuzzy image now—something from a steamy book cover. He had disappeared like the memory of cotton candy at the annual Meadowland fair, replaced by a kid who drove too fast, laying rubber as he sped to the next delivery.

Maggie's children were both in high school. He padded

Magdalena's paycheck with monthly cash bonuses. At first, she refused to accept it.

"Listen, Maggie, you can set it aside for yourself or your kids."

Her English had improved over the years. "Okay. I hide it for my children."

Magdalena never pushed for anything more than what they had. The storage room was a sanctuary. There were times when Ed took his parents to Meadowland for a doctor's appointment. Bill led Magdalena into the guest bedroom. Afterward, they talked side-by-side.

"You felt so good," Bill said.

"I am happy you still like it."

"Why don't you leave Rodolfo?"

"He is a macho. He won't ever let go."

"Wish…."

"What do you wish for?"

"That it could be like this all the time. You know how I feel about you."

She lifted a leg over him. "Show me how you feel."

And he did.

CHAPTER 29
GONE!

Bill was friends with the director of the prune drier in Woodland. He managed to get Rodolfo hired there. Rudy lasted two weeks before he complained of back pain and quit.

Bill's father was ninety-two, living in a rest home now. Gladys wasn't doing too much better. Sometimes she left the stove on, the refrigerator open, and the lights burning. She still collected dead things. Recently she'd found a dried dragonfly and hung it by a string to hover above the rest of the menagerie. Often Magdalena found her sitting on the tree stump in the front yard crying.

"I miss Grandpa," she said.

"I know. You'll see him Saturday."

"He doesn't know who I am."

"Somewhere deep down, he knows."

"Think so?"

"Yes, of course."

"You're sweet."

Gladys never called Magdalena by name because she couldn't remember it. Yet sometimes, her mind became suddenly lucid, and she said things that disturbed Maggie.

"You like my son."

"Yes, he is very nice."

"I see how he looks at you."

Magdalena busied herself, pretending not to have heard.

Then the damp mist returned. "I miss Andrew."

"You'll see him Saturday."

Maggie didn't like dusting near the Museum of Interesting Things. She didn't believe death should be showcased. She thought of the mummies in Guanajuato. She was there once as a child with an aunt and uncle. She remembered the woman under glass, perfectly preserved right down to the pubic hair, and the withered children who would never play together again. So many grisly remains were on display. It was sickening and fascinating.

Maggie walked through the prune orchard to work. A few times over the years, Bill parked his pickup in the middle of it and flipped down the tailgate. She sat on it, and he took her standing. He pulled out on those days, so she needn't walk the rest of the way with an uncomfortable mess between her legs. Bill always carried a clean hanky to wipe her belly with. When they finished, Bill usually made a funny remark.

"No better way to start the day."

Most days, her husband was still asleep when she and her daughters left. The oldest drove her sister to school in a '67 Oldsmobile Cutlass that popped sometimes when you let off the gas. When Rudy got up, he fixed breakfast, sipped a beer, and tinkered in the yard. If it was his day to work for Barbara Koch, he'd put on work clothes and walk over.

Sometimes in the early afternoons, she sunbathed on the back lawn. When Rodolfo came, she put on a beach robe and sat in a lawn chair to read. He watched her as he pulled weeds, raked, and watered. *Never been with a gringa*, he thought. He had a friend that had and warned, "Be careful, 'cause somebody finds out, she'll say you forced her. And who you think the cops will believe?"

Barbara brought him ice tea on the hottest days. She smiled coquettishly and made small talk.

"How're Magdalena and the girls?"

"Good. My wife, she really like work for the missus."

"Think it's gonna be a hot one today."

Rudy shaded his eyes and glared up at the sun. "Yes, you right about that."

"Would you like some more tea?"

"No, thank you, Mrs. Koch."

"Call me Barb."

"Okay."

"Well, I'll let you get back to work."

"Yes, gracias."

Rodolfo took up a pair of hedge clippers to square off a wax-leaf privet. *I'm gonna cut some fresh roses for her*, he mused. *Maybe then....*

***

Bill and Ed discussed putting Gladys in the retirement home with Andrew. With Maggie's help, Ed would be okay by himself. She could cook a few meals and keep the house clean. Ed was fine with the idea.

One Friday afternoon, Bill whispered to Maggie as she cleaned in the kitchen, "I'm goin' through withdrawal."

"Patience, señor."

"Mmm." Bill wanted to lift her to the counter. "C'mon."

"Can't leave your mother by herself."

"She's watchin' Price is Right." He ran a hand over her ass.

"You so bad." She pushed him away.

"Why'd I have to fall in love with such a responsible woman?"

Maggie turned to him. Her eyes were glassy with affection. "You really love me?"

"Sorry, I never said it before."

She wiped a tear from her eye. Then she looked from the kitchen into the living room. Bob Barker was shouting, Come on down! She looked at her watch.

"Rápido." She took his hand and led him into the office. He grabbed the storage key, and they hurried out.

After flicking on the light, the door was locked. It smelled musty, yet the odor represented pleasure. Magdalena lifted her skirt to remove her underwear as Bill drained his pants to the ankles. She placed an old quilt on the cement floor and lay with her knees raised. Bill entered quickly.

"Awww! Damn, you feel good."

"Ayyy Bill, te amo." She fluttered and then clenched around him. "Nnnayyy, oyyy ay-ay-ayyy!"

Less than five minutes later, he spurted. "Jeez! Awwwrrr!"

Bill handed her a blue hanky from his pants pocket, and she wiped.

"You always make a big mess."

"Plenty more where that came from."

After slipping back into her underwear, Maggie fluffed her dress and passed fingers through her hair. She looked around.

"What this?" She pointed to the branding iron.

Bill held it. "It's for marking cattle, so people know they're yours."

"Does it hurt them?"

"Not for long."

"And what that?" She nodded toward a container on the floor.

"Great grandfather's sea chest. Full of crap." He removed a book from the shelf. "*Little Bear's Adventure*. Read this when I was a kid."

"What is there?" She pointed to a box on the shelf.

"I've no idea." He reached for it. "Kinda heavy." He opened it and reached beneath the wadded newsprint. Magdalena took sharp breaths when he lifted out the handgun. "I'll be damned. Heard about my dad gettin' this for my mother. She didn't want it." He turned it over in his hand and scrutinized the engraving. "LadySmith."

"I not like the guns."

He didn't notice the two bullets trapped in the creases of packing material. Turning the weapon, he peered into the cylinder. The four he saw were unoccupied. "Damn thing looks brand new." He pointed toward a wall. In a tough voice, "Hands up, Rocky, it's all over." He pulled the trigger four times. *Click, click, click, click.*

She held out her hand, and he gave it to her.

"You look pretty sexy with that," he remarked.

"What you say? Put the hands up, Rocky?" She aimed at the concrete wall and squeezed the trigger.

CHAPTER 30
ALL THE KING'S HORSES

Renata Corbin lived alone in a gated community north of Tulare. Homes were luxurious Mediterranean. Every room in hers boasted skylights. There was a full bar, spacious living areas, leather seating, and perfectly placed wood furniture. Paintings on the walls included running horses, nude women walking among autumn leaves, and a portrait of Renata, ten years younger, wearing an expression that said, *I know you want me.*

Jimmy felt as though he should shower and wear surgical gloves before coming in to give an estimate about the tile work she wanted done. She met him at the door with a cheery smile, wearing a leotard.

"Sorry," gesturing to her clothing, "just got back from aerobics. Please come in."

She was tall for a woman, bleached blonde, a face nourished with expensive solutions that subtracted ten from forty-eight. Wealthy women of that age often try to retain the appearance of youth by any means.

Standing in the bathroom she wanted renovated, Jimmy held a selection of tiles.

"I adore this one, don't you?" She leaned in close to show him.

"Yeah, that's nice." Jimmy felt silly answering such questions. *How's a guy supposed to answer stuff like that?*

"This one, then."

"Good choice."

"When can you start?"

"Monday morning at 8:00 if that works out for you."

"Perfect. If I'm not here, Maria can let you in."

Renata summoned a middle-aged Mexican woman and explained the situation. The woman looked at Jimmy and nodded. "Yes, Mrs. Corbin."

"Do you work weekends?"

"This'll only take a few days."

"Fine. Maria is off weekends, but I'm usually here just in case."

"Thanks."

"Perfect. See you Monday." She took his hand and kept it longer than necessary.

The phone was ringing when he opened the door to his apartment door and stopped as he picked it up. He went to the refrigerator for a beer and plopped down on a worn loveseat with ripped edges exposing yellow foam padding. He stared at the information card Renata had filled out. Renata Corbin. There was the address, phone number, specifications for the job, tile choice, and her swirling signature. *Renata Corbin, divorced, needy, James Irwin Koch to the rescue.* He tweaked the thought. *Jimmy Kock. Maybe drop more samples by tomorrow, see where it leads.*

The phone rang. It was Michael with a rush of words.

"Been tryin' to reach you. There was an accident at Grandma's. The cleaning lady was shot."

"Wha—?"

"I'll explain later. I'm at the Visalia Police Department. Mom and Dad 're here, and so's the lady's crazy-ass husband."

"How—?"

"Just get here."

"On my way."

"Hurry."

Jimmy's ears were ringing, and the eye-tic returned.

He sat in the van for a full minute before starting. *What's the lady's name? Maria? Monica?* For the life of him, he couldn't remember. The ringing in his ears was starting to ease, but the tic persisted. He drove to Visalia, took Main, and found the station. Mike spotted him out a window and met him at the van.

"What the hell?"

"Let me tell yuh before we go in. Dad was in the storeroom with the lady. There was a gun there. Guess she was foolin' around with it. Ricochet got 'er in the head."

"She's—?"

Mike nodded. "As a door-nail."

Jimmy couldn't hear the rest of what Mike said. Lips were moving, but his words couldn't penetrate the wall of shame and guilt. He only caught the last part.

"Husband wants blood. Went after Dad in the station, and cops cuffed him. They're askin' Dad all kinds of questions."

"Is he under arrest?"

"Nothin' like that. It's just...." He looked at the pavement, trying to gather words.

"What?"

"They did a preliminary exam...."

Jimmy waited for the other shoe to drop.

"Guess her and Dad were...." He couldn't finish.

Jimmy tried to imagine his father with the cleaning lady. "Dad? You're kidding."

Michael nodded gravely. "Wish I was."

"Husband knows?"

Mike shrugged. "Will soon enough."

"What's gonna happen?"

"They wanna question all of us. Uncle Ed's with Grandma."

"Fuck."

"Listen, Jimmy, you know anything about that gun?"

Jimmy's mind whirled. *They'll find my prints, Uncle Ed's too. And the other two bullets. Jig's up. Can't rewrite this.*

"Played with it when I was a kid."

"Played with it?"

Jimmy shrugged.

"And the bullets?"

Think, think, think! You're a goddamned writer! Grandpa Koch has Alzheimer's. "They were in the box. Three of 'em. I tried one out in the barn. It was a dud, so I put it back."

"With the dud still in there?"

"I was a kid."

"Shit. Let's go inside."

"Mom know everything?"

Mike shrugged.

William Koch was exiting the secluded inner offices when they walked into the front lobby. He looked older. Sadness, regret, and hopelessness tugged at his face.

He walked slowly to a chair and slumped down in it. Mike sat next to him, and Jimmy stayed standing. Bill looked up.

"Tell Ed to take Grandma home."

Jimmy did as his father asked. Ed came to offer support.

"Don't you worry, Bill. Everything'll be okay."

Bill stared at his shoes. After Ed left, he looked at Mike. "They got your mom in there now. Twenty-five years down the shitter."

"Mom loves you. You'll get through."

"Don't know her like I do."

The main door to the inner offices opened, and an officer summoned Jimmy. As in a dream, he was seated in a room with a table and three chairs. He repeated what he told Mike. A jowly investigator taped it, seemed satisfied, and said he could go.

"One thing, son."

"Yeah?"

"Your dad and the victim. Did you know they were involved?"

"Just heard."

"The husband lives on your property."

"With two daughters."

"Might be good to keep an eye out."

"Yeah."

"You gonna be around?"

"I live in Meadowland."

"Just sayin'."

"I can stay a few days, I guess."

"Good."

"What's gonna happen?"

The officer shrugged. "If I was your dad, I'd get a good lawyer."

"That's it then?"

"For now."

"I gotta question."

"Yeah?"

"Does my mother have to know?"

The detective shrugged and nodded. "Sorry."

"Shit."

"You're the kid that took that guy down at Mearle's, right?"

"Million years ago."

"I remember that. Like I said, tell your dad to get a lawyer."

"I will."

"Good luck."

"Thanks."

CHAPTER 31
SNAP

Magdalena's husband was named Rodolfo Flores, yet most called him Rudy. His daughters, Elisa and Margarita, arrived at the police station. He followed them to the morgue to identify the body of his wife, he was in the old Chevy pickup, and they were in the Oldsmobile Cutlass. You might imagine Rudy's suffering during this time. The sheet was lifted. He stared coldly at her remains. The hole in her forehead was mobbed clean.

"Yes, it is my wife," Rudy said. Dry-eyed, he gathered his weeping daughters into his arms, and they made their way home. On the way, Rudy's thoughts filled with murder. He thought of the .45 automatic his cousin sold him for cheap after he found the stash of money Magdalena had been squirreling away.

Puta! He knew about his wife and Koch. There was no room in his heart for forgiveness. Macho culture was crystal clear about such matters, and he was well within his rights to despise and disown her. *Whore*! *He'll pay*.

When they arrived at the ranch house, two Chihuahuas circled nervously, darting in and out between their legs with their tongues flickering. He reached down, and they swarmed his hand. One flipped over for a belly rub.

The phone was ringing as they entered the house. It wasn't aunts, uncles, cousins, or his older brother.

Rudy answered. "Si?"

"Hello, is this Mr. Flores?"

"Yeah, who's this?"

"My name's Travis Corbin of Corbin and Associates. I'm a lawyer. Please accept my deepest condolences. So sorry for your loss. I'm here to help."

"Help?"

"Mr. Flores, sources have informed me about the unfortunate event, and I think you have recompense coming to you and your family."

"What this word?"

"Sorry, recompense is a fancy word for money."

"Money." His ears perked up.

"Yes, Mr. Flores. We believe you have a strong case."

"What you want?"

"To represent you, Mr. Flores. Under the circumstances, you probably want justice and recompense."

"Recom—"

"Money."

"Yeah."

"I suggest we meet as soon as possible, strike while the iron is hot. I can meet at your earliest convenience."

"You come here?"

"Yes."

"When?"

"You tell me."

"Up very early."

"Just say when."

"Tomorrow."

"Morning or evening?"

"Morning. Seven."

"Perfect. Won't take any more of your time. Goodnight, Mr. Flores. Again, you're in my thoughts and prayers."

Rodolfo hung up the phone, and a prickly feeling crawled from his neck down his spine. It was the feeling he had when he thought something good was about to happen. Like the time he went to the Five-Hi bar with his friend, Navarro, and they took two girls out to Navarro's car.

Fuck your thoughts and prayers, he thought. I want rec... whatever-the-hell-he-said.

"Who was it, Papa?" asked Margarita.

"A man."

"What man?"

"A lawyer."

She gritted her teeth and nodded to her sister Elisa. "Pinches gringos will pay."

***

At first, Jimmy's mother seemed to be living in a parallel universe. She barely spoke, and there was a look in her eyes, not grief or anguish, but of daydreaming. She began isolating herself soon after her interview with the laconic investigator. Bill drove her home, and not a word was spoken. Jimmy tailed in the van, and Michael followed in a brand new silver Mercedes.

Barbara closed her eyes, and everything was clear. *Bill's slut. I'll be the laughingstock.* Her vision of the future solidified in the mists—a cover for her book of dreams—Del with his shirt open, on fire for her. *Tomorrow I'll find out what's what.*

***

Travis Corbin, wearing a grey suit and a blue tie, sat on the front steps of the old ranch house with Rodolfo Flores.

"Two million seven hundred and fifty thousand dollars," he said.

"Market value, just the land."

Rudy Flores scrunched his forehead together and locked eyes with the lawyer. "Recompense." He pronounced it perfectly, having practiced late into the previous night.

"That's right, Mr. Flores. Recompense."

Two chihuahuas sniffed Corbin's pant leg.

"You think we win?"

"We're very confident."

"What car is that?" He pointed to the gleaming black vehicle parked on the other side of the fence.

"An XJ6 Jaguar."

"How much?"

Corbin nodded, "A pretty penny."

"How much pretty penny I get for my wife?"

"Well, Mr. Flores, let's just say you're in a good position to come out on top."

"Okay."

They shook hands, and the girls offered Corbin a glass of water. He drank it quickly and asked to use the bathroom. As he walked through the living room, his observant eyes took in the living conditions. The bookshelves were lined with mementos given to guests for weddings and celebrations. An empty bottle of Don Julio tequila sat there, along with two ceramic Chihuahuas and a few framed pictures taken of the family. He saw a photo of Magdalena Flores. She was pretty and looked much younger than her husband.

The main bedroom led to the bathroom. The bed was unmade. Several drawers were open, and men's clothes littered the floor. There was a vanity with a hairbrush and various containers of makeup, face cream, and hair products. The bathroom was in need of a woman's touch. As he relieved himself, he looked to his left. His face was reflected in the medicine cabinet mirror. *This's another world. Get in and get out.*

He began working out his piece of the pie as he finished. He tried to flush, but the handle mechanism was broken. He lowered the lid and returned to the living area.

Corbin took out contracts, one in English and one in Spanish, from the inside pocket of his jacket. "This's just a basic representation agreement. It has my fee percentage and other details. I'll need you to read and sign so we can get the ball rollin'."

Rodolfo stared at the legal documents. "Margarita, you read." He was ashamed to admit that he couldn't read in either language. Corbin handed her the contracts, and she sat on a flower-print sofa covered in a clear plastic slipcover. Elisa sat next to her with narrowed eyes.

"You like the tequila?" Rudy asked.

"Sometimes."

"You want?"

"Little early for me. Maybe after this all over, I'll have one with you."

"Okay. I buy."

Margarita handed the contract to her father. "Looks okay."

"Where I put my name?"

Corbin took out a pen from his shirt pocket and made X's where signature and date were needed.

"Here Papa, use this." Elisa handed him a Teen Beat magazine to write on.

As Rudy signed the papers, Corbin added another caveat. "Mr. Flores, I know emotions are running high, but I must insist that there be absolutely *no contact* between you and the Koch family. Do you understand?"

"I got it."

"Good. It's important we show up in court without any incidents like what happened at the police station."

"Yes."

Corbin nodded. "Good. Anywhere else you and your daughters can stay?"

"No."

"Okay. Please remember. No contact."

Rodolfo thought of Mrs. Koch. *En un poco más de tiempo me habría follado a esa señora.* A little more time, and he would have fucked that lady.

Corbin gave Rodolfo a firm handshake. He nodded to the daughters with his most reassuring smile and left.

***

Michael was looking out the kitchen window when Corbin's car drove by, taking Palm Tree Lane out to the highway.

"Come 'ere. Take a look."

Jimmy stood next to him. "What?"

"Jag."

Jimmy shrugged.

"A Jag, Jimmy. Dad better get a lawyer pretty damn quick."

Jimmy watched the Jaguar reach the end of the lane and turn left. "Probably from Tulare or Visalia. Can I use your car?"

"You gonna follow?"

"Yeah."

"No work today?"

"It's Saturday. Gimme your keys."

Bill came into the kitchen. His hair was damp from the shower as Michael handed Jimmy the keys. Bill had slept on a sofa bed in the office. Barbara made it clear she didn't welcome his company.

Bill opened the refrigerator, closed it, filled a mug with coffee, and went into the back yard without a word.

Jimmy caught up with the Jaguar. Corbin had stopped at Jack and Larue's for a bottle of water and a pack of cigarettes. It's not easy following a Jaguar in a Mercedes on a small country road in broad daylight without getting noticed. Jimmy parked off to the side and waited. Travis Corbin finished a cigarette with his back against the car. Casually he blew grey smoke into the dry blue sky.

Gonna make a killing, he thought. *Cool mil'. Gotta head-start. File the complaint with the clerk, get the ball rollin'.*

Jimmy followed carefully until the Jag took the Tulare turnoff at the corner where the Five-Hi bar was. A handwritten sign out front said, Open 5:00 PM to 1:00. It waited for campesinos to spend hard-earned money on cheap tequila and pissy beer. Jimmy followed for a short time, then took an intersecting route. He arrived at another corner a minute before the Jag. Now there was more traffic to hide in. He allowed two cars in front as a buffer.

The Jag drove to downtown Tulare, consisting of nothing more than a well-groomed main street. It parked in front of Corbin and Associates. *Bingo,* thought Jimmy. He opened the glove compartment, found a pencil,' and wrote the address on a corner of Michael's registration card. *Michael hit the nail on the head. Dad's in real trouble.*

Jimmy returned thirty-five minutes later. The Koch household was settling into the *new normal.* Barbara refused to talk with Bill. They barely acknowledged Michael and Jimmy. His mother fixed breakfast, as usual, showered, dressed nicely, and left the house in her recently purchased Buick Electra.

"Where's she going, Dad?" Jimmy asked

He shrugged.

"Dad, we gotta talk," Michael said.

The phone rang. It was Karen. She was getting ready to leave from Bakersfield.

"Dad?"

"Yeah."

"What happened?"

"Everything turned to shit in the blink of an eye," he answered.

"I'm on my way out."

"Suit yourself." He hung up.

"Sit down, Dad." Mike's voice was soft. "We need to talk."

"'Bout what?"

"'Bout you and the cleaning—"

"She had a name, Michael. Magdalena. I called her Maggie. What you wanna know?"

"How did you...?"

"How? Hell, how does anything like that happen? Just does. She filled a void."

"A void?"

"Last few years, me and your mom...." A tear rolled down his cheek. "Wasn't much left. Once you kids were gone, we just kinda stared at each other like strangers. Maggie...she...." Bill broke into sobs. Michael put arms around him.

"We'll figure it out, Dad," Jimmy encouraged. "Keep a clear head. Got a lawyer?"

Bill buried his head in his hands. "Never needed one."

Jimmy and Michael shook heads at each other.

"Where did Mom go?" Jimmy asked again.

Bill shrugged. "She don't talk to me no more."

***

Barbara had found three reputable lawyers in the Yellow Pages. She found one advertisement she liked. At Corbin and Associates, we have your back. She went there first. It looked closed, and she remembered it was Saturday. She tried the door, and it was open. Behind a well-appointed reception area were office doors.

"Hello?"

A good-looking middle-aged man appeared from a doorway. He was wearing a grey suit and a blue tie. "Can I help you, ma'am?"

"I'd like to talk with a lawyer."

He walked to the reception area and took her hand. "I'm Travis Corbin."

"Barbara Koch."

Travis paled yet kept his composure. "Nice to meet you. We're actually closed until Monday, but—"

"I need a lawyer today."

Travis pursed his lips and made his thumbs into a steeple. It was tempting to troll for information that might help his case, yet it would be a clear conflict of interest.

"Sorry, Mrs. Koch. Walling and Associates in Visalia is open, and they take walk-ins."

"Can't you just listen?"

"Afraid not, Mrs. Koch. Legally I'd need to take a proper deposition."

"Do you have the address to the place you mentioned? Never mind, I think I...." She reached into her purse and took out a yellow page. "Here it is. Walling. Thank you, Mr. Corbin."

"You're very welcome. Sorry I couldn't be of more help."

As she left, Travis Corbin heaved a great sigh of relief and returned to his office to work on the complaint.

***

When Karen arrived, they sat around the dining room table. Michael brought her up to speed. Barbara hadn't returned.

"Jimmy found out Flores has a lawyer. Corbin and Associates. Flores's gonna sue."

"It was an accident!"

"You know how it is, Sis."

"Where's Mom?" Karen asked.

"Dunno," said Jimmy.

"Ain't payin' for no blood-sucking lawyer," Bill blurted.

"Dad," Michael argued, "Corbin's gonna try and take you to the cleaners. I'm no lawyer, but I know that's how it works."

"Guess so."

Karen found the Yellow Pages in the office. She turned to the attorney listings. "Shit, guess we know where Mom is." She handed the book to Mike.

"Christ."

"She's gonna abandon ship," murmured Bill.

"Maybe she wants to protect you."

Bill gazed at his children. It was clear that he was right.

Michael looked at Karen and Jimmy. "I'll stay through Monday to find a lawyer. Jimmy, you said you'd stay a while?"

"My next job's in Tulare. I can bunk here for a few days."

"Good. Karen, just keep in touch. Need to stick together."

She nodded.

"Long road ahead," Bill said. "Thanks for tryin' to help."

"We're family," said Michael.

Jimmy winced. "Guess I'll head over to my place to get some stuff."

"Van still runnin'?" Mike asked.

"Seen better days, but it still gets me from A to B."

"I'll come back next weekend," said Karen. "David's parents can watch Charlotte."

***

A steady flow of traffic flowed up Palm Tree Lane and the dirt side entrance. Visitors were going to the old ranch house to support Rodolfo and his daughters. By late afternoon there was loud music and laughter. The two Chihuahuas yipped incessantly. Men gathered out front and boisterously liberated their opinions into the unrelenting heat. They shouted phrases in Spanish, easily translated by anyone who wasn't tone-deaf. Piche güero, hijo de la chingada, puta madre, cabrón, and pendejo drifted across the distance separating the old home from the new.

When Jimmy went into the backyard to burn garbage, he saw them loitering, aluminum cans gleaming in their hands. They threw empties to the ground, and one stood behind the walnut tree to urinate. When they caught sight of him, he was razzed. He returned to the house and looked for his father's .410 shotgun in the laundry room cabinets, but it wasn't there.

CHAPTER 32
CRACKLE

Gum's been collecting beneath tables since the dawn of man. Recently all pretense was dropped thanks to four years of a presidency that celebrated racism and encouraged insurrection.

Cornered, Bill's only allies were conservatives like him—white, privileged, surrounded in a bubble of prosperity made possible by the labor of those less fortunate. The farming community banded together, offering support to a fallen comrade. Words drifted on thermals, and children of laborers listened. Spic, greaser, wetback, beaner, river-nigger—words plow deep, plant seeds, nurture crops of intolerance and irrational thinking for the next generation.

We're reaching the end of our story. Please don't skip forward. As the title of this book floated to the surface, so must the ending sink to the bottom.

***

On Monday, Jimmy was at Renata Corbin's door. He knew her ex was the lawyer who wanted to take his father to the cleaners. He'd keep his ears open.

Maria greeted him at the door. "Mrs. Corbin say she be back soon. She make the exercise."

"Thanks." He assembled the necessary tools from the van along with a drop cloth. In another year, Franey would let him use a service truck, and he'd have two weeks paid vacation.

An hour later, as he chiseled away old tile, Renata stood in the doorway wearing a back leotard.

"Hi, Jimmy." She swiped her forehead and heaved a sigh. "I'm dyin' of thirst. Anything I can get you? Juice, water, a Bloody Mary?"

"No thanks, Mrs. Corbin."

"Renata. Just Renata. How long do you think?"

"No more than three days. It'll need twenty-four hours to cure after it's laid."

She lifted an eyebrow. "Cured after getting laid? Sounds promising."

Abruptly she turned and went into the kitchen. A minute later, she brought him a 7-Up.

"Thanks. My grandmother always has 7-Up at her place. Used to anyways."

"With a splash of Seagram, I could make it a 7-7."

"Better not." He gestured to the tile. "Might end up lookin' like Picasso put this in.

Her unfettered laughter filled the bathroom. "You have a wonderful sense of humor."

At four-thirty, the floor was prepared for tile. Maria left, and Renata talked Jimmy into a drink. She had on a swimsuit covered with a thin beach kimono decorated in cherry blossoms. They went into the back patio to sit side-by-side in a pair of chaise lounge chairs. There was a kidney-shaped swimming pool surrounded by flagstone. The grounds were lush with bright flowers, myrtle, dogwood, tulip, and magnolia trees, surrounded by ten-foot plaster walls.

"Beautiful place."

"It's designed so that something's always blooming. How's your drink?"

Jimmy took another sip. "Real tasty."

"Long Island Iced Tea. Don't let the *tea* fool you."

"Got a gardener?"

"Pedro comes once a week, Thursdays usually. I love skinny-dipping in the evenings."

Jimmy smiled and sipped. *Poke around, see what you get.* "Been divorced long?"

Renata made a sour face. "Such a beautiful day. Let's talk about nice things."

"Sorry."

"It's okay." She was quiet for a few moments. Then, accompanied by a long exhalation, she let the cat out of the bag. "No harm in the telling, I guess. Travis is an asshole. Cheated with his receptionist. I hired a detective who found them shacked up at a motel. I got the house, half the savings, and alimony payments."

"Children?"

"No. He wanted to wait."

"Jeez."

"You may meet him tomorrow. We've papers to sign."

"Hmm." He finished the tall drink. Renata took his glass.

"Another," she said emphatically.

"Really shouldn't—"

"Nonsense." She walked away rapidly, and he admired her toned legs.

A hummingbird hovered over a strand of bottlebrush, and a pair of yellow butterflies journeyed erratically across the yard until one was snapped up by a sparrow. Jimmy watched the wings of the ambushed butterfly float gently to the manicured grass. He heard voices of children playing on the other side of the barrier. In the distance, a siren wailed. He imagined Renata swimming naked.

"Here you go, Jimmy."

"Thanks."

"Let's take these inside, shall we?"

Renata led him into a large bedroom. Light streamed in through gossamer curtains. A California King dominated the space. She set her drink on a nightstand and turned to him.

"What was that you said about being cured after getting laid?"

***

Michael met Jimmy in the driveway. "Let's walk to the old white barn."

"Sure."

"Found Dad a lawyer. Walling and Associates wasn't taking new clients. Found a private lawyer, Louis Crabtree. He was very honest and professional. Said the court clerk'll issue Dad a summons, and he'll have thirty-five days to answer."

"Then what?"

"Gets decided if there'll be a trial." Mike took a paper out of his pocket filled with notes. "There's a couple things Flores's lawyers might sue for. One's personal injury. He didn't think that'd fly. Then there's being unreasonably jeopardized. He's gonna study that more. Negligence. He's pretty sure they'll go with that and get Dad's homeowner insurance to pay off. Better for us 'cause the insurance furnishes a lawyer."

"It was an accident."

"He let her into the storage room. Law says if you're one percent liable, you can still take a beatin'."

"Fuck."

Mike's mouth turned down. They were at the entrance to the white barn. Frayed remains of the rope still hung there. Mike relived the awful day his baseball prospects shattered. He clasped hands behind his neck as he stared up at it.

"Spent a lotta time here," Mike said.

"Lotta splinters."

"Still didn't let you in the club."

"Nope."

"Never said I was sorry."

Jimmy felt like crying. Softly he sang, "Camp'n'wee is Carl, Carl means good...."

Mike joined. "Zemo means bad."

They slung arms over each other's shoulders and listened to the metal roof snap, crackle, and pop.

CHAPTER 33
POP

LadySmith was put on death row. Her metal would either be smelted, shredded, crushed, or segmented with a cutting torch. Seldom did weapons involved in injury or death make it back into mortal hands. She awaited the court's decision. Guilt was not in question. She did what she was designed to do—kill.

LadySmith and her extended family end a quarter of a million lives every year.

***

The next day Maria met Jimmy at the front door, and he began laying tile. Renata arrived in her black leotard and stood at the bathroom door.

"Travis'll be here soon. Once he leaves...." She lifted an eyebrow and smiled. "I gave Maria the afternoon off."

"Be finished in a few hours."

"Cured...."

"After it's laid," he finished.

"Don't tire yourself too much. I might have you tiling the whole house." She spun and left.

Jimmy smiled after her, yet reflected, *Women like her lose interest pretty quick.*

***

Travis Corbin had a loud and commanding voice. Jimmy heard them arguing in the office.

"What else do you want?"

"An apology. You never once apologized."

"Jesus Christ. I'm sorry."

"Save it. I'll never remarry. Two grand every month for as long as I live."

"Accidents happen."

"Is that a threat?"

"Just sign the goddamn papers."

There was a brief silence. Jimmy heard footsteps, and the front door opened and slammed. A minute later, Renata stood at the bathroom door looking haggard.

"Hear that?"

"Yeah."

"All of it?"

"Mostly."

"He threatened me."

"Think he meant it?"

"That man's capable of anything. Anyway, if something happens—"

"Don't say that. Nothing's gonna happen."

"To be on the safe side, write down everything you heard. Would you do that for me?"

"Sure. What about the housekeeper?"

"Her English isn't very good. Doubt she understood half of what she heard."

She led him into the office and seated him in a plush leather chair with pen and paper.

"Put the date and approximate time down too. I'm going to send Maria home. What I need is a good fucking. Think you can manage?"

"Do my best."

"Know you will."

Mike wasn't there when Jimmy returned to the ranch house. He'd escaped back to the central coast. Underground oil tanks had ruptured in a small coastal community, and he was in charge of cleanup.

"Where's Mom?" he asked his father.

"Haven't seen her all day. Your uncle came. We're gonna put Grandma with Grandpa. She tried to burn dry leaves close to the house. Whole house would've gone up if Ed hadn't been there."

"Jeez."

"A guy showed up with this." He handed the summons letter to Jimmy.

"Now we can plan. Did you call the lawyer?"

"No."

"Want me to?"

"Would yuh?"

"We'll need help with the harvest."

"Nobody'll help." Bill gestured in the direction of the old ranch house. "He's got the Mexicans all stirred up."

Jimmy shook his head. "I'll run the catcher."

"Sit a while."

"Okay."

"There's a bottle in the bottom cupboard. Bring glasses."

Jimmy poured a finger for himself and his father.

"Don't be stingy."

Jimmy put two fingers more.

His father took two long swallows, draining half.

"How old's Loftus?" Jimmy asked.

"I've no idea. Don't think he knows either. Goin' on seventy, I imagine." He finished the glass and poured another.

"I'll see if Luis Crabtree's in his office."

"Okay."

Jimmy started to stand. His father caught him by the arm and brought him back. "Jimmy, I'm sorry 'bout this mess."

"It's okay."

"No it's not. I love yuh, son."

"I know, Dad. Love you too."

"Gotta tell yuh something that might hurt."

"Go ahead."

"Thing makes me saddest is losin' Maggie. Goddamn it, I loved her."

Jimmy didn't know what to say. He poured his glass to the top and downed it in one shot. "I'll see if Louis's in."

Early the next morning, Bill was cooking breakfast when the phone rang.

"Who called?" Jimmy asked when he joined Bill in the kitchen.

"Your Mom called to say she's with her mother. Never did like that woman."

"We called her the Mud Dauber."

Bill chuckled. "Lot nicer than names I got for 'er."

Banda music was already blasting from the old ranch house.

"Got that shit goin' day and night," Bill said.

"Just have to finish the Tulare job. Should be home for dinner. How 'bout me and you go into town for somethin' to eat? My treat."

"That'd be nice…." His voice trailed off.

"You all right?"

"Day after tomorrow's July fourth. Al Cloninger invited us for a barbecue. Wanna go?"

"Maybe. Have to see what my schedule looks like?" The schedule had nothing to do with not wanting to go. With time his desire to stay connected to his past was evaporating.

His father gave him a long hug. "You're a good boy."

"See yuh this evenin'."

***

Rodolfo Flores sat on the front steps of the old ranch house at dawn. In his youth, he'd been an early riser. Now that Magdalena was gone, he woke up with the first rays again. While his daughters slept, the two Chihuahuas trotted around the yard, shitting and pissing. One was white and the other brown. The brown one dug beneath the walnut tree. He heard the Volkswagen van puttering in the distance and knew the gabacho boy was leaving.

Rudy thought of changes he'd make after the settlement. Corbin cautioned that a quick settlement was likely to be offered. "Let's not be too hasty, Mr. Flores. We should weigh all options."

Fuck that. Quick is good. I'll drive to Guanajuato in a new truck, get a house, make a business. The girls can stay in Gringolandia if they want. In Mexico, I'll count for something.

The white Chihuahua joined the brown, and they shoveled dirt with their front paws. Two crows settled in the upper branches of the walnut tree and laughed, *Haw-haw-haw*! Rudy thought further into his future. *Women. So many women. They'll see my truck and know what kind of man I am.*

Out of the corner of his eye, he watched the brown Chihuahua carry off somethin in its mouth. The other also had something.

"Come," he ordered, snapping his fingers. They laid in the dead grass chewing. "Come!" They ignored him.

Rodolfo's curiosity made him go to see what they had. They cringed as he approached. "What you got, eh?" The brown dog darted away, leaving its discovery behind. Rudy had to wrestle the other one away, slapping the white one to make it let go. Then he stood holding two pieces of damaged plastic, a blue canoe and a yellow Indian.

Rodolfo was examining them when a loud pop sounded in the direction of the new ranch house. His head jerked up, then he relaxed.

Spray can, he figured. Often they exploded when garbage was being burned. Once he saw a can launched two hundred feet into the air. It sounded like the firecrackers used in Mexico to frighten intruders. His house in Guanajuato was a two-room square of unpainted cinder block. Thieves were known to steal copper tubing running from the water heater into the houses. *They steal anything, even your shoes.*

On Palm Tree Lane, he saw the old man, Loftus, cruising toward the ranch in a run-down '66 Chevy pickup. Loftus loved the truck and washed it once a week. *Been around forever*, mused Rudy. *Wonder how old he is*. The crows flew away, and the Chihuahuas yipped as Loftus parked next to the red barn and went inside.

***

Loftus opened a round container filled with chewing tobacco. He pinched some between a thumb and forefinger and placed it between his lower cheek and gum, ignoring the sting of mouth ulcers. It was dark inside. He opened a large aluminum slider to let in light. Bats fluttered around before clumping together beneath a rafter.

Today was special. On July 3rd, 1910, he was born. It was now 1978. *Sixty-eight*. He'd figured on a napkin that morning as he ate toast with peanut butter. He lived in a ramshackle house bought in Woodland when he was much younger, back when a working man could afford one. His wife was named Cleopatra but preferred Cleo. She died ten years ago of lung failure. Doctors didn't offer any other explanation. He had three children scattered to the winds. *Ain't seen any of 'em for years.*

The red barn smelled like a mixture of everything. By focusing, you could pick out individual odors, yet Loftus preferred breathing them in all together. He'd come into the barn for a reason but couldn't remember what it was. Then he did. *Water canister. Fill it, put it on Johnny-boy*. Johnny-boy was his pet name for the John Deere tractor he'd been using for years. It was parked in the white barn, and the disc was already hooked to it. A round base was welded to the back of the tractor to carry the canister, with a rubber tie-down strap to keep it there.

Loftus filled it with water from the faucet outside the barn and placed it in the back of his pickup. He parked in front of the barn and sat for a moment. *Gonna get drunk tonight. Have me a burger from Ken's Walkup, and watch ol' Cronkite.* He remembered, *Tomorrow's the Fourth. Ain't gotta show up to work with a hangover.* He spit out his chew to replace it with another. The nicotine gave him a pleasant buzz.

He liked working with Johnny-boy. He cared for it like a dear friend, cleaning the oil filter, squirting dust off with a hose, and tucking it in at night. Lately, Bill had talked of planting prune orchards in the open fields. Prices for cotton, beans, and alfalfa were unpredictable. Trees were easier to care for. There was no need for siphon pipes or ditches, just a succession of irrigation pots to flood the borders. He'd miss teaming up with Johnny-boy in an open field.

Loftus was startled out of his reverie by Ed, who pulled up next to him in his pickup. Loftus leaned over and unrolled the passenger window.

"Mornin,'" Ed greeted.

"Mornin.'"

"Helluva thing, ain't it?"

"Yep. How's the boss?"

"Jimmy's with 'im."

"What's he gonna do?"

Ed shook his head. "He don't tell me nothin'."

"How's your mom?"

"Puttin' her with Dad."

"Hmm," Loftus nodded. "Miss your ol' man. Was always good to me."

"Yup."

"Tomorrow's the Fourth. I won't be here."

"Yep. Guy's comin' today to check sugar in the prunes. Ain't even got a crew yet."

"I'll do the shakin'."

"Guess I gotta drive forklift."

"Just need a coupla Mexicans for the canvas if Jimmy runs the catchin' frame."

"He's gotta job in town."

"Yeah, that's right. Forgot."

"Guess I'll water down the roads."

"Yeah, getting' mighty dusty."

"See yuh 'round."

"Yep."

Ed pulled away.

***

The Tulare job was finished. In a few days, he'd do a final courtesy inspection and cleaning. Jimmy gathered his tools and folded the drop cloth. The floor would need twenty-four hours to dry properly. He stood back to admire his work.

He was glad Renata wasn't there to tempt him into another marathon session. It'd been good, but he wasn't in the mood. He used her phone to call Franey, and they told him to return after the Fourth. *Two days off. Need it.*

Before he left, he flipped on her TV. Local news was finishing a recap of the shooting mishap. The incident is currently under investigation, a concise news anchor reported. Before driving to the ranch, Jimmy cruised the streets of Woodland. There were only four. He went by Luz's before stopping a few houses down from Mary's.

Been two years. Wonder what she's up to? He gripped the steering wheel of the red van, which was marinated in memories. One of Mary's brothers, Rafa, came outside. *Must be thirteen*, he guessed. He sat on the front step to put on his shoes. His head twisted around, and he went back inside. He wondered if Mary was a nurse, if she could heal his aching heart, return what was lost in the winds of time.

Jimmy looked up at the sun. *Time to get Dad. Should call Mom. Deserter. Call anyway.*

It was late afternoon when he turned onto Palm Tree Lane. The new ranch house looked natural there at the end of the lane, like driving toward a resort. His mother loved entertaining there. He wondered why they hadn't dug a pool. *Nothin' better after a day in the fields.*

Jimmy parked in the driveway next to his father's pickup. The two-car garage was empty without Mother's car.

"Dad?" His father wasn't in the kitchen or living room. "Dad?" Jimmy left to the back yard. "Dad?" He returned to the house. *Maybe he's in the shower.* He stopped at his father's bedroom and listened. *Nope. Water's not runnin'.* He knocked gently. "Dad?" He tried the door, and it was open. "Dad?" He stuck his head in and found his father. "Dad!"

CHAPTER 34
CONFLUENCE

The river of life takes you further on until it reaches a lake or sea. There are unseen subterranean rivers like the ones inside us. They hold lives in the grip of a current. What we were, what we are—passengers on the river. Dark memories drift toward the bottom, some are buried beneath the muck. Most everything else finds its way somewhere in between. Yet there's part of us that slows down, lets others go by. It sponges morsels from each passing moment, slowing more as it gains substance until, one day, it stops. Gradually it rises to the surface to show what we've become.

You deserve more, patient reader. You've a right to know how Bill died and what became of the surviving members of the Koch family. You're curious as to how things turned out for James Irwin Koch. Shall I offer two or three options to choose from? As I settle on the front steps leading into the old ranch house, I ponder what's best. The answer floats to the surface. Truth will set you free.

***

Jimmy sat on a sofa in the living room. The ringing in his ears dampened the voice on the phone. "Sir, what is your emergency?" The twitch in his left eye made the world jump before him. "Sir, what is your emergency?" He looked at his hands and saw them shaking. He tried to control them, but it was useless.

He managed to choke out the circumstances regarding his 9-1-1 call. He barely heard her assure him that a deputy sheriff would arrive shortly and an ambulance would follow. Her voice sounded as if she were chewing a mouthful of crackers.

The final image of his father was permanently archived in his brain—twisted into an unlikely posture on the bed, half the contents of his head stuck to the headboard and wall. Involuntary reflexes launched the single-shot .410 shotgun hard against the ceiling above the bed, showering him with plaster. The scattergun lay on the carpeted floor. The moment Jimmy's eyes rested on his father, the image was laminated to mitigate the effects of time.

Jimmy heard a distant siren, yet they were just out front. He got up shakily and opened the front door.

"Where is he?" asked a deputy. Jimmy's answer sounded trapped deep inside his head. The deputy rushed down the hallway while his partner stayed with Jimmy. Another siren announced the ambulance. The first deputy was pale looking when he returned from the bedroom. He nodded at the other, who went to see for himself.

"Where is he?" a paramedic asked.

Jimmy pointed to the bedroom door. The second deputy was just coming out. He tried to look stoic, yet it only enhanced the horrified look. Paramedics rolled a gurney down the hallway and disappeared. Deputy one talked in code on a hand-held. He spelled each letter of his father's name beginning with a word, William, Ida, Lincoln, Lincoln, until he arrived at Henry. Deputy two regarded Jimmy.

"Need to sit down, son?"

"Yeah." His hearing was beginning to return.

"Let's sit at that dinner table." He took out a cassette recorder. "Okay to ask a few questions?"

"Sure."

Jimmy answered the deputy's questions, including why his father would take his life. The deputy nodded sympathetically.

"Real sorry for your loss, Mr. Koch. We'll try not to drag this thing out. An investigator's on his way, and he'll probably ask you a lot of the same questions. Got anyone you wanna call?"

Jimmy shook his head. "Not now."

"Okay."

The other deputy joined as the gurney was wheeled down the hallway and out the front door. Jimmy didn't look up from the table. In the next few weeks, he didn't look up if he could help it. The world was too ugly.

***

The funeral was a cornucopia of visages—bittersweet memories waltzed into Jimmy's head and wafted on supple, warm breezes.

There was Marty, his Vietnam vet cousin looking properly dour. Death was no stranger to him. Jack and Larue Ashworth spilled tears. They knew every farmer for miles around. Not many older farmers were there anymore. Some were disabled, others dead, or sold out to corporations. Bill reminded them that life is short. Auntie Dobbs stood with Barbara, her face a mask of indifference. Her daughter kept her lips pursed, and a few tears made their way, yet Jimmy couldn't tell if they were like Sydney's or not. Loftus wore a suit he'd bought forty years earlier. His face was gaunt, lined with the ravages of time. He wondered how much longer he'd have with ol' Johnny-boy. No Mexicans were at the funeral.

Uncle Ed bawled openly, sounding like an extended version of his laugh, "Ugh-huh-huh-huh-huh-huhhh!" Gladys and Andrew didn't understand what was happening. Caregivers stood with them, vacillating between smiles and grimaces before settling on a cloudy look for most of the service. Michael and Karen dripped silent tears, ensconced within the walls of a protective cocoon. Jimmy was reminded over and again that he was in everyone's thoughts and prayers. Matthew Cloninger said, "Sorry for your loss." All of this paled in comparison with his mother's drama.

Barbara executed a perfect swoon, timing it so that Al Cloninger caught her and eased her to the ground. She was the center of attention, solidifying her martyrdom. The Mud Dauber crouched over her daughter. On the fringe, reporters milled around. This was the extension piece they'd hoped for—a continuance of print-worthy sludge to transform the Koch family into cocktail talk for years to come. Yet the entire fiasco didn't have the Doppler effect they'd hoped for.

Karen barely felt a ripple. She lived in Fresno, an hour and a million miles away. Michael was protected by his prestigious employer, helping fuel the country's craving for fossil fuel. Gladys and Andrew were buffered by Alzheimer's. Jimmy quit Franey to move in with Ed. Together they kept the ranch operating as attorneys haggled and fought over the estate. Then one morning, Luis Crabtree called, and everything changed again.

***

Luis Crabtree sat in his office, staring at the last will and testament of William Lester Koch.

Damn it, he thought. *Insurance company was ready with a quick settlement. Bill's premiums would've doubled, but he'd keep the farm.* He'd seen it before—clients slogging through deep mud when the chips were down. They didn't trust him to do his job, to help them out—didn't think he cared. *I do care*, he reminded himself. That was why he didn't have *and Associates*, next to his name.

Luis looked at the date on the will. July 3rd, 1978. Bill changed it just before his suicide. He didn't know much about the family, yet the changes were remarkable, as reflected on line 3.1.

3.1. *I hereby nominate, constitute, and appoint my lawyer, Luis*

Crabtree, as Executor.

> *I bequeath the whole of my estate, property and effects, whether movable or immovable, wheresoever situated and of whatsoever nature to my son, James Irwin Koch. I only stipulate that he should care for his uncle, Edward Koch, and his grandparents, Gladys and Andrew Koch, until the day they die.*

Cut out the wife and other kids in favor of the youngest. Luis picked up the phone, put it down, and picked it up again. He called Jimmy first and asked him to contact the others to meet in his office at their earliest convenience.

***

Jimmy was a full-time farmer for less than five months. Rodolfo and his daughters moved to Woodland to live with cousins until a small settlement was received. Jimmy kept alcohol out of his uncle's house. He didn't want to become a useless drunk.

Jimmy ran the catching frame that summer. Loftus was on the shaker, and Ed worked the forklift. Jimmy found others to help with the harvest—the three Rs. Together they'd decided to turn over a new leaf (so to speak). They were drifting through life, hoping to bump into good fortune. Jimmy treated them with respect and dignity. Often during lunch break, they'd reminisce about the pot-dealing days. When the season ended, Jimmy gave them a large bonus and made arrangements for them to continue with the corporate farm business that bought the ranch at market value.

In late October, Jimmy put personal items in a Meadowland storage facility. He and Ed lived in a motel for a few weeks while Jimmy searched for a house to buy. In early November, Jimmy became a millionaire. On January 3rd, 1979, Andrew Koch died in his sleep, with Bob Barker easing his transition, *Andrew Koch, come on down*! In March, Gladys joined her husband. Before darkness enveloped her, she imagined gazing at the mummified menagerie, reaching for a dried Luna moth and smiling. *Interesting, don't you think?*

Leaves in autumn, thought Jimmy. *Nothing to replace them.*

In April, Jimmy bought a small home for Ed and lived in a modest one for himself on the opposite side of town from Aunt Dobby. He gifted his mother, Karen, Michael, and Ed, with a generous chunk of the inheritance. Then, after visiting Ed one afternoon, he did two things that changed his life again. At three o'clock, he drove to Smith's Market for a few groceries. At three thirty-five, he visited a travel agency on Main Street.

At Smith's Market, he was staring at a box of Wheaties, breakfast of champions, wondering why athletes were no longer depicted on the front of the box.

"Jimmy? Jimmy Koch?"

Jimmy snapped his head around. It was Shirley Hickman.

"Mrs. Hickman! How are you?"

She skipped to the chase. "So sorry to hear about your father, Jimmy. A terrible tragedy."

"Yeah."

"How are *you*?"

"Doin' okay. Still thinkin' about what to do."

Mrs. Hickman's eyes sparkled, and she smiled. She took both of Jimmy's hands in hers and looked at him. "My dear boy. Look at all that's happened in your short time on this Earth. Enough to fill at least three thousand pages. How many times do I have to remind you? You're a writer."

Jimmy's throat grew tight. Within her eyes, he saw his reflection. She'd known all along who he was. He looked at his shopping cart and saw that it was empty. He nodded his head and squeezed her hands.

"I won't keep you any longer. You have work to do." She walked away without looking back.

Jimmy left without buying anything. He sat in the red van. Recently he'd thought to trade it in for something that reflected his wealth. Instead, he took it to a mechanic and had it refurbished from top to bottom. He thought about the central valley. From the ranch, the world seemed flat until it rose up into the surrounding snow-peaked mountains. The sky was blue, and it seemed that summer was getting a head start. *World's bigger than this*, thought Jimmy. *Wanna see how much.*

Jimmy drove to Main Street and looked for the travel agency. It was next to a women's shoe store. Road construction was in progress, and the two-way street was being made into a one-way. Meadowland was changing too. On the outside of the agency were advertisements showing the wonders of the world. The Leaning Tower of Pisa, pristine beaches, ancient ruins, and the Taj Mahal. There were depictions of families splashing in resort pools, couples watching sunsets, and discount offers.

Escape, he thought. *Sort it out, figure out what to do, see what else is out there.* Jimmy stepped inside. Sitting at a desk, looking almost as she had years earlier, was Mary Mancha.

Her eyes grew wide. "Jimmy? Oh my God, Jimmy!"

Jimmy grinned. He blinked rapidly to confirm that she was real. His head reeled with a blender mix of anxiety, joy, and desire. Mary stood to greet him with a hug. He immediately saw that she was pregnant. He hid disappointment as best he could.

"Wow, what's this?" he pointed.

"Yeah." She accepted his outstretched hands.

"Married?"

"No." She changed the subject. "What brings you in?"

"Thought you were a nurse."

She shrugged. "Things change."

"Yeah, tell me about it."

"Sorry to hear about your dad."

"Thanks. How's Rafa and Luci?"

"In high school. They ask about you sometimes."

"Your mom and dad?"

"Same."

When's the baby due?"

"Four months."

"Mind me askin'?"

She shook her head. "Marcus."

"Thought you broke up."

"We did. We are. He was here on break and…." She shrugged again.

"Well, you look great."

She cupped her hands around her swollen belly. "Thanks. So do you."

"How's Marcus feeling about all this?"

"Trapped."

"You guys gonna….?"

"We're finished. Told him I didn't want anything from him." She looked past his shoulder to the parked van. "Still got it."

"Yeah."

"Brings back memories."

"That's why I keep it." He followed her gaze. "I think about us."

"Do you?" Her eyes softened.

And like a dream, when an entire life plays out in seconds, Jimmy knew what he wanted. "Go for a ride?"

Mary pursed her lips and raised an eyebrow. "Seriously?"

Jimmy nodded, "Bought a house. Wanna see it?"

She checked her watch. "Okay." She flipped over the open sign and locked the door.

Jimmy opened the passenger door for her. They drove across town to an established neighborhood with tall trees lining the streets. Homes wore welcoming faces and well-kept yards that exuded tranquility. He pulled into his driveway. The Spanish-style house was spacious, white, with a red tiled roof and an arched entryway. The front yard welcomed them with a beautiful array of flowers.

"It's wonderful. You own it?"

"Paid cash."

Both eyebrows were raised now.

"Dad left me the ranch, and I sold it."

"Oh." She pursed her lips and nodded.

Jimmy turned the engine off.

"Wait a second."

He looked questioningly at her.

"I was wondering, could we maybe drive out to the airport?"

Jimmy's turn to lift his eyebrows. "Been some mountain lion sightings there recently."

"Yeah?"

"Mmm-hmm." Jimmy leaned over, and she met him halfway. Her lips were soft and reassuring. Jimmy started the van and sped away. He no longer felt the need to travel the world. It was sitting next to him—had floated to the surface as a title for his new life.

After they exhausted themselves and lay facing each other, Jimmy didn't hesitate. Words came effortlessly. "Marry me."

"You still want me?" She rested a hand on her tummy.

He kissed her. "More than ever."

"Why?"

"Guess we were too young before. I never stopped lovin' you, Mary Mancha."

"Oh, Jimmy."

CHAPTER 35
WHAT'VE WE BECOME?

How you're raised can mean the difference between genius and sociopathy.

I'm James Irwin Koch. The front porch of the old ranch house is the fulcrum of my life. By burying the yellow Indian in the blue canoe, I attempted to protect what remained of my four-year-old innocence. They were dug up and ravaged by a set of Chihuahuas.

I was bullied simply for being born. I can imagine how Michael felt when Mother announced another *blessing* on the way. School bullies were a piece of cake compared to what awaited me at home. Karen was complicit. I hear her voice imploring Michael to stop. But he didn't. LadySmith was my protection, had my back, and in the end, she offered lasting peace. If not for the dud resting in the chamber of her heart, I wouldn't have written this.

I'll let you choose how it all turns out. Karen's husband is retired. They have a nice house and take short vacations to the central California coast, just like Mom and Dad did. Diehard Republicans. She probably wears a MAGA cap when she's out gardening. Her daughter, Charlotte, is happily married to an occupational therapist. She also has a son who learned accounting and inherited his grandfather's empire. You decide how that will turn out.

Michael retired near Santa Barbara. He's had a hip replacement, but other than that, he's in pretty good shape. He has a son who pitched in the minors and a daughter who teaches art history in Minnesota. No one's ever complained about his second wife. He, too, is a staunch Republican and hits the links as much as possible. You decide.

Barbara Koch stopped reading and focused on seduction. Her powers attracted a series of losers. They took her money, and she ended up mooching off Mike. She's ninety-one and lives in the same retirement home Gladys and Andrew were in. You must decide.

Uncle Ed suffered an epileptic attack and let out a dying fart that lasted three minutes and forty-one seconds. A world record. No one was there to hear it. No one in the Koch family lived more honestly than my uncle Ed. But you decide.

I'm James Irwin Koch. I was Mary Mancha's husband for twenty-three years. We tried to add to the team after my stepson Charles Jr. was born, yet after a third miscarriage, we surrendered. Mary died of breast cancer when she was only forty-four. At the time of her death, we owned three Mexican restaurants. I sold them off. Charles Irwin Koch is dark-skinned like his father. He's smart, humble, and handsome. Charles was a gifted athlete like his father, receiving a full ride to Clemson before playing two years at cornerback for the Cleveland Browns. A leg injury forced him to switch to real estate. He lives in Cleveland. Marcus keeps in contact with Charles, and over the years, they've developed a friendship.

Me? After Mary returned to my life, I attended Fresno State University and received a BA in literature. Then, I earned a teaching credential and taught high school English at Meadowland High School for thirty years. I published a few short stories and a science fiction novel. When I was nearly sixty-four, I caught a break. After self-publishing fifty copies of LadySmith, I snuck them into the bathrooms of a dozen Manhattan publishers. A week later, I received three phone calls and two offers. LadySmith is a bestseller. Go figure.

What I've learned through the years is this:

Mob Mentality = the lowest I.Q. in the group minus 15%. That explains a lot.

Don't rely on others for happiness. Make your own and offer it freely.

Sometimes the majority means all the fools are on the same side.

Self-doubt is creativity's greatest enemy. What's right is right. Vote accordingly.

Life is short, but it's wide. Live it, love it, celebrate diversity, and shine.

Fear + Ignorance = Control. Tame fear, get educated.

A toast...to the Jimmy Kocks of the world. May the yellow Indian inside you survive and prosper.

THE END

Ty Spencer Vossler, MFA, is the Xman (ex-farmer, ex-truck driver, ex-powerlifter, ex-cop, expatriate). He currently lives in Tlaxcala, Mexico, with his BMW (beautiful Mexican wife) and daughter. He has taught English and creative writing for twenty-three years and is currently a professor for the *Colegio ADA* in Puebla, Mexico. His rich life experience has shaped his writings into a reflection of contemporary society. Vossler's published short stories, essays, and poetry have won worldwide acclaim. He attributes his original and creative work to the fact that he shot his television over two decades ago. To learn more about Vossler, visit: www.tyvossler.com.